CHAOS
by D.J. Schuette

Critical Eye Editing
Andover, Minnesota

First print edition, 2017
Printed in the United States of America.

ISBN: 978-0-998-4293-1-1

Critical Eye Publishing
Andover, Minnesota 55304

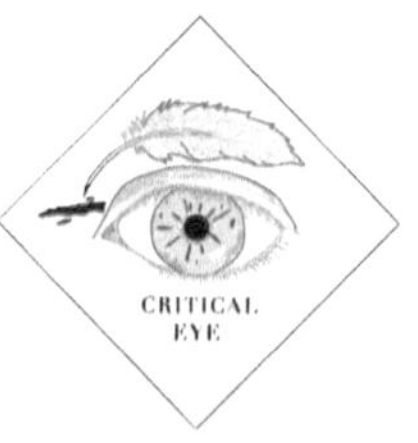

www.djschuette.com

For Colleen.

Far more than I deserve.

PROLOGUE

Baltimore, Maryland
Wednesday, January 23 2013 3:21 AM

Pale light from a gibbous moon filters through the old warehouse's high, dusty windows, bathing the vast and mostly empty space in a dim glow. There's a sharp tinge of charred meat on the air, and something else—something thick and metallic that can almost be tasted at the back of the throat.

A gray rat skitters across the floor, cautious, nose twitching. Stops. Skitters some more. It finds safety for a moment behind a caster then peeks out with its head up. Its nose works some more. There's a smell, faint, worth investigating. The rat paws its way up cold metal until standing on hind legs, stretches as high as it can go against the slick, gleaming surface, and slips back down, defeated. Instead, it scurries over to a small dark puddle a few feet away and dips a nose then a tongue into it. Still warm.

The table is stainless steel. Eighty inches by thirty-six. Not quite three feet high with two-inch deep lips surrounding the entire surface. Atop it is a naked black man. Two glinting quarters cover his open and unblinking eyes. He does not move. Not even to breathe. His dark skin—every bit of it from the soles of his feet to his scalp—is covered with blood and crisscrossed with open incisions. Hundreds of them. Some are shallow. Some deep. Some pink and fresh. Others puckered and scorched. None of them bleed.

But they did. The table is nearly filled to overflowing with blood, black in the moonlight. He is lying in it. Surrounded by it. His hands are partially submerged, his curled fingers breaking the dark, gleaming surface. Hidden beneath are two more quarters resting in the man's palms.

A single drop on his thigh loses its battle with gravity and plops into the pool.

Then, but for the rat the room is silent.

ONE

The wail of a police siren yanked Nicholas Keegan out of a dead but uncomfortable sleep. "Son of a bitch," he muttered and fumbled for his FBI-issued Blackberry. The siren ringtone meant the caller on the other line was someone in law enforcement and it was therefore—unfortunately—not a call he could ignore. It took him a minute to find the phone buried inside of a case file he'd been poring over when he fell asleep in the recliner.

On the bed across from him, Nick's wife flipped onto her side, kicked away the covers and pulled a pillow over her head with a grunt of discontent. For the first time he noticed a slight swell to her usually flat and rock hard stomach. He tried to ignore the anxiety in his own and answered the call.

"Keegan," he said, keeping his voice at just above a whisper. He half-listened with his eyes closed, as a thick fog of sleep tried to steal back over him.

"MPD needs you." It was Bill Quentin, one of the three Assistant Special Agents in Charge of the Minneapolis division of the FBI—Nick's mentor and boss.

Nick held the phone out in front of him and squinted at the screen through bleary eyes and a sigh. 6:26 AM. It didn't matter. He was now up for the day, three hours of sleep or not. Nick extracted himself from the deep cushions of the chair and immediately regretted having spent another night in it when he tried to stand. His lower back punished him with every inch he straightened. "For what?" he asked, wincing. He crossed the room to the bed and planted a kiss on his wife's shoulder.

Connie pulled the pillow tighter over her head.

As Nick headed for the bathroom, he couldn't restrain a grin. It turned to a grimace as he tried to roll his head around another kink in his neck.

"They say they've got the Garbage Man in custody. Pulled plates from one of those GoPros you planted and picked him up a few hours ago. They've asked for you to question him."

"They've got my profile." Nick clenched his teeth against a yawn. "Where's Hicks?"

Quentin uttered a short laugh that sounded like a bark. "Hicks is an imbecile. The Garbage Man is national news, and they can't afford to blow it. They know damn well that nobody's as good as you in the box."

Nick sighed. "Fine. I'll be there in about an hour."

"We don't get requests from MPD brass every day, Keegs. Be nice."

"I'm always nice." He hung up and yawned at himself in the mirror. He ran the back of his hand across the dark scruff on his jaw then squeezed the back of his aching neck. Shaving could wait. A hot shower could not.

Nick stepped into the cramped, featureless room, a steaming cup of coffee in one hand and a greasy McDonald's bag dangling from the other. An equally greasy man sitting at the table glanced up at him through narrowed eyes. His hands were cuffed in front of him and secured to a thick metal eyehook screwed into the table.

"Good morning," Nick said pleasantly as he took the two steps to get to his chair. He slid it out with a foot and set the breakfast down beside a brown folder lying on the table, then sat himself. Nick thought the man across from him looked nervous; his eyes flitted around the room like a pair of insects trying to find a place to land. Not a promising start.

Nick waited in silence until the man's brown eyes finally came to rest on him. He raised an eyebrow. "The Garbage Man, huh?"

"Yeah," the man said with a condescending sneer. "What of it?"

"That's the big time. I'm impressed. But you're not really what I was expecting." He shrugged nonchalantly. "Hey, you hungry?" Nick slid the coffee cup across the table so that it was in reach of the prisoner's cuffed hands. He pulled a bagged hash brown and sausage McMuffin from the bag and pushed them over as well.

The brown eyes narrowed in suspicion. "The fuck you mean, I'm not what you were expecting? Who the hell are you, anyway?"

"Oh, sorry. My name is Nicholas Keegan. FBI." He tipped his head. "And you're Reginald John Barrows. Can I call you Reggie, Reggie?"

Reggie shrugged and began to awkwardly unwrap the McMuffin.

"Just so we're clear, these guys told you your rights and that you're being recorded?"

Reggie nodded, intent on breakfast.

"How about you say that out loud for the camera?"

"Yeah, they read me my rights. Camera's right there, red light blinking and shit. I ain't stupid."

"I didn't say you were. No way an idiot gets away with kidnapping, killing, and cutting up five girls, right?"

Barrows didn't look up from his treasure. "Six. That you *know* of, genius. Don't you watch the news?" He held the sandwich in his right hand and had to lower his head almost to the table to take a bite.

Dubbed the "Garbage Man" by the media, someone had been leaving bags of dismembered body parts along the highway to be picked up and disposed of by the Department of Transportation. They sat innocuously among the bags collected by Adopt-a-Highway volunteers. No one was the wiser until a shard of bone had punctured one of the bags and spilled an assortment of putrefying limbs onto the side of the road. Since then, MNDOT checked every bag before they went into the trucks.

They'd discovered a total of six bodies so far. All were teenage girls from the Twin Cities that had gone missing starting in early spring. But there was no way to know for sure how long the sick bastard might have been using that particular method to dispose of his victims.

If there had ever been any of the perpetrator's DNA in the bags, it had degraded beyond recovery in the heat and sun. No prints. No other reliable forensic evidence.

"Sorry," Nick said. "Six." He leaned forward. "For real, though, how many?"

The sleazeball shrugged again and looked back up at him. "I lost count. Fifteen? Twenty?" he said through a smile and a mouthful of the hash brown. A tiny piece of potato flew from a gap in Reggie's teeth and landed on the table in front of Nick.

"You rape them?"

Reggie shifted in his chair. "Yeah. I raped 'em."

"So you like 'em young and struggling, huh? Or do you knock them unconscious first?"

"It's no fun if they aren't fighting. Crying. Begging for me to stop. Calling out for their mommies and daddies."

That sounded contrived, almost rehearsed.

Reggie bent his head down and tipped the coffee cup just enough to manage a loud slurp.

"How'd you do it? Kill them, I mean," Nick asked.

"Strangled 'em." He took another bite of the sandwich.

"How'd that make you feel? Killing someone?"

"Powerful."

"Yeah? Killing teenage girls makes you feel powerful?"

Reggie broke eye contact. He didn't answer.

"How'd you pick them?"

"They were out alone."

"You have a dog, Reggie?" Nick already knew the answer from the file. Most teenage girls knew better than to approach a strange man without a reason, and he suspected the Garbage Man was using a dog to lure them.

"Huh?" Reggie stopped chewing, rattled by the sudden change in questioning. "Do I have a dog?" Nick didn't miss the flush that crept from his neck into his cheeks. "No. No dog."

"Where?"

"Where what?"

"Where'd you find them? The girls."

"Uh, parks usually."

"How'd you get them to come with you?"

Reggie hesitated and his eyes danced away again. "Liquor. They wanna be cool, ya' know?" He hunched over to take another bite of the McMuffin.

Nick smacked the tabletop sharply with the palm of his hand.

Reggie was so startled that he jerked against his cuffs and dropped the sandwich. It fell apart onto the wrapper, crescent moons of muffin, sausage, and egg. "What the hell, man? Damn!"

"Sorry, I slipped."

"Fuckin' whackjob," Reggie muttered. He worked to put his breakfast back together, but he kept casting quick, nervous glances back at Nick.

"What was it like, cutting them up?"

"Messy. What do you think?"

"I meant how did it *feel*?" He drew the word out a half-second longer than he needed to.

There was a lengthy pause this time.

Nick watched Reggie's eyes drift up to the ceiling. For the briefest of seconds, he pressed his lips together. "Exciting." The pitch of his voice rose almost imperceptibly, and he lifted a shoulder slightly.

"What'd you use to cut them up?"

"A saw—hatchet for the bones." That fit with the autopsy findings.

Nick nodded. "What kind of saw?"

"Hacksaw," Reggie said and popped the last of the sandwich into his mouth.

"Where'd you cut them up?"

"My ba—. My backyard."

"You take any souvenirs?"

"Yeah." He grinned, suddenly all confidence again. "A tooth from each of them. One of the back ones." That tidbit hadn't been released to the press.

"How'd you get them?"

"Pliers." That was also a known fact. A few of the teeth surrounding the missing molars in the girl's skulls had grooves on them from a pair of pliers.

Nick sighed and sat back in his chair. "Listen, Reggie, you're a not a very good liar. But there's a problem. You know some things about this case that you shouldn't. I need you to tell me where you got that information."

"I told you, I—"

Nick rolled his eyes and held up a hand. "Stop. Let me spell this out for you. If you keep up with this bullshit and we can't prove otherwise, you'll go to prison for the rest of your very short and miserable life. They don't like people that fuck with kids in there. You'll get raped every day until your colon ruptures or until someone shanks you in the shower. The guards will happily look the other way while you bleed out. You're as good as dead, Reg." He pointed at the wrapper on the table. "And that was the last McMuffin you'll ever eat."

Reggie blanched and his Adam's apple dropped as he swallowed hard.

"The way I see it, there are two possibilities. There's either a leak in the police department—and I doubt that—or you know him somehow."

"I told you. I'm the Garbage Man." He didn't sound very convincing or confident anymore.

Nick shook his head. "The Garbage Man raped those girls, strangled them, cut them into little pieces and tossed their bodies on on the side of the road. He's a psychopath. You're a sleaze Reggie, but you're no psychopath. You're too soft."

"Hey, fuck you, Fed."

Nick smiled and held out his hands. "C'mon. You're a bundle of nerves in here. You damn near pissed yourself when I smacked the table. Psychopaths don't feel fear like you and me and their startle reflex is virtually non-existent. So who is he?"

"Me."

"Look, I have no doubt that you're a sick little puke who gets off on the idea of raping little girls. Maybe you could even man up enough to kill one of them to keep her quiet, though I doubt you'd have the balls to strangle them. You're more a knife in the back kinda guy, I think. Or a gun. Pills, maybe. You had to make up some things just now, things you didn't have the answers for. But there were a few things that you were trying to remember. The Garbage Man would have all of the answers, and trust me—he knows *exactly* how many girls he's killed. He counts those teeth every night. Who is he?"

Reggie shook his head.

Nick slipped a picture out of the folder and pushed it across the table.

Reggie's eyes started jumping again.

"C'mon, Reggie. You remember Hannah, don't you? Look at her."

He brought his eyes down, but they bounced away immediately. The picture was sickening—a shot of the inside of one of the bags after it had been sitting in the summer heat for who knows how long. Much of her remains were mush.

"Look at her! This is *your* work, right?"

Reggie slowly turned his eyes to the picture. It took a second for him to realize what he was seeing. He retched once and puked up his breakfast onto the table.

Nick stood. "You're such a man, Reggie. Enjoy your brief stay in prison." His hand was on the doorknob.

"The Darknet," Reggie said, defeated. "Some guy's been bragging about it."

TWO

Bakersfield, California
Sunday, July 24 2016 4:20 AM

Aleksandr Zorin stood still and silent, cloaked in the early morning darkness. If Helen Lyman held to her morning ritual (and why wouldn't she—the Non were nothing if not creatures of habit and stupidity), in just a few minutes he'd be drinking in her terror, and a few moments beyond she would be drowning in her own blood. The daughter had snuck out with her boyfriend again in the middle of the night and had not yet returned—another sleepover. That was good. It meant she didn't plan to return until after her mother had left for work. He'd be long gone by then. All the more reason today was the day.

He smiled to himself, ran a thinly gloved thumb over the ridges of a quarter in his left hand and checked his surroundings carefully. The adjacent houses were dark and quiet (as they always were at this ridiculous hour) and spaced far enough away that their occupants were out of earshot. None of them had any dogs to worry about. The Else had chosen Helen for him, but he couldn't have picked a better, *easier* victim had he wanted to.

Over the lazy chirping of distant crickets, Zorin could just make out the shriek of an alarm from inside the house. After a few seconds, it fell silent. His heart rate increased, and his skin tingled with anticipation. He felt his cock twitch against the fabric of his wetsuit. The night was warm and the suit was hot and uncomfortable, but it couldn't be avoided. He was nothing if not cautious, and it prevented the transfer of skin, fibers, and DNA, and would keep much of the blood off of him. The FBI would know plenty about him soon enough, but there was no reason to make their job any easier than it needed to be.

He gripped the straps of the small duffel tighter in his right hand and reached inside with his left, trading the quarter for a small, squishy ball of cheese and then fell motionless again. With his back pressed against the outer wall of the rambler, he could feel her footfalls as she crossed the house and neared the door. There was a brief pause in which Zorin knew she was trying the light switch a few times. The small yard stayed dark—he'd unscrewed the bulb. He heard the first door open, then the storm door swung open a bit and a tiny dark blur raced into the backyard with an excited sneeze.

"Go wear yourself out, doof." Helen's voice was slow and thick with sleep. Zorin heard her yawn as the outer door swung shut.

The dog found him almost immediately and bounded around his legs harrumphing, its fine hair standing in all directions like a mini canine Einstein. Zorin would just as soon have smashed the damn thing's skull under a boot, but he had more important matters to attend to. He gave the Yorkshire the cheese, waited a full minute, then let himself inside.

The heavy, nutty aroma of brewing coffee hung in the air. Helen was nowhere to be seen, but he could hear her in one of the rooms deeper in the house. The terrier danced around his feet and looked up at him expectantly. Zorin suppressed an urge to kick it and got a sense of his surroundings. Then he switched off the light and took a shielded position in the living room.

After a minute, the dog gave up on the hope of more cheese and trotted off down the hall.

Helen's startled cry made him smile and got his cock throbbing again.

"Lindsay?" he heard her call. "Did you let Spazz back in?"

He saw her silhouetted in the light from her room as she came down the hall outfitted for a run.

When she got to the dining room, Zorin heard her sigh. "Honey, you forgot to close the door." She pushed it shut, turned the deadbolt, and absently flipped the kitchen light back on. She took a few steps into the living room.

Zorin stepped out of the shadows. He watched as her body physically registered the shock. Her knees buckled, and she nearly fell. She screamed. It was hardly the best he'd ever heard.

"Lindsay snuck out several hours ago, Helen." He shrugged. "Kids these days."

Her eyes narrowed in confusion as they darted around trying to find an escape. There was none. He'd be on her long before she got to the alarm panel by the front door, and she'd just unknowingly cut off her easiest escape at the back door.

She inched away from him, her eyes flitting to a closed door down the hall. The daughter's room. The dog looked back and forth between them, teeth bared and growling. He could smell the woman's fear, Zorin knew, but wasn't sure where to direct his aggression.

Helen held up a trembling hand. He could see the fast twitch muscles in her arm quivering. So lovely.

"Take what you want and go," she said, her voice shaking as much as the rest of her.

He smiled—something he knew he didn't do convincingly. "Oh, I intend to."

The muscles in her arms and legs tightened, betraying her intent. She bolted for the door in the kitchen.

Her hand was on the deadbolt when he reached her. She slipped sideways down the door, her hands up to shield herself from him. A scream tore from her throat like a siren.

Much better.

At the sound, the dog raced for the back of the house, whimpering.

"Please," she said. Her voice was feeble—childlike—and choked with tears. She shrunk away from him, curled into the least amount of space she could possibly occupy. "Please, don't."

They always begged. He shuddered.

He put a gloved hand on her head. "Shhh."

She tensed against his touch. She wasn't quite done fighting. She leapt at his legs, pushing off of the door. Zorin anticipated the maneuver and stepped back out of reach. He landed a boot in the fleshy part of her side, eliciting another scream—this one ragged and breathy. He was appreciating the sound when she lunged at him again, this time wrapping her arms around his legs.

He respected her tenacity, but she had almost no impact on him at all. She was already weakening, losing adrenalin. He stayed rooted in place as she spent the last of her energy.

"Don't hurt my daughter," she pleaded. "For God's sake, please. Don't hurt Lindsay."

"I'm not here for her."

"Then why?" she asked, tears shining on her cheeks. "Why?" A choked and broken sob escaped her.

"You were chosen." Zorin bent down and put his hand on her head again. He tangled his fingers in her hair and yanked her to her knees.

She keened like a wounded animal.

"It's time. The Else awaits you." He slipped a gleaming blade from his belt with his free hand and stepped behind her.

She put her head in her hands and wept.

The smell of brewing coffee and her dog's frantic barking escorted her into oblivion.

THREE

Columbus, Minnesota
Monday, July 25 2016 4:12 PM

The door to the room was steel and secured by two deadbolts accessible from the outside. The uniforms took up positions and disengaged the bolts. One of the officers slowly turned the knob and, after getting a nod from one of his colleagues, swung the door wide. There was an inhuman shriek, and a naked and filthy blonde girl with wild eyes threw herself toward them, her hands curled into claws.

She spun from side to side as if trying to figure out whom to attack first, still screeching. Then all at once, she seemed to realize what was happening and collapsed to the floor, sobbing. Nick stepped forward, shrugged out of his sport jacket and draped it over the girl's bare shoulders. Then he scooped her into his arms and carried her upstairs and outside into the bright sun and flashing lights of a dozen emergency vehicles. His vision blurred, and his eyes burned as he carried her quaking body toward a waiting ambulance.

Muffled thuds came from the backseat of a nearby squad car as the Garbage Man slammed his head against the glass window in rage as Nick stole away his prize.

As he handed the girl off to the waiting EMTs Nick's phone vibrated against his leg, interrupting a ferocious desire to stride over to the squad and empty a clip into the son of a bitch in the backseat. He drew an arm across damp eyes and checked his Blackberry. Normally, he'd have let the call go to voicemail, but decided he could use the emotional lift that talking to his old friend in Bakersfield would give him.

He walked to a quiet part of the yard, cleared his throat, and answered. "Jim Harris, you piece of shit. How are you?"

"Hanging in there, Nicky. How 'bout you?" Even over the chaotic noise of the scene, Nick could hear the tension in his voice.

"Just wrapping up the Garbage Man case. We literally took him into custody fifteen minutes ago."

"Fantastic! I bet *he'll* have a good time in prison." Jim paused for a beat. "The girl?"

"She's a mess, but alive. Best we could have hoped for."

"Nice. Listen, I know you're busy, so I'll let you get back to it. Think you can give me a call later? I'd like to run something past you."

"Sure. Everything all right? Liv okay?"

"Olivia's great. A goddamn saint to put up with me."

"Ain't that the truth," Nick said. He got a short burst of laughter from the other end of the line, but it sounded hollow and half-hearted.

"I'll fill you in later. Go make sure the case against that fucker sticks."

"Oh, I think this one's a slam dunk. Call you tonight?"

"Sounds good. Tell Con hello."

"Will do."

Nick was glad to have talked to his friend, but he didn't feel better at all. If anything, Jim's unusually dark mood had planted a small seed of dread in the pit of his stomach.

Jack Hicks, the lead MPD Detective assigned to the task force found him in the living room counting the teeth in the little plastic pill container on the coffee table. *Eleven.*

"No dog." He wore a slightly smug expression. "Nice try, though."

Nick beckoned for the detective to follow and led him to the kitchen. Hanging from a nail on the wall next to the refrigerator was a thick leather leash and a key. Secured on the fridge door by a magnet was a small wall calendar filled in by a nearly illegible hand. Nick tapped it with the back of a fingernail.

Hicks leaned forward and squinted to read the scribble on the calendar. He flipped the pages back a few months. The dates that the girls went missing all corresponded with notations on the calendar that said, "Walk Samson."

The detective shook his head in disbelief. "I'll be goddamned."

FOUR

Shoreview, Minnesota
Monday, July 25 2016 7:53 PM

Nick sat on his deck in a plastic chair and watched the sun begin its downward trek behind the rest of the neighborhood. Brilliant oranges faded into pinkish tones as if a stroke of blue paint had been added. Neptune sparkled faintly in a purpling eastern sky. It was as close to a perfect evening as Nick had seen in a long time. There was no humidity, and the temperature had already fallen to a comfortable 75 degrees—perfect for watching the start of a sunset with a cold Nordeast in hand.

Connie was out for an evening run. A small pang of guilt ricocheted in his chest for not getting home in time to join her, but wrapping things up in Columbus had taken longer than he'd hoped. In any case, Nick preferred his jogs in the morning when his testosterone was highest, and Connie liked to burn off her stress in the evening. He knew very little about numbers and mathematics, but he assumed accounting must be stressful in a mind-numbing, put-a weapon-in-your-mouth sort of way. Thank God for her, though. She was a genius at keeping their finances in order.

Nick took a pull from the bottle and watched the twilight slowly devour the dusk. He leaned back in the chair and tried to exorcise the memories of the afternoon. He'd only just succeeded and had started to slip into something akin to sleep when his phone rang. He flirted with the idea of chucking the damn thing over the balcony, but instead sighed and checked the caller ID. He considered it all over again when he saw it was his mother calling.

He thought about ignoring her, but that would only delay the inevitable.

"Hi, Mom."

"Hello, Nicholas."

There was an awkward pause, as there always was. He shook his head and sighed again.

"What can I do for you, Mom?"

"How are you?"

Well, that was new. "I'm fine." He hesitated for a second. "How about you?"

"Just dandy. How is Connie?"

A ball of suspicion formed in his chest. Her consideration made him more than a little uncomfortable.

"She's good. Everything's great. What's up?" he asked, trying to hurry the conversation along.

"I was thinking I'd like to come and see you both. Next week, perhaps."

Oh, Christ. Apparently the thought of becoming a grandmother was bringing out her inner warm and fuzzy. Nick had seen that side of her only a handful of times since his father died, and it was about as soft and cuddly as a brick wrapped in sandpaper. Fortunately, he had a legitimate excuse. "Sorry, Ma. I'll be in Quantico next week. Not the best time."

"I see. Big case?"

What the hell? Nick wondered if she was on new meds. "No. Teaching a class at the Academy on Monday."

"How about this Saturday then? We can do brunch at Hell's Kitchen. I hear it's quite good. I'll pick you both up at ten."

There were few things he'd rather do less on a Saturday. It was amazing, Nick thought, that this woman could so easily annihilate the composure of someone with a psych degree. "Uh, well—"

"Good. That settles it, then. I'll see you Saturday." She hung up before he could object.

"God damn it," he said aloud. At least he had most of the week to come up with a reason to cancel.

The sliding glass door opened behind him. Nick leaned his head back over the top of the chair to greet his wife. "Heya beautiful. You sweaty!" He grinned at her.

Connie wiped her forehead and face with a towel. "Great night for a run. Shame you missed it."

"I know, sorry. I didn't expect to be so late." He caught the dubious look she gave him but diplomatically chose to ignore it. "I'll go in the morning. How long are you allowed to keep this up before my child winds up with shaken baby syndrome, anyway?"

Connie burst out laughing. The peal of it whisked away the dark shadows that the afternoon and his mother's call left in their wakes. It was a perfect sound, like that of a musical chord that vibrates in one's chest. Her laughter never failed to send a little shiver through him.

"As long as I'm drinking enough water and don't overdo it, I can keep going for as long as I'm comfortable, shithead." She arched an eyebrow at him. "But if you're worried about it, maybe we should lay off the sex, too?"

Nick drained the rest of his bottle and rose to face her. "Uh, you just keep running your pretty ass off, then."

"Yeah, I thought so, wiseass. I'm going to jump in the shower quick. Who was on the phone?"

"Nobody important."

"Good, then you're mine for the night." She bent forward and kissed him. "Mmmm, that tastes good. I miss beer." She trotted inside.

They were tangled up on the couch watching *Scorpion* when the local news preempted programming with a special report.

"We have breaking news out of Columbus tonight. WCCO News has learned that the Anoka County Sheriff's Department, in conjunction with Minneapolis Police and the FBI, has just taken a suspect into custody for the recent abductions and murders of six local girls…"

Connie squealed. "Is that what you were doing today?"

Nick grinned at her excitement. "We got him."

"Oh, thank God. You're sure it's him this time?"

Nick nodded, but his smile slipped. "There's video. And souvenirs."

"How many?"

"Eleven. At least."

"My God." She put a protective hand on her belly and her eyes welled with tears. "Those were somebody's daughters. How do people do such things?"

"I wish I had a good answer, babe," Nick said. "They're not wired like we are. They look like us and learn to act like us, but they're missing the stuff that makes us human." He shrugged. "They're perfect predators."

Connie sniffed and smiled at him. "Not quite so perfect as my brilliant husband is at finding them. Maybe now you can get a few nights of real sleep. In the bed." She looked down her nose at him. "Next to your pregnant wife." She said it with a light tone, but he knew she was only half teasing.

"That would be excellent." It wasn't a lie.

She shifted and swung a leg over both of his and straddled him. "I think maybe you should be rewarded for your service, Special Agent." She leaned forward and kissed him.

After a few fantastic minutes, Nick pulled away with no small amount of regret. "Hold that thought?"

Connie pouted at him spectacularly.

"I have to call Jim. He called earlier. Didn't sound like himself at all."

"Harris? In California?" She blew out a breath and got up. "Okay. I'm going up to read for a bit, then. Don't keep me waiting too long, okay?"

"Wouldn't dream of it," Nick told her.

FIVE

Shoreview, Minnesota
Monday, July 25 2016 9:40 PM

"All right bro, what's eating you?"

"That obvious?" Harris asked.

Nick grunted. "I've known you damn near twenty years. And it's not like you're terribly hard to read at the moment."

Harris exhaled a long sigh. "I caught a case yesterday. Was out picking up supplies and responded to a residential alarm in progress in the neighborhood. I was first on scene. Brutal. At first glance it looks like a burglary gone wrong. Maybe a home invasion. That's what the higher-ups are calling it, anyway."

Nick leaned back and put a foot up on the coffee table. "You don't think so?"

Jim hesitated. Nick heard plenty in the silence. "I dunno. It's possible I guess, but it doesn't feel right. Something's off."

Nick caught a hint of desperation in his friend's voice. That bothered him. Harris was no soft rookie and had seen his share of nasty shit. He'd also been an outstanding detective with a record clearance percentage.

"Okay. Tell me."

"I have to be honest, a lot about this does fit the burglary angle. I don't know. It's just… too gruesome, maybe."

Nick's interest was piqued. He trusted Harris's instincts more than Harris himself did. And though it wasn't impossible, interrupted burglaries didn't typically result in "gruesome" crime scenes.

"How so? What can you tell me about the scene?"

"It was a damn mess. Almost looked like the place had been tossed. I can't be sure, but I think the perp covered the vic's face with a kitchen towel. There *were* things missing—her wallet and phone were gone, the jewelry box in her room was cleaned out. But it doesn't look like anything in the daughter's room was touched. Getting an inventory is going to be, uh…tricky."

"Hold on, back up a sec," Nick interrupted. Several bells were going off in his head at once. "You said daughter. Are we looking at two vics?"

"No. Well," Harris cleared his throat. "Yes, but no."

Nick dropped his foot and sat up a bit straighter. The hesitation marked a significant source of his friend's distress.

"The girl wasn't home at the time. From what we've been able to gather, she snuck out in the middle of the night to meet up with her boyfriend at the college dorms. Frat party. According to the boyfriend, she passed out about three in the morning and didn't get back home until about 10:15. Couple other kids confirmed they were both there all night. She's the one that found the body. She's uh…" Harris trailed off, his voice wavering. Nick heard him take a deep breath and clear his throat again. "She's a wreck. In a catatonic stupor that the doctors aren't sure she'll come out of."

Nick remembered his own overwhelming emotions while carrying Amber out of her personal hell earlier in the day and felt for his friend. Cops were taught to keep themselves detached, but it was often much easier said than done. "You said your vic's face might have been covered but you couldn't be sure. Was the scene contaminated?"

"Total clusterfuck. Goddamn dog was all over the place, bloody paw prints everywhere. It'd been licking up her blood—his fucking eye was plastered shut with it. I thought he was blind at first. And the girl, Lindsay…"

Harris trailed off, stuck in the memory of the moment, Nick knew. He'd seen it many times in those he'd interviewed. Their eyes would lose focus, and they'd stop recounting, momentarily trapped in whatever trauma they'd experienced. Nick wished he could spare him. If this were an official request, Nick might be able to convince his boss to send him out to assist the Bureau guys from Sacramento, but for the moment it was just two friends shooting the unofficial shit. Then an idea came to him.

"Jim," Nick said, "didn't you guys just get body cams a few months back?"

"Yeah."

"Perfect. Send me everything you've got, and I'll take a look."

SIX

Shoreview, Minnesota
Monday, July 25 2016 10:32 PM

Nick opened his laptop, logged into his secure email, and clicked on the video attachment Harris had sent. His desktop was clean, adorned only with his laptop and Blackberry, a few faded pictures of his father with the guys from the Jacksonville PD, and a brightly painted gold-colored brick. An American flag in a triangular wooden shadow box hung on the wall in front of him, a gold badge tucked into the corner. The memorial flag was from his father's funeral, the brick a souvenir from the FBI Academy for completing an optional—and hellish—six-mile run-cum-obstacle course designed by some seriously sadistic Marines. It had come to be known as the "Yellow Brick Road," thus the unusual trophy. It was, in fact, the same course Jodie Foster ran during the opening scene of *Silence of the Lambs*.

Nick absently clicked a pen on his thigh and resisted the urge to open the supplemental .jpeg files on his screen while he waited for the video to finish downloading. He wanted to see the scene exactly as Harris had first seen it before he looked at the photos.

When Nick first joined Violent Crimes, he'd been required to study a seemingly endless barrage of the most horrific crime scene photos and videos ever recorded. He'd watched the trophy recordings of killers as they tortured, raped, and butchered for the camera. Many were terrors a typical cop wouldn't come across in fifty lifetimes on the job. It gave him a perspective that he hoped his old college roommate would never have to experience.

A chime alerted him that the file was ready. He pulled a pair of headphones from a desk drawer, plugged them in and put them on. He double clicked the icon.

The interior of Jim's squad filled the screen as Harris pulled into a driveway alongside a late nineties model Mercury Cougar that looked to be on its tenth of nine lives. His hand and arm came into view, and he made a handful of keystrokes on the mobile data terminal. Running the plates, Nick assumed. A few massive bags of ice sat on the passenger seat. Moisture trickled down the plastic. The squad's A/C emitted a constant dull roar. Nick's skin prickled as if he were sweating.

"Ten-ninety-seven, dispatch. I'm Code Six Adam," Harris said into his radio, relaying that he'd arrived on scene and might need further assistance.

The rambler beyond the windshield was small and well maintained, but out of place among the newer contemporary two-stories that made up the rest of the cul-de-sac. It wasn't without a quaint appeal, however. Jim got out of the SUV and went around to the Mercury and placed his palm on the hood. Then he rounded the corner of the attached garage and approached the front door via the adjacent walk.

Nick listened for the klaxon wail that sometimes accompanied tripped alarms. He heard none. Instead, he could just make out the sound of a ringing telephone from inside the house—probably the alarm company trying to make contact with their clients.

He was about half a dozen virtual steps away from the front door when he realized it wasn't closed.

"Shit," Nick murmured to himself, an instant before he heard Jim say the same thing in the headphones.

The perspective changed as Harris took up a position with his back against the side wall of the garage. An arm crossed in front of the camera lens again as Jim keyed the mic on his shoulder radio.

"This is Item Robert One, I've got an eleven-four at previous address," Harris whispered, requesting backup for a potential emergency. "Send them in quiet. Out."

There was a pause that lasted about five seconds, during which Nick imagined his friend gauging the situation before resolving to continue. Nick's view slipped left as Harris sidled along the wall toward the house until he reached the corner. The orientation of the image changed so quickly as Harris swung around to the left side of the door, it made him slightly dizzy. Instinctively, Nick looked at the jamb for marks that might indicate forced entry. There were none that he could see. The phone had, for the moment, stopped ringing. He heard no voices, however, and assumed the caller had hung up.

Jim's left hand came back into view and rapped on the door. It swung open about three inches. Harris leveled his pistol to chest height, aimed through the gap. It was dark inside, and it was hard to make out much, but things looked to be in a state of disarray.

"Hello? Ms. Lyman? It's the police." He was answered by the high-pitched and rapidly approaching yips of a small dog. Within seconds, a tiny reddish-brown snout poked through the breach, making far too much noise for something so small. His fur was a flattened, matted mess. As the dog struggled against the weight of the door, trying desperately for the one more inch it would need to escape, Harris called into the home again.

"Hello? This is the police. Can anyone inside hear me?" Nick wondered how Harris could hear anything himself over the ear-splitting yelps of the dog.

"Would you shut up?" Harris snapped, just as the dog managed to get its entire head through the door. At the rebuke it retreated into the gloom, still barking. He left behind a rust-colored smear on the white paint of both the door and the frame.

"Fuck," Harris said in Nick's ears. He took up a two-handed grip on his weapon, crouched low, and leaned his left shoulder against the door. He followed its swing with a neat sweep of the gun, clearing the room beyond in one fluid motion.

The place was ransacked. Overturned furniture cluttered the living room to the fore and the dining area to the right rear. Shards of glass littered the floor, glinting in the sunlight streaming through the door.

The dog—a Yorkie, Nick thought—regained his courage and approached, barking incessantly as if he were the most ferocious little beast that had ever existed. He disappeared from the camera's view for a few seconds, then popped back onto the screen as Harris bent over to take a closer look. Wet-looking, dark-red tufts clung to him in clumps. His eye was caked shut with gore. It looked as if blood had either been poured—or shed—in copious amounts all over the little guy. Nick could see why Harris might think the dog had lost an eye.

"Bakersfield P.D. Ms. Lyman?" He took a few more slow steps inside, gun leveled in front of him. Two days and two thousand miles removed, Nick willed Harris to use caution. Potential evidence was everywhere: broken glass, toppled furniture, tiny paw prints stamped in varying shades of brown and red on the beige carpet. The darkest of those prints were nearest what he assumed to be the kitchen at the back of the house.

Harris chose the path opposite the dining area for his approach, and headed toward the left-most entryway. The terrier, finally quiet and looking like something out of a bad horror movie, entered the frame again and bounded on ahead. At the threshold, it turned and gave them a last look through its good eye before disappearing into the obscured room.

Nick thought he heard something in the headphones. He rewound the video a few seconds and turned the volume up as high as it would go. He could just hear a faint whisper over the clicking of the terrier's nails on the kitchen floor.

The screen stilled as Jim went motionless, and Nick knew he'd heard it too. He closed his eyes and tried to make out the words, but they were unclear. The angle of the video allowed Nick to see a small triangle of white linoleum and the furthest wall of the kitchen. It was covered with dark speckles. Nick's own nostrils filled with the heavy copper smell of blood. He could feel the weight of a Glock in his hand. He sensed Jim's dread.

The wall approached quickly, and the world spun again, so Nick was looking back at the front door, then at the wall of the den as Jim pressed his shoulder against it. The voice coming from the kitchen was clearer now—a female's, but he still couldn't make out what was being said.

Nick heard a vehicle outside. The perspective changed again, and a woman in uniform appeared, silhouetted in the doorway. Her eyes swept the room and stopped on him. Jim's arm came up and briefly filled the frame as he motioned to her. The woman nodded once. She moved deftly through the mess and took up a position at the opposite corner of the wall.

"Miss, are you all right in there?" Jim's voice boomed in the headphones.

The whispers continued unabated.

"This is the police. Can you hear me?"

No response. Just the whispers and the clicking of little paws on tile.

"I'm coming into the kitchen. If you have any weapons, slide them across the floor toward the sound of my voice." Nothing. "I have a gun, and strongly suggest you don't make any sudden movements when I come in. Are we clear?"

The dog peeked its head around the corner and gave a single yip, then disappeared back into the room.

Jim turned toward the female officer, and Nick watched as he clicked off a three count with his fingers, then whirled around the corner and into the room, gun leading the way.

The kitchen was bright with sunlight pouring in from the windows above the sink. It took a fraction of a second for the camera lens to adjust before the footage became clear. Nick's chest tightened, and he inhaled sharply. Blood painted nearly every surface in the small room. Nick noted a very clear arterial spray pattern on the door of the refrigerator.

Jim retched. Across from him, the female officer puked onto a somewhat clear patch of tile.

A girl of perhaps seventeen knelt on the floor in a large pool of blood. She rocked back and forth, with a woman's head resting on her knees. Tears spilled down her cheeks. She spoke the words, "I'm sorry, Mom," over and over, while using a small, once-white towel to try to wipe the blood from the ashen face of her mother. She was succeeding only in making a smeared, sticky mess.

The dead woman's arms were outstretched to either side of her, left palm up and the right down. Something glinted in her left hand. A dark, gaping slit ran along her throat from just beneath one earlobe to the other, plainly visible despite the downward tilt of her chin.

There seemed to be long minutes of silence and stillness in which they took in the scene in its entirety, but Nick knew it was no more than a few short seconds. Time moved differently in crime scenes.

"Miss?" Harris inched forward amidst the spatter. He lowered himself into a crouch about eight feet from the girl, her mother's body between them. Any further progress was barred by copious amounts of blood.

"Miss," he repeated, "are you hurt?"

The girl continued to wipe at her mother's face with the stained towel, the only response her ceaseless apologies to the dead woman in her lap.

"Kaitlyn, go outside. Call it in," Harris said. "Wait for Lejas, and have him rope off this entire lot. Front yard, back yard—all of it. Bring the digital with you when you come back in. I want you to take images of everything from the door to the kitchen until CSU and the ME get here. I'll secure the rest of the house."

"Yessir," she said, looking pale and more than a little relieved. She vanished around the corner.

Tiny paw prints were scattered throughout the kitchen—some red on the white un-splattered tile, some white on red where the dog had pranced through the blood as it began to dry, and many others were just shallow impressions on the now tacky surface of the blood pools.

Nick made mental notes of the position of the body, and what appeared to be coins at seemingly random points in the room. One lay on the floor on the edge of a large blood smear to the right of the dead woman's shin. Another, just visible under the lip of a cupboard door, lay atop a puddle of congealing blood. A third sat in the open palm of the vic's left hand—quarters, he judged by their size.

Nick shivered, and his stomach knotted uneasily. He pushed back against memories better left in the past and forced himself to stay focused on the video unfolding before him.

"Miss," Harris said again. His hand came into view, and he snapped his fingers in the air over the body. "Miss Lyman? Hey! Listen to me. I need you to let go of your mother, and move back so I can take a look at her, all right?" Jim's voice was unsteady.

The girl just continued to look down into the vacant eyes of the corpse that had been her mother and tried to clean her face with the bloody rag.

"Dammit," Harris muttered. He rose. "I'm going to go take a look around the house, okay? You just stay here with your mother."

He backed out of the room and crossed the main living area. As he reached the hallway leading to the rest of the house, he turned back. Jim blew out a long, shaky breath that wobbled the feed on Nick's screen. The camera stayed put for a few seconds that felt like an hour, focused on Lindsay as she rocked and wiped at her mother's face, surrounded by a sea of blood.

SEVEN

Nick smelled coffee. And bacon. His stomach growled. He opened an eye and found himself not where he expected. He'd watched Jim's video twice more before he'd gone upstairs, intending to take a look at all of the .jpegs before crawling into bed. He'd never made it any further than the chair. Again.

The bedroom door swung open, and Connie came in with a mug in one hand and a plate in the other, both steaming. She set the plate down on the arm of the recliner and handed him the coffee. She sat down on the bed facing him. She smiled, but Nick could see it was forced. His face got warm. A stab of guilt punched him in the gut.

"Oh shit, babe. I'm sorry."

"Don't apologize. This isn't about me. You can't keep doing this. You're not sleeping more than a couple hours a night. It's been at least a week since you've even slept in the bed."

"Jim had a case. He—"

"There's always going to be another case, Nick. You can't possibly keep up this pace. I'm worried about you."

He heard her unspoken words beneath the spoken ones. *I'm worried about us.*

Nick took a swallow of the coffee. It burned the back of his throat. "You don't have to worry about me. I'm fine. But you're right. I can't keep doing this." He hoped the *to you* was adequately implied. He stood and went to her, setting the coffee mug down on the end table. He sat and took her hand. "I'll work on it."

She squeezed his fingers. "I get that what you do is important, and you're great at it, but there's only so much one person can do. Nobody expects you to rid the world of all the crazies on your own, and there has to be more to life than your work, you know?" Her free hand strayed to her stomach.

He nodded. "I do." He slipped a hand around her neck and pulled her into a kiss.

She moaned softly, but pushed him away after a few seconds. "You missed your chance, Romeo. I've got to get going, and you'd better get ready yourself. Don't forget, we're having dinner with Mindy and her new boyfriend tomorrow night."

Nick collapsed back on the bed. "Ugh."

Connie gave him a stern look. "It's not going to kill you. Besides, you can spend one evening profiling someone who isn't a serial killer."

"Knowing your sister's taste in men, it's entirely possible that he *is* a serial killer."

Connie punched him playfully in the stomach. "All the more reason for you to be there, jackass."

He groaned. "Fine."

"No work, okay? One night."

He figured he owed her a lot more than that. "No work."

She leaned back and kissed him again. "Maybe I'll even let you make up for last night when we get home."

He sat up. "Now *that's* a deal."

Connie grinned at him slyly. "I've got to go. Eat." She rested a hand on his chest for a second. "I love you."

"Love you too, babe. Have a good day," he said as she left.

Nick sat back down with his coffee and munched on a crispy strip of bacon, thankful for his ever-forgiving wife. As he ate, he opened the pictures he hadn't made it through the night before. Most told him nothing new, though there were a few things he found interesting: A knife found in the top rack of the dishwasher, with blood on the blade. An image of a kitchen block with an empty slot that appeared to match it. Pictures of the victim's empty and overturned jewelry box. Another of the daughter's room, the jewelry box apparently untouched. A desk in a small office with a dust void where a laptop likely sat. A purse, contents spilled on the kitchen counter—gum, tampons, cheap sunglasses, wrappers, makeup, a few pennies—but nothing of real value. No cell phone, no wallet, no cash.

Nick shoveled a forkful of eggs into his mouth and clicked on another icon. He stopped chewing.

What the fuck?

It was a picture of four Minnesota statehood quarters partially stained with blood.

EIGHT

The morning sun crested the tallest of the concrete, glass and steel towers of 6th street and flooded the street below in a blaze of blinding fire. Thousands of downtown employees, on foot and jockeying for every bare inch of sidewalk, donned sunglasses or shielded their eyes against the sudden brightness.

Zorin, dressed the part in a well-tailored, three-piece suit, maneuvered easily through the crowd. He masked his malachite-green eyes behind a pair of expensive Serengetis—a favorite prize from one of his previous undertakings. A small smile teased at the corner of his mouth, a product of his amused contempt for the Non. Cattle. Sheep. Worker ants. Moving through their daily worthless existences, beholden to the wills and desires of others. *Disgusting.*

He casually lofted a gleaming quarter a foot or so into the air. It fell in a lazy arc back into his palm. He knew it was tails again without needing to look at it. He heard the Else murmuring in his ear just as clearly as he felt the ridges of the eagle under his thumb.

At that same moment, a handsome man in a sharp, grey Armani suit brushed up against Zorin's arm as he made an attempt to pass against the onslaught of Non crowding them on all sides. The man shot him a quick, unapologetic glance after the bump. Zorin made eye contact over the frame of his sunglasses. Exhilaration passed through him. Another victim had been chosen.

Zorin fell in behind him and slowed, allowing a few ants to fall into the gap between them. He kept the man in sight, and followed. After a moment, Armani veered off toward the curb and stopped at a coffee cart near the corner of 2nd Avenue and 6th Street. Zorin got in line behind him and took the opportunity to commit everything about him to memory, down to the very smallest of details.

He was probably in his early-fifties, with salt and pepper hair. He was about 6'2 and looked to be in good shape—a physical challenge, perhaps. He set a high-end, Italian leather laptop bag worth an easy grand on the sidewalk in front of him while he reached inside his sport coat—wealthy. His Gucci shoes were polished to a high shine— wealthy and meticulous. He had a small scab just underneath his jaw line, probably courtesy of a morning shave—not *too* meticulous. A quick glimmer of sunlight reflected off of his left hand as he handed the girl a crisp twenty—married. A gold Rolex peeked out from underneath his right sleeve when he took a quick sip from the steaming cup she handed him—wealthy and left-handed.

Zorin got himself a small coffee, but kept his target in sight as he crossed 2nd Avenue amid a small crowd and headed toward U.S. Bank Plaza. He closed to within about fifteen feet just as the man chose a door. Zorin dropped the coffee cup into a garbage can just outside the entrance and slipped his wallet from the back pocket of his slacks.

A pretty blonde at the information desk greeted Armani with a smile and a few words as he crossed to the elevator bank on the east side of the atrium.

Zorin timed it so he arrived at the desk just as the elevator doors slipped shut.

"May I help you, sir?" the receptionist asked with a smile as he approached.

"I hope so, miss." He slid his sunglasses off and gave her his very best rakish grin. "The gentleman that just got onto that elevator over there—about fifty, graying hair, grey suit, very distinguished looking? I think he may have dropped this." Zorin held up his own wallet. "I was hoping to compare his name to the ID to be sure it was his before I have to get in to work myself."

"Oh, that was Mr. Wainwright. Scott Wainwright. With Ernst and Young on the fourteenth floor," she said. "If you'd like, I can have it taken up to him."

Zorin made a show of flipping the wallet open and pretended to check the driver's license. He frowned. "Damn. Not my guy after all. Oh well, I appreciate your help, anyway."

"Sure, I hope you find him."

"I'll make sure it gets back to the owner. Thanks again." He tipped her a wink, dropped the wallet into his jacket pocket and headed back out the way he came. When he was outside again, he slipped the shades back on and shook his head, amused, as always, at how painfully simple people made his work.

NINE

Brooklyn Center, Minnesota
Tuesday, July 26 2016 2:49 PM

Nick was preoccupied but tried not to show it. His mind kept slipping back to Jim's videos and images. Fortunately, his boss wasn't quite as adept at reading people as he was.

"Nice work yesterday," Quentin said. "That's one fewer piece of shit child rapists and murderers that we have to worry about."

"Wasn't just me, but I'll take it no matter how we got it."

"Bullshit, you and I both know that dipshit Hicks couldn't find his dick if it was in his goddamn hand." Nick knew that Quentin and the lead detective from the MPD had locked horns a number of times in the past.

Arrogant prick though he was, it was hard to be pissed at a guy that he'd walked into hell with the day before. "He said he'd call us next time. Maybe he's grown up a little."

"Right," Quentin scoffed. "I'll believe that when I see it."

"That's what I told him. You'll have my report by the end of the day."

"Good. You ready for Quantico?"

"Piece of cake," Nick said with more confidence than he felt.

"You can bet O'Neill will be watching," Quentin said, referring to the Executive Assistant Director. Beyond his investigative duties with the Minneapolis Bureau, Nick served as liaison for the National Center for the analysis of Violent Crime (or NCAVC), which required him to report to the EAD on matters of national importance.

Though he'd been surrounded by law enforcement his entire life, Nick had a hard time convincing himself that O'Neill didn't make him nervous. The man was as sharp as anyone Nick had ever met, and he had a storied history with the FBI that was decidedly badass. It didn't help that he held Nick's future with the Bureau in his hands.

Quentin wasn't blind enough to miss his hesitation. "Don't sweat it. You're his golden boy. ViCAD is your baby, and closing the Garbage Man case won't hurt. You'll do fine. Besides, I've taught you everything I know."

"That's what I'm afraid of."

Quentin flipped him off. "Get out of here, smartass. Go write my report."

"What do you think?" Jim asked. His face hovered on Nick's monitor.

Nick *thought* his friend looked tired and suddenly old. Gray was creeping into the dark hair around his temples, and his eyes were dark-rimmed and haunted. "I can't say for sure yet. But I see why you're skeptical."

"What about the quarters? That's a goddamn signature."

"Maybe. But there's no way to know where they were before the girl got there and fucked up the scene, so it's hard to say for sure. I only saw three of them in the video. Where was the fourth?"

"Underneath the fridge door."

"Any prints on them?"

"Nope. Some blood, but otherwise clean as a whistle."

"Hmm. If they'd come from your vic's purse, there'd almost certainly be some latent partials on them. What'd your ME say?"

Jim huffed out a harsh breath. "Both carotids severed. She was damn near beheaded. Arterial spray on both sides of the kitchen. But get this—she was drowning while she bled out, Nick. There was blood in her stomach and lungs. There are three spots of high-velocity spatter that were consistent with her trying to expel it by coughing."

"If both carotids were severed, she almost certainly would have bled to death before she drowned."

"That's exactly what the doc said. But he also told me there was more than enough blood in her lungs to call it a drowning. Said it was the first time he'd ever listed multiple CODs. He couldn't determine a primary cause."

Nick pushed back in his desk chair and rubbed at his temples with his eyes closed. He tried to visualize how such a thing would be possible. "If your vic was coughing up blood and it was expelled from her mouth, her trachea had to be somewhat intact. Otherwise, it would have just been propelled straight upward as her diaphragm was in spasm." Nick opened his eyes and frowned as he came to the only possible conclusion. "He held her head in place, so the blood could pour down her throat and severed windpipe. He wanted her to experience the sensation of drowning. That was important to him."

"Jesus fucking Christ. That sound like a burglary to you?"

Nick absently slipped off his wedding ring. He began to turn it over his knuckles as if it were a coin. An old habit he'd picked up when he quit smoking that gave him something to do with his hands besides hold a butt. "If it was, there's almost certainly a personal element. What did your M.E. say about the knife?"

On the monitor, Jim upended a can of Diet Dr. Pepper. His Adam's apple bobbed three times in quick succession. "Seven-inch Santoku. Positive for the vic's DNA, but he can't be sure that it's the murder weapon. He said the blade isn't entirely consistent with the wound, and he'd have expected to find more tissue on it. More blood on the handle."

Weird. "Entry?" Nick watched his ring glint and gleam as he turned it back and forth over the back of his hand. It was almost hypnotic.

"Two main points, front and rear door. Neither forced. There's an alarm pad at the front door. Deactivated just before 4:30 AM. ADT said that's normal. But they did say that it was disarmed and then immediately rearmed about eleven-thirty. We assume that's when Lindsay snuck out. The panic alarm was tripped at 10:16 AM. That would have been when she got back home. I was there ten minutes later and her car was still warm."

"CSU?" Nick asked.

"Not a goddamn thing. No prints, fibers, hairs. No blood other than the vic's. They think they isolated a depression in the backyard and estimated it at size 11. Nothing castable. It's been hot as hell here, so the grass was mostly dead and rigid."

"You ping her cell?"

"Yep. Nothing."

"I'm guessing the girl's father isn't in the picture?"

"In the wind. We're trying to track him down."

Nick frowned. If anything, it was the absence of evidence and the apparently intentional misdirection that was bothering him. It was overly elaborate for a burglary or home invasion.

He stopped the ring's momentum, and spread his fingers. It dropped onto his desk with a soft ping. He slipped it back on the proper finger and returned his attention to the monitor. "How are you doing? You all right?"

"Fuck no," Harris said through a long sigh. He dropped his elbows onto his desk and laced his hands behind his neck. "You know how if you stare at a bright light then close your eyes, you can still see it? That afterburn?"

"Sure. Of course."

"Every goddamn night since, when I close my eyes I see that kitchen. The blood pools, the spatter, the paw prints. And the paw prints are the worst somehow. I can't say why. But it's like it's all seared onto the back of my eyelids. And when they took Lindsay away… My God, Nick, I've never heard a human being make a sound like that. I could still hear her shrieking outside as they were loading her into the bus. I hear it every time I wake up. It's like I'm fucking surrounded. I can't escape it."

"I know this doesn't help, but it gets better."

"I think that's actually worse somehow."

"I know, but it does. If it didn't, there's no way we could keep doing this without losing our shit. How *is* the girl? Lindsay? She still in the hospital?"

"Yep. No change."

Nick shook his head. "Jesus. Poor kid." Nick thought again of pulling Amber out of the Garbage Man's basement the day before. He wasn't convinced that it was always better to survive such nightmares.

"Yeah."

Nick heard the pain in Harris's voice, and he wished there was something more he could do for him. "You talk to your department shrink?"

Harris grunted. "Fuck that. I don't need anyone else in my head."

It was the response Nick expected. Cops were notorious for holding onto their demons with both hands, and Jim was no different. He changed the subject. "I'm guessing you still haven't run this through ViCAP," he said, referring to the Violent Criminal Apprehension Program database.

"Not yet. An official inquiry will probably get my ass into hot water. Chief has his eye on a political seat. He wants the case closed and swept under the rug A-sap."

"I've got orientation on Monday for ViCAD in Quantico. I'll run this past one of our analysts. We'll see if anything pops. If it does, then you can key it, knowing you're going to find a link."

"That'd be excellent. I need to be able to give that girl some answers. Some kind of closure."

"I get it, Jim." He remembered Amber quaking in his arms. "Trust me, I do."

Nick tried to transcribe the endless minutiae of the past several weeks into the digital form on his monitor, but he instead found himself scrolling through Jim's images again. He kept returning to the close-ups of the Minnesota statehoods. He chewed at the inside of his cheek, something he did when he was deep in thought or uncomfortable. Right now he was both.

The coins were newer, the blood brighter, but it didn't matter. His mind had already made the inevitable leap back in time.

Those shitty blue Whitman folders. The ones with the coin-sized cutouts. He remembered how it hurt his thumb to force the coins into them. He also remembered how he and his dad would hoot like fools and high-five when they found a date or mint that they didn't already have. It was something only the two of them had shared.

Not long after Richard Keegan was murdered during a traffic stop gone horribly wrong, his personal effects had been returned to Nick and his mother. Among them were four quarters, stained with his father's blood. He'd needed every one of them for his folder. Without understanding exactly why, he'd carefully pushed them into their respective places without cleaning them off. After, anytime he wanted to feel close to his dad, he'd flip open that cheap cardboard folder and stare at them. Once in a while, when he couldn't talk to his mother, he'd talk to the quarters instead.

He'd even taken the folder with him to college. It sat for more than two years on a crummy Ikea desk in his dorm room, where Nick spent countless hours in pursuit of his law enforcement and psych degrees. In a way, his father had been right beside him while Nick followed in his footsteps.

Until it disappeared during a wild all-night rager.

TEN

Minneapolis, Minnesota

Wednesday, July 27 2016 7:03 PM

Nick liked Mindy Peterson well enough. She was endearing in a not-quite-obnoxious way, blonde and pretty with angular features very similar to Connie's, and the same hazel eyes. She was every bit as smart as her sister too, at least as far as IQ went, but she had the emotional intelligence of a grapefruit. She never had a problem picking up men; she was always dating someone new. The problem was the kind of men she was attracted to—overbearing, manipulative, controlling assholes who would show their true colors after a few months. She'd escape one bad relationship, only to jump right into the next. One of these days, she was probably going to get the shit kicked out of her by one of these abusive pricks.

This guy was no exception. He acted the part well enough, but his smug confidence was off-putting and he was handsy in a way that Nick recognized as a sign of possessiveness and dominance. He only touched Mindy when he perceived someone was looking at her, then he'd put a hand over hers, or slide a little closer and slip an arm around her. She was his prize.

At least dinner was good. Fogo de Chao was one of Nick's favorites, and he looked forward to the meat coma that was sure to follow the meal. Connie rested an easy hand on his thigh under the table and led the conversation like a masterful musical conductor. "What do you do? Do you have family here in Minnesota? How did you two meet?"

"What do *you* do?" The guy asked him.

Nick smiled. He rarely shared what he did with people, but telling jackoffs like this gave him a little secret thrill.

"Law enforcement," he said and took a bite of tender, fire-seared rib eye. Connie gave his leg a little squeeze under the table. *Behave.*

"Yeah? I've got a buddy who's a cop. Where at?"

"The FBI. I'm a forensic criminologist."

"Cool. What's that exactly?"

Nick grinned. "I catch bad guys by analyzing and anticipating their behavior."

Nick was the only one at the table who noticed Mindy's date blanch slightly, as it dawned on him that he was probably under a microscope. He also let go of Mindy's hand.

Connie jumped in and changed the subject. "Min, how's Mork?"

"He's such a sweetie. I just wish I could get his barking under control. He's getting worse."

Something flitted around the edges Nick's mind. He narrowed his eyes and tried to pluck it from obscurity.

Douchebag had regained a bit of his composure. "Little shit still barks at me like he's Cujo whenever I come over."

"Son of a bitch," Nick muttered under his breath. It was so obvious he was pissed at himself for not catching it sooner.

"What, honey?" Connie said.

"Excuse me, I need to make a few phone calls." He pushed back from the table and stood.

He kissed his wife on the cheek, trying to ignore the set of her jaw and the flush that had risen in her cheeks.

He leaned over and kissed Mindy on the cheek as well. "Dump him," he whispered.

"Harris."

"Any luck finding the ex-husband?" Nick asked him.

"Not yet. Where'd that come from all of a sudden?"

"The dog. He went nuts when you went into the house. He should have alerted Helen to an intruder. She should have armed herself somehow, or had her phone ready to call the police, or made a beeline for the panic button on the alarm—anything. All indications were that she'd been surprised by her attacker, and that doesn't make sense unless the dog didn't bark at all. That means the dog was familiar with Helen's killer. If it wasn't the ex-husband, it was someone who'd been around enough to befriend him."

"Shit. I'll put more people on it."

"All the extra noise at the scene would make sense if someone was trying to hide the fact that the murder was personal."

"Yeah, it would. Be great if I could just ask Lindsay. And if it's not someone close to the family—"

"Then it's someone who spent some time stalking her. I'm calling one of our BAU analysts to see if she can expedite this for me. I should know something on my end in a few days. I'll let you know. Hang tight."

The drive home was painful. Connie hadn't said a word to him since they'd left downtown, and when he glanced her way, he thought there was a little too much reflection from the passing streetlights in her eyes.

"Mindy's date was a dick," he said.

She said nothing and stared straight ahead.

After another minute of the silent treatment, he couldn't take it any more. "I'm sorry, Con. Something just hit me. It couldn't wait."

She didn't answer, and pretended to check her phone for messages.

"I know you're pissed. I don't blame you. But this stuff is life and death. Sometimes minutes matter."

He saw her shoulders rise as she took a deep breath. Then she sighed and relented. "I know. It's just hard for me sometimes. You're *always* preoccupied. There's always something going on in your brain that has nothing to do with me. Is this how it's going to be when the baby comes?"

For the second time in as many days, Nick thought about his dad—somehow, *he'd* managed to be both a good father and cop. Could he hope to do the same? As an FBI agent, the stakes were often much higher for Nick, and the idea of bringing a kid into the world knowing the true depth of the darkness in the shadows scared him. How could he possibly strike a balance between protecting a little life while trying to hunt those that would take it without remorse or hesitation?

It was Nick's turn to sigh. "I don't know, Con." After several more seconds of silence, he added: "I hope not."

Nick relegated himself to the couch for the night.

ELEVEN

It didn't matter how late it was. Nick was almost always awake and waiting for him. Tonight was no exception. Nick heard the footsteps approaching, too heavy to be Mom's. It was dark in his room, but the glow of Nick's eyes in the light from the hallway always gave him away. He sat up expectantly.

"Hey, buddy," Dad whispered. "You sleeping in here?" He pretended to fumble blindly around the room until he "tripped" onto the bed. This routine led to a bout of tickling that left Nick breathless with laughter.

"Okay, okay. I'm awake!" Nick said gasping.

When Dad finally let up, and he got over his giggles, Nick exhaled a huge satisfied gasp. He asked, "How'd it go today?"

"Ooooh, today was very exciting. A few of the guys from the drug team called for backup, and Burt and I got into a foot chase with a suspect."

"No way!" Nick said.

"Yes way! The guy was quick too. He ran like a cheetah. Burt got winded after about a quarter mile, so I signaled for him to cut across

a few yards. Marty and Frank are pretty fast, so the three of us kept on running after the guy, figuring he'd tire out eventually."

"Did he?" Nick whispered.

"Well, not exactly." Dad laughed. "He tried to get sly and ducked between some houses, probably trying to find someplace to hide, ya' know?"

Nick nodded, rapt.

"The guy looked back to see where we were and ran smack into Burt who was standing on the corner with his hands on his knees trying to catch his breath. We heard this big 'Ooof!' from up ahead then Burt was yelling, 'Don't move, scumbag!' The two of them were all tangled up on the ground. They wrestled for a minute, but this guy was no match for Burt. Once he got an arm behind the guy's back it was all over. Burt had himself a pretty good bloody nose though."

"Cool!"

"It was kinda cool, bud. Better than a day of paperwork, that's for sure." Dad ruffled Nick's hair. "How was your day?"

Nick shrugged. "School. You know. Boring."

"Are you still bored with it because it's too easy for you?"

Nick shrugged again. "I guess. Most of it's pretty easy. Except math. I hate math. We're working on multiplication tables, and that's just a bunch of memorization. But when am I ever going to use that stuff anyway?"

"You'd be surprised. And you're still growing up. What if you get a job as an accountant or an architect or a construction worker? Math is super important in those jobs."

Nick shook his head. "I'm gonna be a cop. Like you. You know that."

"You still want to be a police officer, huh?"

Nick nodded. "It sounds like fun."

"Well, it has its moments, but it's very serious work too, kiddo. You have to be very careful and pay attention to everything around you all the time. There's tons of paperwork. And math.*"*

"Nuh-uh."

"Uh-huh," Dad mimicked and poked Nick in the chest softly. "The good news is that you have plenty of time to learn it, and plenty of time to decide what you want to be. You don't have to know that yet."

"But I do know. I want to do what you do. I want to catch bad guys."

The light from the hall illuminated his father's nod. "You can be anything you want if you work hard for it, Nick. But it's not all about catching bad guys though either. It's about protecting innocent people. It's about teaching kids about how bad things like gangs and drugs and violence hurts the people around them. Sometimes, we even save lives. We do lots of stuff."

"Will you take me to shoot soon, Dad?"

"Soon, son. That's a really big responsibility. The biggest. In a few years, I think you'll be ready, and I promise I will take you if you still want to go then, okay?"

Nick nodded sullenly, then thought of something. "Why didn't you just shoot that guy today, Dad? That would have been way easier, right?"

Dad stretched his legs out on the small bed next to him and looped an arm around his shoulders.

"Do you know that I've only drawn my gun on the job one time— ever?"

Nick shook his head.

Dad nodded. "It's true. And I've only fired it to practice. You should only pull your weapon if your own life or someone else's is in immediate danger. It's not like a cartoon, you know? If you shoot someone in the head or chest, they're probably going to die, and killing somebody changes you forever, even if it's an accident. So, unless I'm trying to save you, me, your mom, or someone else, my gun will always stay holstered."

"Why does it change you?"

"That's a really good question, and one I'm not sure if I can answer right. But I think it's because there are some things that hurt good people inside. Like stealing, right?"

Nick nodded, remembering a particularly unfortunate incident at a 7-11 the previous summer.

Dad thought for a minute. "You felt pretty bad for taking those fireballs—guilty and ashamed?"

"Yeah," Nick said, both his voice and head dropping low.

"Well, stealing someone's life is one of the most serious things there is. Something like that can make a good person feel guilty and ashamed forever. It makes them sick inside. And they never forget it."

"What about a bad person?"

Dad smiled and gave him another poke. "You don't have to worry about bad people, right now. That's my job."

"Richard, your dinner's reheated," Mom called from the hallway.

"Thanks, babe. I'll be there in just a minute."

Her silhouette disappeared from the doorway.

"The only thing you need to remember Nicky, is that people— even people who do bad things—always do them for a reason. Their reasons may seem crazy to us, but to them they make perfect sense. Sometimes people hurt so much they get broken inside, and that makes them all confused and backwards. They don't feel bad for doing bad things, and sometimes doing them even makes them feel

better. They may not think like you and me, but they're still people. Does that make sense?"

Nick shook his head.

"It will someday. But for now, it's way past your bedtime. You've got school tomorrow, and my dinner's getting cold." He kissed Nick on the forehead. "Now get some sleep."

Nick wriggled himself back under the covers and lay down again. "Love you, Dad."

"I love you too, buddy."

TWELVE

Stafford, Virginia
Monday, August 1 2016 7:23 AM

Nick parked his loaner in front of the north building of the Aquia Commerce Center in Stafford. The two non-descript brick buildings were situated four miles southeast of the sprawling FBI Academy campus on Quantico Marine Corps Base and housed the Bureau's Behavioral Analysis Units, the ViCAP analysis team, and the Critical Incident Response Group.

Nick managed to get through security in a record-setting nine minutes while they verified his Minnesota credentials then made his way upstairs to BAU.

He knocked on the frame of an open office door, grinning from ear to ear.

Valerie Shianco looked up from the stacks of documents and case files covering her desk. Only a black coffee mug with the DOJ seal peeked out of the mess like a solitary lifeboat floating in an exhausting sea of tedium and ugliness.

"Keegs!" she squealed, and rose to give him a hug, knocking a folder off the desk on the way. She ignored it and reached her ample arms out for him. "How are you, hon?"

"I'm good," he said, giving her an affectionate squeeze. "How 'bout you gorgeous?"

She smacked his arm. Her smile made her eyes crinkle and sparkle. Valerie was in her late-fifties and had been with the Bureau for the better part of thirty years. She and Nick had formed an unlikely and unbreakable friendship when he was in the Academy and working a subsequent organized crime stint at FBI Headquarters in D.C.

"You headshrinkers always know how to flatter a lady. I can't believe a damn word you say." She looked Nick up and down, like a proud mother. The dichotomy between Valerie and his mother was painfully apparent. "You look real good, sugar." She nodded. "Real good. The field and that pretty wife of yours must agree with you."

It wasn't lost on him that she'd avoided answering his question.

"C'mere, sit, sit!" She brought him to a chair, took a stack of folders off of the seat and tossed them onto the mess on the desk. "It's been what? Three years now?"

"About that, yeah." Nick slid the chair around so he could sit next to her. He laughed aloud when he saw her computer monitor stashed in the chair well. He picked up the folder on the floor and pointed it toward the discarded monitor. "You do realize all of this is on there?"

Valerie waved at her desk dismissively. He set the file down atop a stack with a smirk.

"This is what you might call organized chaos, smartass. I have a system." She tapped her temple and sat. Her chair protested with a shriek. "I can find any file on this desk a damn sight faster than any on that computer. How d'ya think I've kept my job all this time?"

Nick shrugged. "I always thought you had something juicy on the EAD."

She smacked him on the knee, and he laughed again.

"Oh, I've missed you, Val."

"And I've missed you, darlin. How's Minnesota?"

Nick raised an eyebrow, leaned in to her and whispered, "It took three winters for my nuts to crawl far enough out of my abdomen to stop shooting blanks."

Valerie was in mid-snicker when she got it. She emitted another high-pitched squeal that sent her into a coughing fit. She held up a finger while she tried to clear her lungs.

"Jesus, Shianco. You should really lay off the Camels. Shit'll kill you."

She switched the finger she was holding up to him as she finished hacking. Nick laughed again.

"Connie's pregnant?" she asked when she could finally breathe again.

Nick smiled, but it felt forced. He knew it was a weak attempt. "I haven't told anyone else at work yet."

"And why the hell not?"

"I'm not entirely sure I'm ready for this."

"Well you'd better goddamn get ready. Why on earth wouldn't you be? You'll be a great father."

"I don't know about that. How would you have liked for your parents to know damn near everything you were thinking?"

Valerie had a good sarcastic laugh at that. "Trust me, hon, it doesn't work that way with your own kids. You might be able to get inside the twisted brains of the most horrific psychopaths, but when it comes to a hormonal teenager? That shit can't be profiled. Still, you'll be just fine."

"I hope you're right. It's not like I had the benefit of a *normal* upbringing."

"No such thing, sugar," she drawled.

After a few seconds of hesitation, Nick gave voice to the one fear he couldn't shake. "I can't turn it off, Val," he said and motioned toward the files on her desk.

"Now *that* I understand." She smiled ruefully. "We don't have the luxury of ignoring what's out there. But Nicky, don't let this become your everything. There's gotta be more to life than just these goddamn files. They'll eat you and anything you care about alive, otherwise."

Nick knew her thoughts were wandering into dark territory. He didn't really feel any better, but for her sake he changed the subject.

"You have a chance to run a query on the statehoods?"

"I did. First, tell me where that came from."

"Bakersfield. My old college roommate, a lieutenant in the BPD called me off-book about a case he caught early last week. His superiors are calling it a home invasion, but he wasn't convinced. I took a look at it, and neither was I. Did you come up with anything?"

"Your class is at nine, right?" she asked.

Nick nodded.

"Let's go outside then. I need a smoke to get into this."

Valerie grabbed three folders from the madness on her desk and led him downstairs and out the back exit. The two walked to a series of benches overlooking a small pond that abutted the north wall of Commerce 1. A pair of wood ducks rippled the surface of the water as they preened. A thin barricade of trees muffled the sound of passing traffic on I-95 not even fifty yards away.

"I can't exactly say I miss this place," Nick said, recalling the nearly six months of grueling and intensive training he'd endured just a quick jog from where they were sitting. "But it sure feels like coming home."

Valerie lit her cigarette, pulled a long drag and exhaled.

Nick leaned into the cloud surrounding her and breathed deep.

She noticed and grinned. "Never goes away completely does it?"

"No, it really doesn't," he said, savoring the sharp, familiar smell and even the slight sting in his eyes. A full decade hadn't completely erased the occasional pangs.

"Okay," she began. "I got four hits on my initial query on the statehoods. I also ran a keyword search for the word 'quarter' pre-2009, which is when Treasury finished minting the statehoods. That netted me another twenty or so files. Most I was able to eliminate right away. These three," she put a hand on the stack sitting on her lap, "looked more promising. Victimology, geo, and M.O. are all *completely* different in each of the cases—it's a damn good thing I didn't add any other parameters, or they would never have flagged." She opened one of the folders and handed it to Nick.

He scanned the file while she recited the bullet points from memory.

"Amanda Taylor. March 2014. Albany, Georgia. White female, dark hair, twenty-two years old, in college. Big girl. 180 pounds, 5'8. She was found in her apartment less than a mile from the campus. She'd ingested root of water hemlock, of all things—'Cicuta Douglasii.' Very nasty. Fatal in even the smallest quantities. Her stomach contents indicated she'd consumed quite a lot of it as part of a meal of asparagus and parsnip pasta. There were two finished plates on the dining room table. Trace of the toxin was found on only one of them."

Nick looked up from the file and tilted his face to the sky. For a second he allowed himself to just enjoy the mild warmth of the morning sun and a kiss of breeze that whispered a constant sigh through the leaves. One of the wood ducks searched underwater for something, its ass pointed skyward. When it righted itself, it gave a "maaaaack" to its mate, and they flew off toward the highway.

"It's interesting to note," Valerie continued, "that hemlock root smells a lot like parsnip, so any unusual odors would have been masked by the meal. She died horribly. The seizures were so violent she broke her neck. I had to look that up; I didn't believe it was possible. Turns out it is, but requires convulsions of tremendous force. Her spinal cord was severed at the C-3 vertebrae, and she suffocated. I can't even imagine the agony. Four quarters were found at the scene, one in each palm and covering her eyelids. All of them were Pennsylvania statehoods. No transfer, no trace, no prints."

Nick flashed back to the video of the Lyman scene and the quarter in her hand. He was willing to bet the other coins had been positioned similarly, but had been displaced when the daughter moved the body. It was what Nick had expected, but he frowned nonetheless. "That's him. Did either of the other two cases files you found come out of PA?"

"No."

"So the states change, but we still don't know what it is this unsub is trying to communicate to us. Where he's been or where he's going, maybe?"

Valerie shrugged. "That'd be my guess, but there are significant time gaps between each of these cases. I doubt we have anything consecutive to make that determination yet." She handed him the second folder. "I also have a case from October of '09 that matches the signature. The quarters were standard eagles, but found in the palms and over the eyes just like the girl. Sergio Diaz Peña. Hispanic male, 62 years old, 5'7, 135 pounds. Corpus Christi, Texas. Blunt force."

Nick raised his eyebrows at her.

Valerie nodded, and dropped her smoke into a receptacle next to their bench.

"He died from internal injuries sustained by a savage beating that the coroner said must have gone on for many hours—if not *days*—based on the extent and coloration of bruising. He had seventy-two broken bones from fingers to ribs and his skull was shattered along the orbital bone. That one blinded him in one eye. They found traces of vitreous humor on his right cheek from when the eyeball burst. And a collapsed lung."

Nick winced.

"The coroner said he'd never seen a body with so much physical trauma. The murder weapon was never found, but one of the perimortem bruise patterns on his chest was 'roundish' and had circular shaped voids about an inch in diameter. They think it was made by a bowling ball."

"God damn." That was an MO Nick hadn't seen before.

"Oh, just wait." She held up the third folder, and Nick took it from her. "Darien Jackson. African-American male, 5'10, 210 pounds. 2013. Baltimore. They found him in an abandoned warehouse in early February, but they're reasonably sure he died in January sometime. He was well preserved because of cold temps. He was found on a stainless steel hospital style table in the *precise* center of a monstrous room. Some astute detective took the measurements."

"That's interesting." Any time an unsub took the time to demonstrate such a measure of meticulousness, it suggested something of importance.

Valerie nodded her agreement. "Sharp force trauma this time. Over and over and over. In all they found *exactly* one thousand incisions. Literally, death by a thousand cuts."

"Not possible," Nick interjected. "He'd have died from shock or bled to death long before that."

Valerie held up a finger and lit another Camel. "Not so fast, hotshot," she said, exhaling another white cloud. "He was bled slowly over a period of *days*. And, many of the wounds were cauterized to prevent him from bleeding out. He was lying in solidified blood over an inch deep—almost three gallons worth. Too much for a man his size, so the M.E. did some deep diving and ran several panels on the blood. It was in two distinct layers and was, in fact, *all* Jackson's. The lower levels showed traces of a paralytic called Pancuronium Bromide. He'd have been totally immobilized, but able to feel every cut and cauterization. Like your worst possible fucking nightmare. The upper layer was anemic and had high levels of adrenaline in it. Considerably more than the body is capable of producing on its own."

"Hold it," Nick said, trying to access his memory of physiology. "So they think, what, that he was bled, then allowed to recuperate, then bled again? That's how he ended up in three gallons of his own blood?"

"Not only. The M.E. concluded that he probably *did* die on that table. Maybe more than once. There were signs that he'd been paddle shocked with a defibrillator to bring him out of V-Tach. Conductive gel on the chest and the evidence of adrenaline in the blood. Plus there was an obvious difference in the blood layers. The lower was shallower and had dried long before the other. They could see the striations from the side when the victim was *peeled* from the table."

Nick wrinkled his nose.

"Their words, not mine. And there's more."

He sighed. "Because that's not enough?"

"COD *was*, believe it or not, exsanguination. His femoral artery was severed clean and he then bled out quickly. They think that was forty-eight to seventy-two hours after the first series of cuts were made. They also believe that a tilt feature on the table was used to even out the blood like cake batter in a pan. Once they got Jackson off the table, and the M.E. had taken his samples, they decided to try to melt away the blood from the top down with hot water. When they got to the lower layer of blood they found the statehoods. All of them."

"You mean all four? They were in the blood and not in the palms and over the eyes?"

"No, I mean *all* of them. All fifty states. Twenty-five on either side of the body, about two inches apart, running the entire length of the table, all tails side up, in order of statehood. He had coins in his palms and over his eyes too. Nevada. Obviously, we don't have a similar case file for them either. But if we're talking about Vegas, they're notorious for skipping ViCAP."

Nick was silent, his throat dry. A breeze blew mist from the fountain onto his neck and face. He shivered.

"Anyway, those copies are for you. Have your boy in Bakersfield key his case file, and I'll add it to the pile and forward the bunch to the EAD. I'll let him know it was your find. Since the Cali quarters were Minnesota statehoods, maybe he'll let you run the case."

Taking the lead on a serial case like this was rare. And just about as big as it got in the Bureau.

Valerie stood with a groan and a wheeze. She put a hand briefly on Nick's shoulder and started to walk back toward the door.

"Hey, dinner tomorrow night?" Nick called after her. "Before I have to head back home?

"I wouldn't miss it." She tapped her watch. "You've only got about thirty minutes before your orientation, sugar. You'd better get a move on. I'll sign you out with security." She dropped him a wink and headed back inside.

As he ran back to his car, Nick grabbed his Blackberry and shot a text to Harris.

THIRTEEN

Quantico, Virginia
Monday, August 1 2016 8:53 AM

Little had changed in the Academy building in the years since Nick was a student. He was reasonably sure some of the very same posters adorned the walls in classrooms that he passed, the fluorescents having faded many of the colors to a sickly yellow. He even recognized one or two of the instructors from his own Academy days, and Nick thought they too seemed faded somehow. They no longer shared the same bright-eyed enthusiasm and naivety of the students that roamed the halls, or the ferocity and intensity that he remembered from his training days. By now, the vast majority had been replaced with a newer, sleeker, and more digital breed of animal.

The auditorium was at capacity. Clustered together on the left near the front was a group that Nick immediately pegged as the Academy's NATs—New Agents in Training. He could identify them as much from their youthful eagerness and optimism as by the drab Bureau-issued garb they wore. At this stage of their training there were only about thirty NATs left—still twice the size of the graduating class of 2009 to which he belonged. Not all of them would make it, Nick knew.

The bulk of the remaining seats were filled either by law enforcement officers from local P.D.s—a handful of whom he recognized—or men and women who had the erect posture, bearing and attentiveness of military personnel.

A cameraman hovered in front of the riser fiddling with his equipment. Today's presentation would be broadcast to nearly ten thousand law enforcement agencies all across the country, and recorded for future use.

No pressure, Nick thought.

The cameraman shot him a thumbs-up.

"Good morning," he began and waited the second or two it took for the idle chatter to die down. "Welcome to the orientation for ViCAD. For those of you that don't already know me, my name is Nick Keegan."

An excited murmur ran through the cluster of recruits. Some of the cops looked around obliviously and whispered to people next to them. Nick saw a few headshakes and shoulders raise in shrugs. A few shushes went up as did a handful of fingers to lips. For his part, Nick was shocked and somewhat amused that his reputation still preceded him at the Academy.

"Before we begin, let me tell you a little about myself. I was born and raised in Florida, an only child. My dad was a cop—and my hero—so naturally that was all I ever wanted to be as a kid. I'm sure some of you in here can relate. I have a master's in Criminal Justice and a bachelor's in Psychology from UMD College Park. When I got out of school, I went back home and served with the Jacksonville Sheriff's Department for three years, then applied to be an agent.

Some of you know the drill—twenty-one weeks of push-ups, running, and firing ranges."

That got a laugh out of the NATs, who, Nick was certain, knew the drill. The average agent fired nearly 4,000 rounds during their time at the Academy and probably did twice as many push-ups.

"I spent two years at DC HQ working organized crime and am currently serving as Special Agent and primary NCAVC liaison at our Minneapolis Field Office.

"A few years back, I was asked to be part of a ViCAP task force that had nothing to do with solving a crime. Instead, we were tasked with finding ways to improve it. Over the last several months, we've been rolling out bits and pieces of the changes we came up with, but today marks the real beginning of the new system."

Nick scanned and profiled his audience. Many of the cops sat back in their chairs with their arms folded across their chests. Those were the hard sells, the ones that ViCAP had failed in the past. Most of the NATs were leaning forward in their chairs, totally engaged. The military vets were motionless and intent on his every word.

"The Violent Criminal Apprehension Program was created in 1985, though it was first conceived in 1956. An LA homicide detective named Pierce Brooks came up with the idea while investigating two similar cases. Brooks had to cull through newspaper clippings from all over the country at the library. It took him eighteen months to find what he was looking for. What he envisioned was a warehouse of data that could be more easily cross-referenced.

"A great idea in theory, but in practice what we got was a cumbersome pain in the ass. ViCRAP, I think many of you call it," he said with a smirk.

Many of the recruits turned to look at the LEOs around them accusingly. To them, this was blasphemy, Nick knew. Some of the police shifted uncomfortably in their seats, like children caught eating a booger.

Nick laughed. "It's okay, it's true. ViCAP is almost entirely worthless. I say 'almost' because just this morning it helped me link four separate cases to single serial offender. It *can* work, but it needs to work *a lot* better."

As he scanned the room, one of the NATs caught his eye. She had long red hair pulled back into a ponytail and was sitting ramrod straight with a look of concentration so intense he couldn't help but wonder what she was thinking. Nick guessed that she'd probably grown up in a military family, but beyond that he couldn't read her at all. He knew better than to try to tell himself that he was simply intrigued and had not singled her out only because she was gorgeous—he was a guy after all, and he well understood the defective psyche of the human male. She never made eye contact with him, but Nick was sure he saw a slight twitch at the corner of her mouth as he looked at her.

"ViCAP now houses stats for over 90,000 violent crimes, and more than 4000 LEAs have used it at one point or another. A blazing success, right?"

Most of the cadets looked impressed, the cops just looked pissed off. They already knew what the NATs did not.

"Anyone care to guess how many law enforcement agencies there are nationwide?"

"I bet I've personally talked to 4,000 different departments in my goddamn career," someone scoffed.

That elicited a burst of laughter from the LEOs in the room.

The stunning redhead that Nick had noted a few seconds before spoke up when the room quieted. "17,000, give or take," she said.

Nick smiled, but at the room, careful not to direct it at her exclusively. He stayed silent for a few seconds to let that sink in.

"17,000," he repeated. So less than a quarter of all available agencies have ever used ViCAP. And that doesn't tell us how many of those are using it regularly or just once before they abandon it. Every year, there are more than 100,000 cases of murder and forcible rape that should be entered into the database. That means that a system that has been around for more than thirty years now houses less than one year of real data. And that says nothing of the other 1.2 million lesser violent crimes that occur annually.

"And therein lies the problem. ViCAP only works if we feed it. You guys try to use it, it fails to give you good data, so you stop using it and thus there's nothing there for the next user to find. It's a self-perpetuating problem. We realized pretty quickly that data entry needed to be our primary focus.

"At the same time, we kept hearing about military vets returning home from the Middle East to find their regular jobs gone. A light bulb went off. A lot of those brave men and women had already seen the very worst humanity has to offer. Provided we could get the funding, we could employ many of them with temporary government positions where they'd have the opportunity to continue to serve their country.

"ViCADETs, please stand up." Nick said.

Roughly a hundred men and women rose. The cameraman panned the audience.

"This is but a small number of those that served honorably and have joined the program. All told, we've enlisted more than 15,000 across the country. Many are watching right now via live feed. Thank you all for your service, and welcome to the team." Nick led an applause that turned into a rousing minute-long ovation interspersed with whistles and "Ooh rahs!"

After everyone calmed, Nick continued. "As of today, ViCAP is no more. It will henceforth be known as ViCAD, the Violent Crime Analysis Database. And these men and women will be Data Entry Temps, thus ViCADETs." He tipped his head toward the back of the room. "You can take your seats.

"Technically, they will be federal employees working with their local law enforcement agencies. Their salaries will initially be taken from the cost savings of getting out of the Middle East. Their primary function will be to enter both open and cleared violent crime case files into ViCAD in reverse chronological order. This will assure we're putting the most emphasis on active or recent offenders.

"A lot of our soldiers already have some level of security clearance, and all have signed non-disclosure agreements stating that they will not discuss anything in the files with anyone outside of the law enforcement community. They have tactical and combat knowledge, and because they are," Nick made quotes in the air with his fingers, "feds, they can serve as consultants for your departments in virtually any way needed. The hope is that eventually some of them will take permanent positions as law enforcement officers, or Special Agents, or analysts, because God knows we're probably going to need them when we find out what's really happening out there."

A uniformed MPDC officer that Nick recognized said, "Some poor bastard at the NYPD is gonna be busier than a constipated mathematician trying to root it out with a pencil."

Laughter erupted again.

"Now there's a visual I could have lived without." Nick said through a chuckle of his own. "But you're right, captain; some stations will be much busier than others. We've asked for estimates on the number of files we'll be dealing with for each division, precinct, station and satellite. Temps were assigned to each accordingly. In some cases, it might take years to get all of the files keyed, even with a fairly good-sized team. But some of the smallest satellites might not need any more than a single person for a day or two, so we can shuttle files to them from larger jurisdictions.

"Over the next few hours, we're going to go over the new ViCAD questionnaire, and talk about how it's going to be integrated into your existing systems over the next several months." Nick smiled. "Once that's done, our documents will self-populate, which means you're only going to have to key your case files *once*."

A cheer exploded from the police in the room.

FOURTEEN

Minnetonka, Minnesota
Monday, August 1 2016 4:16 PM

Zorin waited until the door was nearly closed before he stepped out from behind the topiary and slammed his body into it. He felt it connect, and a satisfying "oof" came from the other side. As the door swung back open, he saw Scott Wainwright collapse to his knees and barely get a hand out in time to prevent a total faceplant. Mail skittered across the polished wood floor.

He stepped inside and closed the door behind him.

Scott Wainwright jerked around. "Who the hell are you? What are you doing in my house?" He started to rise, but after getting a good look at Zorin, seemed to think better of it. Instead he scooted back a bit and held out a hand. "Take anything you want. Anything. I won't report you."

Zorin sighed. This part was tedium. He leaned back against the door and folded his arms across his chest.

"I can make you a rich man," Wainwright said.

"I'm already rich, Scott. In *so* many ways."

A blank look of confusion passed swiftly across Wainwright's features. "There's a safe in my office." His voice trembled, and he looked terrified, but Zorin suspected it was partly manufactured. People like Wainwright weren't cowed quite so easily. He'd be running through the options in his head, debating between flight, negotiation, and fight.

"Of course there is. Would you care to share the combination with me, or shall we just get right to this afternoon's real entertainment?"

Wainwright recited a series of numbers without hesitation. A bit too eagerly, Zorin thought. It would almost certainly be a panic code that would sound a silent alarm. He wasn't born yesterday.

Zorin could see the wheels turning as Wainwright tried to come up with a play. There was none, but he didn't need to know that just yet.

"My family," Wainwright tried. "They'll be home any minute."

"No. They won't," Zorin said. "Your wife has a standing appointment at the spa for a facial and massage, and your daughter is at ballet practice. They won't return until after 7:30. We have plenty of time. About that safe? You were saying?"

"It's biometric. It requires thumbprint identification. I'll take you upstairs and we can open it."

Zorin sighed and pushed off the door. "How about you drop the act, Scott. You can't manipulate me." He despised Non who assumed they were of superior intellect. They were *always* wrong.

"I'm not. Really. I think there's more than $150,000 in cash, plus bearer bonds. It's yours. All of it. Unmarked. Untraceable."

Zorin lifted one eyebrow but said nothing, encouraging Wainwright to continue. He didn't need the money, but only a fool would pass up that kind of opportunity. He was no fool.

Zorin watched Wainwright fumble for a few seconds, then his eyes widened slightly. "I can get you more," he blurted. "We can set up an untraceable account in a non-extradition country, and I can transfer it to you. Maybe as much as a million. Just don't hurt me." He paused. "Or my family."

Zorin smirked. "You're a piece of work, Scott. Why exactly would I need to go to a non-extradition country if I don't have to worry about you turning me in? And your family is little more than an afterthought. If I had to guess, I'd say you're a high-functioning sociopath."

"I—"

"Enough," he said with enough authority that Wainwright shrunk back from him a bit more. "Here's what's going to happen. You're going to stand up slowly, face forward with your hands together behind your back, and walk slowly into the living room. I will follow. If you deviate… well, I don't suggest you deviate."

"Aren't we going upstairs?"

"In a manner of speaking, yes."

"What does—?"

"Move."

The investment banker got to his feet slowly. This was a critical moment. As long as Wainwright believed he still had a say in the ultimate outcome of events, he could be controlled until he was completely subdued. Hopeless men could be very dangerous. Scheming sociopaths out of options even more so.

Wainwright was apparently stupid—and arrogant—enough to think he had a handle on things, because he obeyed. As they crossed the threshold into the first living area—a huge room filled with light mocha-colored furnishings, Zorin slipped a large zip tie and a hypodermic from his pockets.

The thick white carpet sucked at his feet like spongy moss. High-backed chairs sported polished frames and thick cushions that matched the couch and two recliners perfectly. A Steinway piano sat in the far corner, varnished to an unusual caramel shade that blended with the other furniture. In the center of the room was a large marble coffee table shot through with streaks of beige, brown, tan and chocolate-toned specks. A floor to ceiling bay window with drawn fallow-colored drapes adorned the south wall, and a marble-mantled fireplace the east. The room smelled of cocoa.

Ridiculous, Zorin thought.

"Listen," Wainwright said. Before he could finish the word, Zorin cinched the zip tie around his wrists. A second later he sank the needle into Wainwright's right triceps.

"Hey! Ow! What—? Damn it, I told you I'd cooperate. This isn't necessary. And I can't use the fingerprint scanner with my hands like this. Untie me and we can still work this out."

Ever the salesman, Zorin thought, entertained by Wainwright's continued attempts to negotiate his way out of the situation. But he could see the cracks in the façade of Wainwright's bravado now. The pitch of his voice had risen, and there was a genuine waver in it. The muscles in his arms trembled, though he supposed that could be the Pancuronium too. It happened sometimes before the muscles stilled altogether.

He led Wainwright to the back corner of the marble table.

"Sit down on the floor."

"I'd rather thtand."

"What you want is irrelevant. You're going to sit. I suggest you do so under your own power. Otherwise, when your legs give out you might crack your head open on the table, and that just won't do, Scott."

Wainwright made his way awkwardly down to the floor. He tried to use an arm to support the process, but it collapsed beneath his weight and he tipped over sideways.

Zorin laughed and jerked him upright. He used a second zip-tie to strap his arm to the thick leg of the table facing the bay window.

"Whath hathening? The thafe." Wainwright's face was a mask of confusion, his eyes narrowed. He shook his head as if to clear it, but it wouldn't move like he expected it to. It tipped to and fro as the muscles in his neck failed him. Zorin thought he looked a bit like a shaken bobblehead.

Amused, Zorin watched him struggle to control his body for a moment. "Oh, yes. The safe. Of course." He knelt down behind Wainwright and pulled a knife from his belt. With a swift slice, snap, and twist he removed Wainwright's left thumb at the second joint with ease.

Wainwright's screams of pain didn't begin for a full second. Zorin ignored them and left him to bleed on the carpet while the Pancuronium did its work.

Zorin ascended the staircase to the richly appointed second floor. Everything had a Romanesque feel. Mock pillars appeared to suspend the high-arched ceiling of the main hallway. Artwork adorned the walls. By the time he found the office, Wainwright's screams had stopped. His diaphragm would now be incapable of forcing adequate air through the larynx to produce sound. He'd be able to draw enough air to breathe, but only just.

The office was monstrous, filled with dark oak bookcases and two large, matching desks adjoined to form an L-shape. Three flat screen monitors were angled to face the brown leather chair behind.

Zorin stepped behind the desk and looked at the bank of dark monitors and a wireless laser mouse sitting to the left of a large calendar blotter filled with a month's worth of doodles. He heard the soft whirring of fan motors cooling the computer in a cabinet under the desk. From this vantage point, he could see the entire room. The bookcases covered the entirety of the walls to his left and right and a fair portion of the wall behind him, separated only by a large, draped window. On either side of the door on the far wall were two large paintings with leather loveseats beneath them, and two more comfortable-looking leather armchairs sat at an angle in front of the desk.

It took him longer than anticipated to find it. A very slight height difference in one of the bookcases betrayed the casters underneath that allowed it to swing away from the wall. The safe was behind—a high-tech, high-end unit that would be impossible to crack without a code and fingerprint. Fortunately, he had both.

He set Wainwright's thumb on a shelf for now. He'd come back to it when his work downstairs was complete. If he were going to trigger an alarm, he'd want it to be the very last thing he did before leaving. Delivering Wainwright to the Else was the only thing that absolutely mattered.

The quarters had demanded suffocation. Easy enough, if boring. He needed a way to liven things up a bit. On the way downstairs, he noted a small panel embedded in the wall, and he smiled as it came to him.

It took Zorin a few minutes to find the hose in a utility closet downstairs and another to find the panel in the living room. Wainwright waited for him patiently, perfectly still but for a barely perceptible rise and fall of his chest. A small but lovely red pool bloomed like a rose from the thick white shag beneath his hand.

Zorin plugged the hose into the round outlet in the wall, and the vacuum hissed to life. He tested the suction on his wrist.

It left a most satisfying raised, purple circle on his skin.

FIFTEEN

Nick slipped the empty clip from his Bureau issued .40 caliber Glock 22. It was his "POW," or personally-owned weapon, but the one he was most comfortable with and the one he would draw first if shit ever hit the fan. Though requalification with his Bureau-issued .40 caliber Glock 22 was mandatory, he also needed to show proficiency with the 17 if he planned to carry it in the field. He'd just aced the round with it—a rare feat that earned him a place in the FBI's honorary elite firing group known as the "Possibles." Fewer than 2000 shooters in the Bureau's history had qualified on pistol with a perfect round.

"Nice shooting Keegan," the instructor said. "Don't see that every day."

Nick grinned and swiped an arm across his forehead. The morning was humid and still. It was going to be a scorcher. As he switched to the .40 cal, the inside of his bag lit up. Valerie had texted him.

Get over here right away when you're done. Big news.

Valerie wasn't the melodramatic type. To her "big news" could only mean one thing—another body.

Valerie's impatience had apparently gotten the better of her. When Nick finished up with the M16 and grabbed a towel from his duffel he saw her seated on the grass, ashing into a paper coffee cup about twenty yards back from the long gun range.

She waved at him, smoke drifting all around her in the still air like a shimmering, ghostly cloak.

"You really couldn't wait?" he asked.

"I'm on my lunch. I figured I would come and fetch you personally. O'Neill wants to see you." She nodded toward the range. "How'd you do?"

"I passed." He shed his ballistic vest and finished drying off. "What's so urgent?"

She took a manila folder from her lap and waved it in the air in front of her face like a fan. "Another case came through last night. Same signature."

Nick knelt down on the grass beside her and frowned. "I figured as much. Only dead people get you that worked up. Why does O'Neill want to see me?"

"Probably because you know what's happening here more than anyone else. And maybe because I told him I thought you should take point."

Nick's stomach flipped. He couldn't say no to something this big, even though he knew it would almost certainly cause more problems at home. "Thanks, Val."

"Don't let this swell that pretty head of yours, but you're damn good, Nick. ViCAD is brilliant, and will do more to advance the Bureau than anything in the last thirty years. Maybe ever. I've been around a long-ass time, and I've never seen a more promising agent come through."

Nick felt his neck and cheeks warm. He watched in silence as an ant crawled up and down a blade of grass next to his bag.

"I love you, Nicky. You're like the son I never screwed up. A second chance for me, maybe."

Nick reached over and touched her arm to let her know he felt the same. It was perhaps most ironic that this broken and screwed-up woman was more a mother to him than his own broken and screwed-up mother. Sometimes water really proved to be thicker than blood.

He stood and held out a hand to Valerie to help her up. "Well, I suppose we shouldn't keep the EAD waiting."

She let him pull her to her feet, wiped the grass off of her skirt and bent to grab the contaminated coffee cup from the grass. She gave him a sly look and held the folder out to him. "Did I mention this murder took place in your neck of the woods? Twenty miles west of Minneapolis."

"Son of a bitch. That could be the link to the statehoods. He's using them to tell us where he's going next. Where specifically?"

"Minnetonka. Rich guy. Let's get over to Commerce 2. I'll fill you in on the way."

They walked to the parking lot where Valerie loaded him into her Ford Fusion for the five-minute drive. He'd have to come back later for the loaner. He wanted to have as much information as possible before he met with O'Neill.

Valerie lit another Camel once she was settled in the car and rolled the window down.

"What were the statehoods?" Nick asked without consulting the folder. Valerie could just as easily give him what he needed in two minutes. It's what she did best.

"Minnesota. Again."

"So it would appear we're in for an extended visit. How nice."

"I've never seen anything quite like this unsub, Nicky, and I've seen lots. If you take this case, be careful."

"Tell me."

"Scott Wainwright. White male, mid-fifties. 6'2, 180. Married, with a nine-year-old daughter. The wife and girl were out when it happened. Witnesses corroborated their whereabouts. There is a pretty tight window for TOD, they put it at about 6:00 PM. Initial COD is suffocation; the M.E. identified petechial hemorrhaging on scene. He also found a needle mark in the back of Wainwright's arm. Full autopsy is underway as we speak."

Nick stayed quiet. He had questions, but knew Valerie well enough to know she'd probably get to them on her own.

"They found him strapped to the leg of a heavy marble table with plastic zip ties. His left thumb had been amputated. It was later used to open a biometric safe with a fingerprint pad in the vic's office. Blood pooling indicates the thumb was removed after he was secured to the table. Just like before, the unsub raided the wife's jewelry box but doesn't seem to have touched anything in the daughter's room. As I mentioned, they had serious bucks, so the daughter did have some valuable pieces, but the unsub ignored them. He saved the house safe for last. He used Wainwright's thumb and a six-digit panic code, designed to immediately alert the monitoring company. Police were dispatched in less than a minute, and on-scene in just over ten. There was no sign of the subject when they arrived. The wife said she believed there was a significant amount of bearer bonds in the safe and at least a hundred grand in cash."

Nick whistled. "So we now have a loaded unsub too. Spectacular."

They turned off of Jefferson Davis Highway and into the Aquia Commerce Center lot.

"This guy is smart, Nick. I've seen enough case files to know the difference. He killed Wainwright *before* he tried to open the safe. That was the last thing he did before he left."

Nick nodded. "Which means he knew or at least suspected that Wainwright had given him a panic code. It also tells me that he really didn't give a damn whether or not he got the money. What was important was the kill, not the payday. Otherwise, why not keep him alive long enough to make sure he could open the safe?"

"Who's got the case currently?" he asked her.

"A detective Nguyen is the primary and the one who keyed the case into ViCAD last night. I think there was a Morgan Bates listed in the file as well."

Nick smiled. "Oh, I know Chief Bates."

"What?"

"He's a damn colossus and swears like a sailor. Ex Spec-Ops. Scariest black man you'll ever meet until you get to know him. Total media whore and funny as hell. Can you put in a call to him and let him know I'd like to meet with Nguyen at the scene tomorrow, say 2:00? I'll need to see the M.E. ahead of that if possible. Any time in the morning is fine."

"Sure. I'll do that while you're in with the EAD."

"We still on for dinner tonight?"

"Wouldn't miss it, darlin'. You'd better get on in there."

As Nick headed for the stairs, he regulated his breathing and forced down his nerves. It wasn't just his imminent meeting with O'Neill that was weighing on him. He was starting to get a feel for the capabilities of this unsub. He had, thus far, completely controlled the scenes and predicted his victim's actions. He wasn't just stalking them. He was *profiling* them.

SIXTEEN

Terrence O'Neill wasn't where the buck stopped in the FBI, but he was certainly one of the final resting points. As leader of the venerated criminal branch, he was widely considered to be the third most highly ranked official in the Bureau. He was also known for a no-nonsense attitude that Nick appreciated. He was the kind of man who commanded respect, but also wanted straight shooters on his teams, even if that meant a challenge to his authority.

"Special Agent Keegan." The EAD stood to shake his hand. "Nice shooting today."

Nick figured he probably shouldn't be surprised, but found he couldn't help it. He checked his watch. "It's been less than an hour, sir."

O'Neill smiled shrewdly, a twinkle in his eye. "Yes, yes it has."

"I had a good day, thank you."

O'Neill motioned to a chair in front of his desk and returned to his own. His desk was immaculate. Only a computer monitor and keyboard, phone, and a thick, solitary folder sat on its surface. Nick assumed—correctly—that it was his personnel file.

"It's been a while."

"Yes, sir. Almost two years since we met to talk about the changes to ViCAP."

"Goddamn bureaucracy. Ask to take a shit, and it takes a month to get approval. I trust your orientation went well yesterday?"

"I think so. The NATs and ViCADETs are up to speed and the LEOs seemed excited about the changes. Getting their buy-in has always been the hard part."

"I suppose anything must be better than ViCRAP. Right, Agent?"

Nick flushed. "I apologize, sir."

O'Neill laughed. "No need, Keegan. We both know it's been called much worse. ViCAP needed this overhaul, and if you'd tried to bullshit a roomful of cops, you'd have lost them. Well done."

"Thank you, sir."

"How's Minneapolis?"

Nick recognized O'Neill's attempt to put him at ease. He was even surprised to discover that it was working. He had a feeling the EAD was once an exceptional interrogator.

"Cold. But otherwise, very good. We've got a great team."

"And your wife?"

Nick smiled just thinking about her. "She's a saint."

"Well, I'd suggest you hang on to her then. Those are hard to come by."

"She's a rarity, no doubt."

O'Neill nodded. He leaned forward and rested his bulging forearms on the desk.

Nick couldn't help but notice the faded black scars on the brown skin of his hands. He knew the story—everyone did. Some twenty years earlier, O'Neill had gone to question the neighbor of a suspect believed to have been involved in a high-profile bank robbery. He was invited inside and ambushed by three men armed with knives and a Louisville Slugger. But they'd fucked with the wrong ex-Marine. When backup arrived, the three men were already face down on the floor in varying states of consciousness, their hands cuffed or tied behind their backs.

"So tell me about this serial case. SA Shianco told me you discovered it, and ViCAP linked three cases with the same signature. Yet another this morning. In Minnesota, in fact."

Nick filled him in on the events that had led up to their meeting. "With your permission, I'd like to talk to the Hennepin County M.E. and coordinate with the BCA and Minnetonka Police."

O'Neill nodded. "Sounds reasonable. What can you tell me about this unsub?"

The interview phase of the meeting had begun.

"I haven't had a chance to look at the files in their entirety yet. But my assessment is that we're dealing with a highly intelligent and organized white male, most likely in his late twenties to early thirties. He is extraordinarily versatile and enjoys challenging himself by switching up his M.O., geographic profile, and victimology, which has had the added bonus of keeping him off our radar. He's an opportunist; he steals from his victims, though that is secondary to the act of killing. I suspect he has some kind of medical background. He's demonstrated the ability to effectively use paralyzing agents to subdue and control victims, has used an I.V. on at least one occasion, and appears to have revived one of his victims—maybe multiple times. I get the impression that he revels in exploring the limits of the human body. And mind."

O'Neill steepled his fingers under his chin. His eyes were closed, and his head bobbed slightly as he listened.

Nick went on. "He has an antisocial personality disorder—a psychopath with a nasty sadistic streak. He enjoys making people suffer. He lacks empathy and emotion, but his actions aren't impulsive. Rather, they're well thought out and meticulously planned and executed. He has obsessive traits, but seems capable of keeping them under control. He relishes the kill more so than the method, which indicates that the power, challenge, and signature are sufficient to sate his appetite. That's a bit unusual, but not unheard of."

"What do you make of the signature? The quarters?"

"Unless there's a case we haven't seen between Bakersfield and Minnesota, which is unlikely given the timing, I think he's using them to communicate to us where he's going to kill next. It could be meant as a challenge or a taunt to law enforcement. But they're also important to his fantasy in some way. They have meaning to him, a purpose."

"If you're right that means there are more vics out there."

"Yes sir. We know he's been operating since at least '09, so it could be *a lot* more. I think ViCAD will flush out the scope of what we're dealing with here pretty quickly."

"It's interesting that he'd surface now, of all times, but I agree. ViCAD coming online is going to play to our advantage."

"I hope so. If nothing else, it will be a good test of the new system."

"Do you think he's escalating or devolving?"

Nick thought about it for a second. "That's hard to say. In Bakersfield, he sacked the place. That's what had them thinking that it was a home invasion. That might be a sign of devolution, but I'm more inclined to think it was intentional misdirection, since this most recent scene required such precision and control. Because we don't have any identifiable pattern yet, I can't say for sure—but a week between kills is fast. Really fast. That's not really enough time to establish someone's habits with any degree of certainty. It seems unnecessarily risky."

O'Neill nodded again.

"He stalks his victims, but I think there's more to it than that. He has a very good understanding of psychology and human nature. I think he profiles his victims in much the same way that *we* would profile *him*."

"Why's that?"

"Several reasons. He was able to charm his way into dinner with one of the vics. He's used a paralytic in three of the five cases, so he seems to know when he can control the situation and when he might need a little extra help. And I have to take a closer look at the case from yesterday, but he murdered the vic *before* he went after the safe. That suggests to me that he had at least some idea that he'd been given a panic code. Those are signs that he's reading and anticipating people's behaviors."

"Not exactly a pleasant thought."

"No," Nick agreed. "Everything I've seen so far is very...*chaotic*, for lack of a better word. But to him, it makes perfect sense. There's an order to it. We just need to find it."

O'Neill pushed back from his desk and settled into the chair. "So here's where I'm at, Special Agent Keegan."

Nick held his breath.

"By all accounts, you're one of the best agents we have in the field. I don't, for one minute, doubt your ability or your commitment. What I need to know is if you *want* this case. Serials aren't easy to begin with, much less mobile ones. You may be required to travel at a moment's notice. It could take months or years to capture him—look at BTK. You'll be managing a task force of dozens, if not hundreds, of agents and officers across the country as this unfolds.

"I've sat where you are now, and had I known what kind of monumental task a case like this was at the time, I'm not sure if I would have taken it on. There's *always* a ticking clock. There's always a life hanging in the balance. Every time another body shows up, you can't help but take it personally. It takes a toll—first on you, then on those that love you. It can be dangerous. This is not something everyone can—or *should*—do."

Nick thought of Connie and the baby and everything he had to lose. Could he carry the weight? Could they? Did he really have a choice?

O'Neill said, "I decided a long time ago that I would never assign someone a case like this without making sure that they knew the potential costs first. It has cost some everything. Are you prepared to risk that?"

He wasn't.

But he answered "yes," anyway and immediately felt sick to his stomach.

"Okay then." O'Neill nodded once as if that settled the matter. "You're going to need support from BAU-4 for this," he said, referring to the Behavioral Analysis Unit specializing in crimes against adults. "I'd suggest Indra Tandon and David Xavier. Indra has exceptional skills and is probably one of the most experienced agents in BAU. Her specialty is crime scene analysis. She was with the Evidence Response Team for almost ten years. Xavier is a goddamn savant. Brilliant beyond imagination, but he can sometimes be…a *challenge* to deal with. Asperger's or something like. But he can see patterns and links in things that will blow your mind. He and Tandon work together most of the time. She gets him."

Nick nodded. "I'll stop downstairs and introduce myself."

"One more thing, Keegan. If this explodes, you're going to need ORION to coordinate your task forces. We'll activate it if you feel it necessary. I'm here to support you in any way you need."

"Thank you, sir. I appreciate that. And your confidence in me."

"You may not be thanking me for long, son. I've been chasing these bastards for a long time, and I've got a bad feeling about this one."

SEVENTEEN

Stafford, Virginia
Tuesday, August 2 2016 1:21 PM

Nick entered BAU-4 and was directed to Xavier and Tandon, who were sitting together at a table reviewing the five case files that Valerie had sent over during his lunch. Indra Tandon stood to greet him. Xavier stayed seated and continued browsing the files, either ignoring or oblivious to his presence.

"Special Agent Keegan, I gather?" Tandon had a thick accent, her voice exotic and soothing. She was impeccably dressed, her graying hair pulled into a tight bun. Her wide-set, penetrating brown eyes and striking aquiline features accentuated her evident intelligence. She stepped forward with a hand outstretched, her eyes directly on his, assessing—always assessing. Nick doubted they missed much.

He took her hand. Her grip was firm and confident. "Ms. Tandon. Please, just call me Nick."

Her eyes never left his, but he noted a slight softening of her steady gaze that he recognized as an indicator of some modicum of trust. In those few seconds, he suspected she saw as much a kindred spirit in him as he did in her.

"A pleasure, Nick. Truly. What you have done with ViCAD is most impressive. I'm eager to see what will come of the changes. And you may call me Indra." She spoke deliberately, and seemed to choose her every word with care—a perfectionist certainly, perhaps with a touch of OCD. Nick imagined the hangers in her closet evenly spaced, her house immaculate.

"Thank you, Indra. But believe me, ViCAD was born through the efforts and ideas of many, not merely mine. I just hope it helps us to do our jobs more effectively."

"As do I."

David Xavier appeared the polar opposite of Indra. He wore wrinkled khaki-colored cargo pants, a forest-green plaid flannel shirt, and a pair of bright orange Converse high-top tennis shoes that Nick could see under the table. He had near set eyes, the palest shade of blue Nick had ever seen, almost colorless. His curly, murky-dishwater blonde hair struck out at seemingly impossible angles in a manner similar to Albert Einstein's. His mouth moved constantly, forming silent words that only he could hear or comprehend.

"Mr. Xavier," Nick said, acknowledging the seated man. He held out a hand and leaned toward him.

Xavier's eyes widened and he focused them on Indra in a panic. He pushed back in his chair and made a low keening sound of distress.

Indra gently pushed Nick's arm down and Xavier calmed. "Chiraptophobia," she said. "David prefers to maintain his personal space. He does not like to be touched."

"I see," Nick said, somewhat shocked. "I apologize, David."

Xavier appraised Nick for the briefest of instants, then his eyes began to dart around the room until they finally came back to rest on the screen in front of him. After a few seconds, he fell back into his rhythm, his mouth moving in silence, a finger on his chin.

"Eccentric, yet incredibly effective," Indra explained. "He does not speak often, so please do not be offended. You can be sure he hears and understands everything you say, probably better than you yourself do, if that's possible."

"Valerie said I shouldn't play chess with him."

Without looking away from his monitor, Xavier said, "King's pawn to E4." His voice was high-pitched and soft, though not timid. When he spoke, he did so with an unusual cadence, but with a surety that belied his other nervous behaviors.

Indra laughed. It was a wonderful sound, like the song of wooden wind chimes. "I would not recommend it."

Nick took her advice. "I surrender, David. Another time, maybe."

Xavier shrugged.

"Have a seat, Nick," Indra said, indicating a chair that would put her between the two men, presumably to keep Xavier comfortable. Her protectiveness toward him was apparent; she clearly had a maternal instinct. "We're looking over the case files that Valerie sent us now. I'm sure there is little need to tell you so, but this unsub is particularly imaginative and very dangerous."

Nick nodded. "By constantly changing his M.O. he's less likely to get bored, complacent or have a chance to 'perfect' his crimes, which is when most serial murderers get sloppy."

Indra acknowledged the fact with a grim smile. "He's supremely confident. That might cause him to make a mistake, but I rather doubt it. His confidence comes from practice, preparation, and an abundance of caution."

"I agree." Nick said, watching Xavier scroll through ViCAP questionnaires with extraordinary speed. "Does it seem to you that this guy has an unusual amount of control over his actions? I get the impression it's more than just a psychological need that drives him."

"There is always something uncontrollable about what they do. A need that is more primal than conscious. He is living inside a fantasy that is absolutely real to him. Where his actions are justified and have a purpose. That fantasy obviously does not require a certain type of victim, or relate to a particular geographic area or even necessitate a specific modus operandi. It is, therefore, not the 'how,' the 'where,' or apparently even the 'whom,' unless we find some nebulous link between the victims. It's the 'what'—the kill itself, and the 'why' that are important to him."

"I'd like to have the two of you start looking for potential connections between the victims, just in case that link is there. I hear that's one of Xavier's specialties. There are no immediately obvious commonalities, but that doesn't mean there aren't any."

Indra nodded. "Indeed. We will look into it."

"I'm planning on taking a detailed look at all five files on my flight back to Minneapolis tonight. I've not had time for anything other than a quick review with the exception of the Bakersfield scene. I'm not nearly as quick as Xavier."

"Not many are," Indra said with a reassuring smile.

"I expect to hold a conference call with all the affected LEAs to set up task forces before the end of the week. One of the first orders of business will be to cross-reference airline, car rental, and hotel records in the vicinity of each of the known crime scenes. We'll probably want a federal subpoena that gives everyone blanket authorization to acquire those records. It will save everyone some time. Can you handle that for me, Indra?"

"I'll make the call as soon as we're done here."

"We might need to partner with Cyber to access some of their filtering programs to help speed up the search. There's going to be a shitload of data to weed through, especially since there are significant gaps in our timelines right now. Our best chance is probably going to be to focus on California and Minnesota since those are the closest together from a time perspective, but who knows what may show up?

"And as long as we know he is operating in Minnesota, I'd like to have you both there to assist, if you can swing it."

"O'Neill made it clear that we're at your disposal."

"Just let me know when you can make it happen. If you get me your flight info, I can probably pick you up."

David angled his monitor toward Indra. She smiled, her eyes crinkling with humor. In turn, she showed it to Nick. "How about tomorrow at 3:13?"

The screen was split, half of it dedicated to several tabs of case files, the other the Delta website. He'd already picked a flight. Nick's eyebrows went up, and he glanced over at Xavier. "You might just be the most efficient asset in the Bureau, David. I'll probably still be at the Wainwright scene at 3:13, but I can have one of our agents pick you up."

"We'll be there," Indra said and gave Xavier back control of his monitor. His fingers flew across the keyboard as he presumably booked the flights. Nick had never seen anyone type so fast—it was very nearly superhuman. After less than a minute, he went back to reading, using his roller mouse to scroll rapidly through the screens.

Nick lifted his eyebrows again and shook his head. "Wow."

"One of his many talents," Indra said, still grinning with amusement at Nick's awe.

"All right then," he said. "Am I missing anything?'

Nick and Indra were both surprised when Xavier spoke. "The quarters."

"What do you mean, David?" Indra asked.

He shook his head without looking away from the screen.

Nick prodded a bit. "I'm open to speculation."

"Nothing is unintentional," Xavier said. "Everything is deliberate. *Especially* that which seems random."

Nick looked to Indra for help, but she just shrugged. "He sees something. That is all I can say. David rarely speculates. When he can quantify a pattern, he'll identify it."

Nick couldn't hide his disappointment. "Great."

"Trust me, Nick. It's always worth the wait. And I've come to appreciate the way his mind operates. Conjecture may sometimes point to truth, but it misleads just as often."

"And yet, conjecture is my forte."

Indra smiled warmly at him. "And often mine as well. That is why this team will work well together. Each of us has a unique process and perspective."

Nick hoped she was right. "Okay then. I think that takes care of everything for now." He stood. "Call me when you get in tomorrow?"

David didn't move, but Indra rose with him. "Of course," she said.

"Hopefully you won't need to be in Minneapolis long. His last kills were just over a week apart—"

"Eight days, fourteen hours," Xavier corrected. His eyes never left his monitor.

Nick wondered if they even had that long.

EIGHTEEN

Quantico, Virginia
Tuesday, August 2 2016 4:21 PM

The Wall was hallowed ground to Nick. Nearly two hundred photographs hung along the corridor, some well known and others barely spoken of: Gacy, Ridgeway, Kemper, Gein, Lucas, Rader… It seemed endless and felt profoundly impossible. Bundy, his thin lips curved into a knowing smile, his eyes as lifeless as the young women he'd left in his wake. Ramirez, his black hair wild and jaw set, with his head tilted slightly down in a contemptuous, predatory stare.

Nick stepped back and took in as many of the photos at once as he could. He'd never told anyone, but from here he saw evil. He *believed* in it. It was like one of those puzzles in which a collage of thousands of tiny images was used to make a larger picture that was related in theme. He knew and understood that individually the images represented nothing more than one dysfunctional brain that he could define and comprehend, but taken together as a whole they were something altogether different. Therein lay something ferocious and fearsome with gnashing teeth that was hungry in a way that could never be sated.

The power Nick felt here wasn't borne of the empty gazes staring back at him, but the sound of the deafening screams of the thousands of victims that The Wall represented—the ones who were not on The Wall at all. A lump rose in his throat. His chest tightened, making it hard to breathe. He felt like he might drown in the tears of the dead.

"You hear them don't you?" a woman's voice asked from immediately behind him.

Nick damn near jumped out of his skin. He'd been so drawn into The Wall he hadn't even heard her approach. "Jesus *Christ!*" he hissed and spun to see who had snuck up on him so stealthily.

It was the redhead recruit that had caught his attention at the ViCAD orientation the day before. She stood ramrod straight with her hands behind her back and her chin raised slightly. Up close, he could just barely see a splash of pale freckles on either side of her nose. Instead of his pulse decreasing from the initial scare, he was pretty sure it jumped again.

"Sorry," she said. "I guess I should have known better. This place will do that to you."

"I think you might be lucky I'm not armed," Nick said.

She smiled. "I checked."

He couldn't help but laugh as his heart rate came back to normal.

"I'm Addison Lange. Addie. I was at your presentation yesterday."

"I remember seeing you there. How'd I do?"

"Well, no one shot you. So, fairly well under the circumstances, I'd say."

"We made everyone check their weapons beforehand. Just in case."

Lange's hazel eyes twinkled with amusement. "Ah. That explains it." She paused, looking at The Wall. "That was the first standing ovation I've seen in a classroom setting since I've been here. Kind of a big deal, ViCAD."

"It could be. We'll know soon enough, I guess. What division, Ms. Lange?"

"Cyber. I've always had a...*thing* for computers."

The way she said it made Nick want to change all of his passwords.

Addison sat down on a bench across from The Wall. After a quiet minute she said, "I'm sorry about your father."

Nick was only slightly taken aback. "He died a long time ago. But thanks."

"Traffic stop, right? Early 1993?"

Nick sat a few feet away from her on the same bench. "You've been doing some research." For some reason he couldn't explain, it didn't really bother him.

"Most people call it stalking," Addison said with a wink.

Nick laughed again. "I was trying to give you the benefit of the doubt. But yes. I was twelve—just turned, actually. Dad pulled some guy over for a busted taillight. He took two in the vest, one in the leg then another to the head."

"I imagine that was tough."

Nick had a suspicion that she spoke from her own experience. "It was. But in some ways, I was also pretty lucky. The guys from my dad's station took me under their wing, so I had a terrific support system. And there was a charity drive. The people of Florida were very generous; we never had to worry about money."

"Did they get the son of a bitch?"

Nick looked at Addison Lange. She appeared genuinely interested, but Nick had little doubt that she already knew the answer. "Yes. He ran, but they grabbed him in Albany, Georgia the next day.

Some small-time gangbanger. Cruz, his name was. He hung himself not long after. Never went to trial."

Addison looked down and nodded.

"Not that I mind," Nick said, "but why are you asking?"

She met his gaze again and shrugged. "I'm always curious what motivates people to do this. You've got more reason than most."

"I suppose so, but it's really all I've ever wanted to do. Even before my dad died. Other kids had Batman or Superman, but my dad was always my hero." Nick wasn't entirely sure why he was telling all this to a complete stranger, but he found it came easily nonetheless. She was affable and non-threatening in a way that very few people were. Between her looks and stoic charm, he imagined there weren't many that could resist telling her anything she wanted to know. *She'd be great in the box*, Nick thought. "What about you? What's your motivation?" he asked.

She looked at Nick for a long moment before answering. "Finding justice for those who can't get it for themselves."

Nick smiled at her. "That's all the reason any of us should need, right there."

"Can I ask you something that may be a bit personal?"

Nick gave her a playful sideways look. "I'd say that ship has already sailed, wouldn't you?"

The pale skin on her neck and cheeks flushed, but she grinned at him. "What does The Wall do to you?"

"Now *that's* an interesting question." He stood back up and regarded the many dozens of photos. "And I'm not sure if I can adequately answer it. You asked if I could hear them? If you mean the victims, yes. I hear them. The pictures themselves don't really do anything at all to me, I guess. The Wall though…as a whole…that's different." He put his hands in his pockets and shrugged. "It makes me wonder. Each of them is a monster, but the beast is all of them taken together. There's something in the darkness that has broken them and turned them loose on the rest of us."

Lange frowned. "It's strange. Everyone sees this place, but few seem to really *see* it. A lot of people walk by and don't even look up. Even when I pass and try not to look, it makes me shiver."

"I bet that's more common than you realize. Here there be tygers," Nick said, quoting one of his favorite stories.

"And ghosts."

"Yes, and ghosts," he agreed.

Addison stood.

For a moment the two of them just looked down the incredible length of The Wall.

She turned to him. "Well, it was nice to meet you, Special Agent Keegan," she said and extended a hand.

He took it. Her grip was strong and confident. *Definitely military,* he thought. "Nick. And you too, Ms. Lange."

"Addie," she reminded him.

"Addie, then. Good luck with the rest of your training."

"Thanks. Good luck with ViCAD."

She strode off, a long ponytail of red hair swinging across her back like a pendulum as she went. Nick suspected she'd be a good agent. The ones that heard the victims usually were.

NINETEEN

Nick took his seat aboard a surprisingly empty 727 bound for Minnesota. He scrolled through e-mails on his Blackberry and sent Connie a text message while the small parade of passengers fumbled with their carry-ons and double-checked their boarding passes. In short order, the pre-flight announcements began, and Nick breathed a silent sigh of relief that the window seat next to him remained vacant.

Once airborne, Nick raised his armrest and scooted over to allow for some maneuvering room and privacy. The 300-pound gentleman in the aisle seat looked more than a little relieved and raised his own armrest to allow his considerable bulk to settle.

Nick pulled out his laptop and a small Moleskine notebook. He decided to review the cases in reverse order from most recent to oldest. He also chose to start with the crime scene photographs first, so he wouldn't be swayed by any of the officer's notes or findings. In addition to the photos of the Wainwright scene, Detective Nguyen had attached two panoramic videos of the kill room and the office, plus one regular video, which walked Nick from the semi-circular drive through the entirety of the house.

Nick traveled virtually up the drive to the convertible BMW parked at the topmost arc and proceeded through the home. He jotted notes along the way and paused and rewound the video in several places, especially in the living room where the body was found. He supplemented the videos with photos for close-ups and angles the video didn't provide. All in all, Nguyen and the techs from the Bureau of Criminal Apprehension had done a good job documenting the scene in its entirety.

He noted the small blood pool on the floor behind Scott Wainwright's body, the Minnesota statehood quarters in his palms and over the eyes, and the blood droplets leading away from the body and up the otherwise immaculate stairs. The video followed the drops into the office, around the desk and then focused on the bookcase, detached thumb, and hidden safe. The video's final moments walked Nick through the rest of the Wainwright home, which, with the exception of an empty jewelry box in the opulent master bedroom, appeared to be untouched.

Nick then watched the 360° panoramic videos and was able to gain some perspective. The house was quite large, somewhere in the ballpark of 6500 square feet, Nick guessed, and probably worth a few million. He watched his view spin slowly around the living room and used his arrow keys to change direction. After several reversals back and forth, he frowned and narrowed his eyes in concentration. His intuition whispered something in his ear that he couldn't quite hear. He stopped the rotation altogether and focused on the victim—the *back* of the victim. The camera had been positioned in the approximate center of the room to capture the panorama, which meant that Scott Wainwright had been left facing *away* from the entryway.

That didn't make sense at all. It would present the least amount of emotional impact. Nick jotted down *remorse?* in his notebook. He looked at the monitor again and shook his head. It was incongruous and out of character. From what he knew so far, this unsub was all about impact, killing in the most shocking and unimaginable ways. He seemed to take a perverse pleasure and pride in it, yet here he had essentially tucked his work away into a corner. Nick made a few more notes and moved on to Jim's case file from Bakersfield.

There wasn't much more to see that he'd missed during his first look at the case. It was a heartrending scene, and he couldn't help but think of Lindsay Lyman stumbling upon her mother's body. He wondered how she was doing and understood how Harris had become so emotionally involved. He felt for his friend.

The differences between this case and the Wainwright scene were many and far from subtle. If he didn't already know better, he'd never have linked this case with the one in Minnesota. The house was small and quaint, less than 1500 square feet, and there were far more promising targets on the same block. Obviously, though he wouldn't walk away from an opportunity, this unsub was choosing his victims in a way that had nothing to do with their potential for financial gain.

The Bakersfield scene was far bloodier, more intimate, and hands-on. The two scenes were halfway across the country from one another, and the victims couldn't have been more different. This scene had been trashed as if the unsub was seized by a fit of rage, while the Wainwright's was relatively pristine. At this point, only the presence of the statehood quarters linked the two cases.

Nick was somewhere over Michigan when he dug into the next case. He had yet to review this one in any detail, so it was new except for what Valerie had shared with him. In March of 2014, a twenty-two-year-old female college student had been poisoned in her dorm apartment, apparently during a dinner date.

Amanda Roberts wasn't particularly popular, and none of her neighbors, classmates, or limited group of friends had anything to add to the investigation. By all accounts, Amanda was an excellent student—smart but shy, and to the best of everyone's knowledge hadn't been on a date in years. She was overweight, but otherwise healthy. She was found on the floor five days after her death near a small, square card table that had served as her dining table, set for two. No one had bothered to check in on her until the smell had become unbearable for neighboring students. By that time the maggots had begun to feast. The pictures were dramatic and unpleasant, even to Nick, who'd seen plenty worse.

Amanda Roberts was a low-risk target for the unsub, which was how he'd managed to kill her without attracting any attention. If Nick was right about the unsub's age, he'd have been considerably older than Amanda, yet he was still able to gain her trust and a place at her dinner table. He therefore might look younger than his age, and was likely charismatic, or both. It was also possible that he knew the victim, but for reasons Nick couldn't really articulate yet, that didn't seem likely.

As Valerie had told him, Amanda had broken her neck during the violent convulsions caused by the cicutoxin. The resulting paralysis had caused her to suffocate. He took a look at a separate toxicology report in Amanda's file on the effects of cicutoxin poisoning. It indicated an onset of symptoms 15-90 minutes from the time of ingestion with death typically occurring within three hours. Nick hoped to God it didn't take that long.

He looked at a photograph that showed Amanda Roberts's greenish and bloated corpse lying on the floor with the statehood quarters sitting in her putrefying palms and sunken eye sockets. Nick realized the unsub must have sat there and watched as Amanda collapsed to the floor while vomit and froth oozed from her mouth, nose, and eyes. She might have reached out to him for help as her body convulsed and her bladder and bowels released. Then her body seized so violently, it snapped her spine. He gloried in watching her suffocate and succumb. Only then could he have placed the quarters without them having been thrown all over the room.

Nick shuddered at the thought. This was one sick, cruel bastard.

The other two case files did nothing to change that opinion.

While not his first victim, Nick believed that the murder of Darien Jackson in Baltimore, Maryland from 2013 represented the "birth" of his unsub. Thus far, it was the first case in which statehood quarters were used as a signature. The medical table had been placed in the exact center of a vast room in an abandoned downtown warehouse—none of the other crime scenes necessitated such obsessive behavior. The kill was exceptionally sophisticated and precise. Who actually counted *exactly* one thousand incisions? The coroner hadn't been able to say definitively, but he was reasonably sure that all of the cuts had been made peri- or ante-mortem, meaning the femoral artery was likely the final and fatal wound, and Mr. Jackson had been kept alive for the entirety of that horrifying ordeal. And the unsub had buried one each of every statehood in two inches of the victim's pooled blood to be found during the autopsy, almost like a magician revealing the secret behind a new trick.

The last of the five victims was a small Hispanic male, so horribly disfigured Nick could barely make out his features. His arms, hands, fingers and feet were all bent at abnormal angles, and shards of bone had torn through his skin in half a dozen places.

Nick studied a close up of what had once been Sergio Peña's face. His jaw, smashed and swollen, distorted his mouth into a horrible angular grimace. His ballooned and bloody lips hung open just enough to reveal fragments of shattered teeth. The right eye was obscured behind a mass of pulpy flesh. The left was gone; the optic nerve dangled inside the empty socket. Shredded sclera hung there, white against the black hollow. The only word that adequately described what was left of Peña's countenance: *mush*.

Bile pooled in the back of Nick's throat, and he fought off a wave of nausea and light-headedness. He flagged down a flight attendant and handed her his credit card. A moment later she handed him a whiskey. He quickly replaced the burn in his throat with one in his stomach before returning to the file.

COD had been listed as blunt force trauma to the chest, which had crushed his internal organs. A splintered rib had punctured a lung. Crime lab recreations suggested a sixteen-pound bowling ball had been dropped on Peña's chest from a height of eight to ten feet.

"Goddamn," Nick said aloud.

The man in the aisle seat took out an earbud. "Hmm?"

Nick tried to smile apologetically, but knew he didn't quite get there. "Nothing. Sorry."

The big man shrugged and went back to his in-flight movie.

Nick shifted in his chair and took a deep, shaky breath. He slipped his phone from his pocket and absently scrolled through a few favorite pictures of he and Connie and waited for the liquor to steady his hands. What the hell had he gotten himself into? Never before had his resolve wavered. He'd never questioned his ability. The cruelty of those he hunted had never shaken him like this. Now he wondered if he could face off against someone this sadistic. Could he get inside of his head? Did he want to? This wasn't just one of the killers on The Wall. This felt like the dark dragon that murmured in their ears.

And worse. He'd betrayed Connie. Their child. Again. He'd bitten off far more than he could chew, knowing full well that it would probably mean neglecting them at the most critical time. And might that have been the point? No one had any idea how much the thought of bringing a child into a world filled with these monsters haunted him. No one knew how much his need for justice consumed him. It was relentless. He wasn't sure there was room for him to both be a decent husband and father and a good cop. He'd never spoken the fear aloud to Connie—the only person who'd ever even remotely tempered the fire in him.

Nick leaned back in the chair and took several long, slow breaths and told himself to get a grip. He heard Xavier's awkwardly confident voice in his head. *Nothing is unintentional. Nothing.* Something about those words sang to Nick. Someone who dropped bowling balls on people possessed an innate cruelty that didn't really allow room for something as human as remorse. If he took that a step further, it meant there was a purpose for the misdirection and destruction in the Lyman home. That voice in the back of his mind was whispering again, still too quiet to hear. He tried to let it go. It would speak up in its own time.

Nick stowed his laptop, then closed his eyes. He ran the crime scene photos through his mind like a slideshow, hundreds of them. He wasn't blessed with a photographic or eidetic memory, but these images were much more difficult to forget than to remember.

CODs were different in every case. Victims were different in every case. Location was different in every case. Nick mentally tossed image after image away, purging the irrelevancies. He compared the positions of the five bodies. Three of the five were found in exactly the same positions—lying on their backs with their palms up. Helen Lyman may well have been in the same position before her daughter had moved the body. Wainwright's head had been tilted back to rest atop the coffee table's surface. His hands had been freed from the zip ties that had bound him to the table and were left resting on the carpet facing up with the coins in his palms.

As the plane began its descent, Nick had his gruesome mental slideshow down to five images. Each was likely the very first to have been taken on scene—the ones capturing the full effect of the bodies as they were found. The posing of the bodies couldn't be coincidence, and it was clear that the statehoods weren't either. Because Wainwright's body wasn't left in the same position as the others, the pose itself wasn't what was important—that was simply a means to an end for the coins. *That* was what mattered—maybe the *only* thing that mattered.

Nick's stomach lurched as the plane dropped suddenly. Over the intercom, the captain instructed the flight attendants to prepare for landing, but Nick only heard Xavier's voice. *The quarters. Nothing is unintentional.*

Xavier had seen in minutes what had taken Nick hours to understand fully.

"Son of a bitch," he said under his breath. He slipped the paper files from his laptop bag and looked more closely at the images, focusing on the quarters. He opened his Moleskine and started jotting down notes.

Wainwright: H, H, T, T

Lyman: H, unknown, unknown, unknown

Roberts: T, H, H, T

Jackson: T, T, H, T

Peña: H, T, H, T

That's a fucking code, he thought.

TWENTY

Minneapolis, Minnesota
Tuesday, August 2 2016 9:48 PM

Before Connie even had a chance to say hello, Nick reached across the console, put a hand behind her head and pulled her to him. He kissed her deeply, enjoying the taste of her lip-gloss and tongue. He felt the tension slip from his muscles as oxytocin did its thing. The disturbing images finally began to fade away.

"I've missed you," he whispered against her lips, his forehead pressed against hers. He felt a slight tickle when she smiled that ran through his body like a current.

"I missed you too, baby." She pushed a stray lock of dark hair back over an ear, and her eyes gleamed.

Nick kissed her again, longer and slower this time. He let his right hand wander up her stomach and cupped her breast. His thumb found her nipple through the thin fabric of her blouse.

Connie shivered beneath his hand. "Mmmm. Keep that up and we'll get a ticket for parking, among other things," she said with a mischievous grin. She gave his thigh a squeeze as she pulled away from the curb. "How was Quantico?"

"Good. Orientation was a success," he said. "We should start seeing some of the case files come through tomorrow. How was your little vacation?"

Connie told him about her Monday and Tuesday for several minutes. "Oh! Did you hear about the rich guy in Minnetonka?" she asked. "It's all that's been on the news here since last night."

"Yeah. I've been asked to lend a hand tomorrow." Nick felt like an ass for not telling her the whole truth, but he wasn't ready for her disappointment yet. Right now, he needed her. "How's Mindy," he asked, changing the subject.

Connie looked across the seat at him, perhaps sensing his deflection. If she did, she didn't say anything. "Good. She broke it off with Tim. We hung out, drank wine, and watched girl flicks." She slipped him another playful glance. "Magic Mike was great."

Nick rolled his eyes. "I'm sure it was. Didn't that win best picture?" he teased.

They made it as far as the kitchen. Nick pulled her to him and kissed her again with an urgency that she responded to immediately, her body relaxing against him in silent acquiescence. He helped her shed her clothes, and pressed his mouth on the soft, flawless skin of her neck and shoulders while she took her pants off and then worked on his. He stepped out of them and kicked them away, scooped her up and carried her into the living room.

Nick slipped his hands over her in the dark letting her intensifying sounds be his guide. She shuddered against him and made a soft hungry sound that he could only describe as a growl. Then she pushed him back and took over. She shifted her position and slipped onto him effortlessly. The sensation made him catch his breath. He lifted himself up and found her nipple with his mouth, pressing it between tooth and tongue. He held the small of her back and countered her movements in the ways that he knew she liked best. Her paced increased, and he could feel her body beginning to tense.

Nick closed his eyes to the pleasure and let Connie work herself toward her climax. Then, unbidden and without warning, Peña's demolished face came into his mind. He instinctively pulled back, and opened his eyes wide in something close to terror.

In the midst of a building cry, Connie grunted slightly and slowed her rhythmic motions.

He was diminishing inside of her. *What the fuck?*

"You okay?" she asked him, placing a hand on his chest.

A glimmer of light found its way inside from the window and glinted off of a bead of sweat on Connie's arm. Nick focused on it and tried to slow his breathing down. "Yeah, I'm good. Sorry."

"What's wrong, babe? That's never happened before." He sensed her disappointment, but she managed to keep it from her voice. Just.

Nick felt heat in his cheeks. He tried to swallow, but his mouth was too dry. He sighed instead. "I took the case. The Wainwright case. It's linked to the one Jim called me about last week."

Connie was still and quiet for a few seconds that felt like a lifetime. Then she pulled herself up off of him and stood. She lingered over him for another brief eternity. The anger and disappointment on her face was utterly concealed by darkness, but he saw it plainly nonetheless. Then she walked off toward the kitchen without a word.

He didn't try to stop her.

TWENTY-ONE

Shoreview, Minnesota
Wednesday, August 3 2016 6:48 AM

Nick felt the cushions of the couch shift slightly. He was normally not a heavy sleeper, but this morning, making his way to consciousness was like digging through several feet of packed earth. The smell of coffee helped bring him the rest of the way. He opened his eyes to a mug sitting on the table in front of him casting swirls of ghostly white steam into the air.

Connie sat a few feet away, motionless, looking down at the floor. He wondered for a moment if perhaps she was there to make peace. That hope shattered when it dawned on him what she was doing. *Oh shit.*

He sat up quickly. "Hey."

Connie flinched and drew in a sharp breath. She turned her head toward him slightly. Though her eyes were red and puffy, the blood had drained from the rest of her face. Furrows creased her brow, a terrible mixture of horror and concern. The corner of her mouth twitched.

Nick took a deep breath, caught someplace between anger—whether toward himself or her he didn't know—and regret. "I'm sorry. I didn't want you to see that. I'm an idiot." He swung his legs off the couch, sat forward, and took a photograph of Darien Jackson from her hand. He gathered the folders and photographs together in a pile and put them on the coffee table.

She shook her head slightly and stood, taking the mug with her. Nick felt an irrational pang of disappointment—he was apparently on his own as far as coffee was concerned. He reached out and took her hand before she could walk away. "If it makes you feel any better, I feel the same way. They don't get much worse." It was a small but necessary lie. "It's why I had to take this case."

Connie pulled away, her fingers slipping through his. She walked around the back of the couch and started toward the kitchen, but paused and looked back at him.

"Just go get that sick son of a bitch," she said.

TWENTY-TWO

Few things amused Aleksandr Zorin more than churches. Such abundant foolishness. The worshippers. The structures. The trillions of dollars. Entire *nations*. All devoted to an epic myth. His very existence should be more than enough proof for anyone that it was all complete and utter nonsense.

The Basilica of St. Mary was an impressive example of the Non's boundless stupidity. Zorin arched his neck and gazed at the soaring vaulted ceiling, the massive arches, and the stained glass windows that provided the majority of the chapel's dim light. It was mostly empty inside, a few dozen people spread throughout, seemingly spread as far apart from one another as possible.

He chose an empty pew near the rear of the church, a few rows back from a woman's bowed blonde head and hunched shoulders. The soothing voice of the bishop conducting the mass carried through the vast space to him. Zorin listened for a few seconds then rolled his eyes. Absurd.

He spun a quarter on the wooden pew next to him. It bounced off of the backrest and started to flutter, rising in pitch as it collapsed. He spun it again. The woman in front of him turned, annoyance etched into her brow. Zorin looked down his nose at her, and the corner of his mouth rose in a smirk. Her brow smoothed as her eyes widened, and she quickly returned her attention forward. He nearly laughed out loud when she crossed herself.

He watched the quarter finish its fall. Not even they were cooperating today. He would very much have enjoyed burning the eyes out of the nosy cunt in front of him. He supposed he could just kill her anyway—the idiots at the FBI would never put it together—but there was too much at stake to start being reckless now. He set the coin in motion again, smiling when he saw the woman's shoulders rise slightly. It was the little things.

Apparently the fourth spin was the charm. She got up with a loud sigh of exasperation and stormed past him without casting another look in his direction.

"Sorry," he whispered sarcastically as she went.

Zorin wasn't much for reflection, but the way the bitch looked at him reminded him of the disapproving scowl a mother might give her child. Not *his* mother, of course. Her gaze had always been a tad more glassy and vacant…

He'd been an unforeseen consequence of his mother's "business" at a time before she'd been a hopeless addict. Once, she'd been a well-paid call girl with several affluent clients. She'd also been beautiful. He couldn't remember a time when that had been true, but he'd seen pictures.

His sire might have been any of a few dozen men who had paid for their time with his mother by the hour. Why she'd decided to keep him, he'd never been able to figure out, but maybe she had hoped he might provide her with some kind of salvation. Incentive to turn her life around, perhaps.

Instead, she'd become a second-rate whore. At some point after he was born, she hooked up with a small-time gangbanger who fancied her milk-swollen tits and pretty face. He fucked her when she suited him, sold her when she didn't, got her hooked on coke, then—to establish complete control—married her. Over the several years that followed, that bastard built his own little circle of hell in their small house on Lone Star Drive.

There was physical abuse, hooking, a constant supply of drugs, and raucous parties where his mother was either gangbanged or passed around like a joint. Zorin spent almost all of his time in a small room at the back of the house occupied by little more than a mattress and beat-up dresser, listening to the sounds of his mother being smacked around or fucked.

When Zorin was ten, not long after his stepfather suddenly stopped coming home, he and his mother had gotten stoned together. They laughed so hard tears streamed down their faces, and snot dripped from their noses. It was among his most vivid of childhood memories. That was the night when she told him the little bit he knew about his life. It was also the night she showed him how to use his cock for something other than pissing. She'd been so fucking wasted she didn't remember anything afterwards, which was probably just as well. Though he wasn't burdened by guilt or shame, on some level, Zorin recognized that there was something forbidden about what had happened between them.

From that point on, he'd sometimes watch his mother whoring through the keyhole, or from a slightly cracked bedroom door. And occasionally, after her johns went home and she lay passed out and naked on the couch, he'd sneak in and touch her while he jerked off all over her face, like he'd seen a few of them do. There was something incredibly gratifying and bestial about it that he didn't comprehend until much later in life.

Zorin gazed around the vast chamber, looking at the images on the ten main double-arched stained glass windows. Dust motes hovered in the muted light filtering through them. One of the depictions caught his eye. Two men stood on either side of a boy. He didn't know who they were supposed to depict, but it would have been irrelevant information to him anyway. It did, however, trigger another memory…

It was the end of summer break before his freshman year. He was hot and bored, and spent most of his afternoon chucking rocks at mailboxes and birds when they got close enough. Two juniors caught him on the way home and offered to show him around his new high school campus. It was deserted. They took him around back on the premise of showing him the track, baseball diamonds, and football stadium.

As the first of their punches rained down on him, it began. It started with a shudder in his stomach. An incredible heat and tension spread through his chest, back, and shoulders, as if great flaming wings were trying to burst out of him. A pressure built inside, blooming with a force unlike anything he'd ever experienced. It was as if he were being reborn. No. Born. *It was exhilarating. It was power.* Was *this what it was like to* feel?

They didn't see the smile start to form on his face as they beat the shit out of him. They didn't sense the change that he felt—a fundamental shift from prey to predator. Zorin dropped to the ground beneath the hail of blows. His fingers found and curled around a brick.

He smashed it into the sandaled foot of one of his attackers. He heard and felt the satisfying crunch of bone. He roared and whirled around, driving himself and the brick upward as he went. He caught the second one squarely under the chin—the fucker's teeth clacked together like a gunshot, and his head snapped back. As it came forward again, Zorin saw only the whites of his eyes. Zorin spun again, and leapt atop the first teenager before the second had even hit the ground.

He was yowling in pain from his shattered foot. Tears coursed down his cheeks. He held his hands out, pleading. Zorin raised the brick above his head. The boy screamed and turned his head away, tensing for the blow. Zorin slammed the brick on the sidewalk, inches from the sniveling shit's skull. It broke into half a dozen ragged shards and red dust. The kid slowly turned his head back to him, eyes wide with terror. Zorin grinned at him and leaned forward, pinching off his next scream with a forearm to the throat. After a blissful half minute of panicked thrashing, the kid's body went limp.

Zorin took a sharp piece of brick and went to work. He carved the words, "I EAT COCK" into the flesh of both boys' chests. Then, feeling gloriously alive, he stood, dropped the bloody shard on the ground next to them and walked home with a raging hard on throbbing in his shorts.

No one came for him. And he never saw the two boys again. But Zorin was willing to bet that, wherever they'd gone, it was a rare occasion indeed that they went shirtless, much less showered after gym.

Zorin smiled at the memory. A small choir appeared at the front of the church and began to sing beneath a suspended statue of the crucified Jesus. Ah, yes. Crucifixion. A handy technique that could be used as a means to a wide variety of ends—or simply as a way to immobilize the Non while he did his worst to them. He made a mental note to work it into his repertoire again soon.

Between the incident behind Robert E. Lee High and the dozen or so small animals he'd reveled in killing, Zorin had a reasonably good idea of what he was, even as a teenager. At the very least he knew he was fundamentally different—people's pathetic sensitivities and spineless behavior constantly baffled him. He quickly came to understand that he'd have to be careful. Very, very careful.

His mother became a worthless tramp. By the time Zorin was sixteen, she was perpetually strung out on some combination of booze, marijuana, cocaine, meth, or heroin. When she started taking drugs as payment for services rendered, he barely managed to keep them afloat with paper routes and the small paychecks and stale leftovers from the greasy burger joints he worked at.

It wasn't a pretty or easy existence, but it shaped him. Made him strong. It taught him the self-reliance he would eventually use to survive. In high school, he turned his terrible grades around and forced himself to enjoy learning, realizing that it was a necessary means to his end—or more precisely—the ends of others.

Now he was the perfect predator, capable of astounding things. He'd gone more than sixteen years dispatching soul after soul into the Else, and to his knowledge he'd never raised even the slightest suspicion.

One way or another, that was about to change. They would hold him in awe soon enough.

TWENTY-THREE

Nick put Brian Mulvaney in his late fifties. He was short and rotund, and sported an exceptionally thick, white moustache that Nick suspected was made up of more hair than was on top of the man's head.

The Medical Examiner led Nick to a covered table in a chilly examination room that smelled of equal parts formaldehyde and ammonia. He drew back the sheet without preamble, exposing Scott Wainwright's pale corpse from the waist up. He also lifted up the sheet to reveal his left arm, sans thumb.

"This one was interesting," Mulvaney said. He pushed a pair of wire-rimmed glasses further up his nose. "I spent a good portion of yesterday trying to make sense of it. As a matter of fact, I brought in someone from Anoka County to consult with me."

"Were you the one that responded to the scene?" Nick asked.

"Yes. I arrived just after eight Monday evening." He held a blue-gloved hand out over the corpse as if to introduce them. "Scott Wainwright. 53 years. I determined prelim COD at the scene." He took a penlight from his lab coat pocket. With a practiced thumb he raised one of Wainwright's eyelids and shone the light inside for Nick to see. "Petechial hemorrhaging. Suffocation."

Nick nodded.

The ME closed the eye again and pointed the penlight towards Wainwright's neck. "His hyoid bone was intact, and as you can see there was no obvious bruising or discoloration on the throat."

"Not strangled," Nick said.

"Correct." Mulvaney moved down the length of the table a bit, slipping the penlight back into his pocket. He lifted Wainwright's left hand. "Sharp force removal of the left thumb at the metacarpophalangeal joint. The cut is quite clean but the cartilage is torn. My guess is that he cut first then twisted it off the rest of the way." He pointed to the flesh that remained around the base of the thumb. "Fairly precise positioning of the blade right over the joint. No hesitation marks."

"Is that unusual?" Nick asked, squeezing the based of his left thumb with his right hand looking for the joint. It wasn't terribly easy to find.

The ME shrugged. "I'd say it was fairly confident cut." He raised the arm up and pointed to a small bruise on the back of the triceps. "I also found this at the scene. Two-centimeter hematoma, injection mark at the relative center. New, probably within a few hours of death based on coloring." He lowered the arm and covered it again with the sheet.

"How long for tox?"

"I've asked for priority. Two to three weeks minimum."

"Tell them to check for Pancuronium Bromide. That might speed things up."

"A paralytic." Mulvaney nodded slowly, a small toothy grin barely visible beneath his bushy moustache. "That would make sense." He took a small notepad from his breast pocket and jotted down a note, then replaced it. "He has another roundish perimortem hematoma about five centimeters across on his lower back, left lateral." He turned and placed his hand on the small of his back a few inches from his hip to illustrate.

He opened Wainwright's mouth and motioned for Nick to take a look. "I found what looked to be a mixture of vomit, blood, and particulate in his mouth and throat, as well as severe swelling and discoloration around the oropharynx. That was pretty much all I could determine at the scene. A Death Investigator transported the body here, and I performed the full autopsy the following morning—yesterday—at 08:23.

"Both of his lungs had collapsed. It wasn't until we got confirmation of the particulate in his mouth that we started to hypothesize what had happened to him."

Nick was almost afraid to ask. He did anyway. "What was it?"

"Shredded lung and sinus tissue."

Nick grimaced in empathetic reflex and confusion. "Jesus. What would do that?"

"A vacuum."

After a few seconds of silence, Nick realized his mouth was hanging open. He closed it and tried to swallow, but there was no saliva in his mouth. His throat responded with a dry click.

"It took us some time to reach that conclusion," Mulvaney went on. "None of us had ever seen anything like it, but it made sense. If a vacuum hose with sufficient suction was affixed over the oropharynx, the tissue would initially stretch and swell to fill the hose, and the trachea and esophagus would collapse but not completely. Air would be drawn in through the nose, but if the nose were pinched off, then it would first pull air from the lungs, then tissue. Small amounts of stomach content would likely travel up the esophagus as well."

"So he quite literally had the life sucked out of him?"

"That was our assessment, yes."

"Were you able to confirm it?"

Mulvaney nodded. "I contacted Detective Nguyen and asked him to look for a vacuum at the Wainwright home. They have a central unit—the kind where you plug a hose into the wall. A fifty-foot hose was found in a utility closet. Positive for blood, bile, and particulate. It's in evidence with the BCA."

"Good Lord."

"We assumed he must have been unconscious. It was otherwise difficult to imagine that anyone would remain still under such circumstances. Paralysis would explain it, though that's disturbing on another level entirely. Death would have taken a few minutes minimum and would have been excruciating."

Nick didn't doubt it.

TWENTY-FOUR

Minnetonka, Minnesota
Wednesday, August 3 2012 1:38 PM

Nick spent some time driving around the area of the victim's home before his scheduled meeting with Detective Nguyen. It couldn't have been a much better location for a murder site. The Wainwright house was reasonably secluded in an area where backyards were measured either in acreage or how many steps you were from the lake. Nick knew that the odds of someone having seen anything were close to nil—none of the neighbors were close enough or within line of sight. The best Nick figured they could hope for was someone having noticed an out-of-place car parked in the neighborhood. Or maybe a jogger had run past the Wainwright residence at the time in question.

That might not be such a stretch. He'd long since stopped counting the taut, shapely women in straining sports bras and spandex shorts he'd seen running during his drive around the subdivision. This was where the beautiful, expensive people lived. He had to admit that the scenery was top-notch. The gorgeous homes and expansive Lake Minnetonka were fun to look at, too.

As Nick approached Wainwright's house for the third time, he saw a cruiser in the drive and pulled in behind it. A small Asian man in police uniform got out of the squad and leaned against the open door. He gave Nick a curt nod.

Nick put the Ford Escape from the Bureau's motor pool in park. Though he didn't expect to need it, he'd chosen it because there was a Crime Scene Collection Kit in the back. Just in case.

Nick exited the vehicle and introduced himself to Detective Nguyen. Despite his small stature, Nguyen's grip was like a vice, and he carried himself like someone who might be a little bit dangerous when shit went down. Nick liked him immediately. Unfortunately, Nguyen didn't seem to share the sentiment. His eyes had a hard, challenging edge. It was a look that Nick had seen many times from locals who felt the Feds were stepping in to take over their investigations.

"Good to meet you, Special Agent Keegan," Nguyen said unconvincingly.

"Nick."

Nguyen stood with his arms crossed and nodded again, but didn't bother to give him the courtesy of his own first name in return. "So what can I do for you, Special Agent? Was something wrong with my ViCAP report?"

Nick could have played it tough, but in his experience it just made things more difficult. He decided to grease the wheels instead. "On the contrary, it was very thorough. The panoramic videos were a big help."

Nguyen stared at him.

Nick figured the man's diminutive size gave him a bit of a Napoleon complex, and he probably overcompensated a bit because of his ethnicity as well, so he bit off a smart-ass comment. "They gave me a pretty good idea of how things went down here on Monday, but I'd like to walk through it with you, if you don't mind."

The detective pursed his lips and shrugged. "Knock yourself out."

"I'm going to do this a little differently than you may be used to. I want to walk the scene as if I'm your perp. I may need you to play the role of Wainwright for me and maybe fill me in on a few details as we go."

Nguyen's eyes narrowed ever so slightly, as if he thought Nick might be criticizing his work after all.

Nick sighed internally. "I just got a look at the file last night on a plane from Virginia, so there may be things I've forgotten or overlooked," he said.

"You talk to the ME?" Nguyen asked.

"A few hours ago, yes."

"This is one fucked up prick."

"Yes, he is. Listen, Officer Nguyen, I'm not here to bust your balls. We've got five bodies attributed to this asshole, each worse than the last. There's almost certainly more to come. By the end of the day, you're probably going to be part of a multi-state task force charged with bringing the guy in. I don't give a damn if you like me, but we're going to be working together, so…"

Nguyen pushed off the car. "Fine. Let's do it."

Nick said, "Your cruiser looks reasonably close to where Wainwright's BMW was found, yes?"

"Close. Hang on." Nguyen got into the squad and pulled it forward a few feet and put it in park again. "About here."

Nick looked around and focused on the large torpedo-shaped topiaries adjacent to the entry that he'd seen in the photos. Nick walked over to the single step in front of the front door and peeked behind the shrubs.

"BCA's been back here, I assume?"

"Yep. The mulch and dirt matched what was found in the entry. Nothing more than depressions back there. Not enough for a size or casting."

Nick shrugged himself behind the topiary. "What do you see?" he called.

"Not a damn thing. Just a sec." He ran down to the end of the drive and returned in less than a minute. "From the front side, I might have just seen your shoes, but I was looking for them. Driving in, I doubt Wainwright would have seen anything."

"Okay, so you'd have gotten out of the car and went to the door."

Nguyen went to the door and let himself in with a key. He disabled the alarm using a pad just inside the door. "If you didn't move, I still probably wouldn't have seen you," he said.

"You didn't," Nick said.

"How do you know that?" Nguyen asked.

"The bruise, lower back. Wainwright was probably going through his mail and closing the door from the inside when it swung back open and slammed into him. Caught him totally off guard. He'd have fallen off the riser and pitched forward into the entry, scattering the mail on the floor. There's any number of ways I could subdue you from there."

Nguyen grunted, noncommittally conceding the possibility.

"What did the family's schedule look like?"

"Vic left work just before 4:00. That was pretty normal according his employer. He rarely worked late."

"Must be rough," Nick mused.

"Yeah, no shit. Monday, Wednesday, and Friday the daughter has ballet class at 4:30. Mom goes to the spa, gets a massage and a facial, or whatever the hell it is they do there, and picks the kid up around 6:30. On Mondays they go out for dinner and get home between 7:30 and 8:00. Scott went to the gym those same days and got home around 9:00."

"Where's his gym?"

"Here in Minnetonka."

"*Four hours*?"

"We're looking into it. Supposedly, he played tennis. I assume he ate dinner somewhere in there, but that seemed like a long workout. We're all over the adultery angle. The wife too."

"I'm not telling you how to run your investigation, but I wouldn't waste a lot of time on the wife."

"She could have hired someone. Plenty of motive. He's worth several million."

Nick shook his head. "No. Killing is very personal to our guy— an art. Murder for hire is beneath him. Do your due diligence, but it's almost certainly a dead end." He ignored Nguyen's disapproving frown.

"I knew their routines. I'd been watching," Nick muttered, taking in his surroundings as he imagined his unsub had. "He was in California Saturday before last. He'd need at least a week and preferably more to establish the family's routine. The murder was on Monday. He was most likely watching every day from the previous Monday. It's not much, but your team can use that when questioning neighbors about anything unusual: vehicles in the area, people they'd never seen before, suspicious behavior."

Detective Nguyen nodded and made some notes in his tablet.

Nick stepped down off the landing and looked into the living room. He saw the blood stain on the carpet about four inches from the table leg where Wainwright has been strapped. He thought again about the strange location of the body.

"All right," Nick said. "You're Wainwright. You've just been blitz attacked and are on the floor. You're startled, but a pretty fit guy. What do you do?"

"If you didn't have a weapon and I wasn't seriously hurt, I'd attack and beat the shit out of you."

Nick smiled at Nguyen's confidence. "What if I was bigger than you? Twenty plus years younger?"

"Fight or flight, right? Same answer. I'd take the chance."

"Be Wainwright, Detective. There are no cuts or contusions on your body other than those we can account for, right? No blood from anyone other than you."

"No," Nguyen admitted. "So he probably didn't fight. I still think a weapon is the best way to control the scene, though."

"Okay, I can accept that possibility. So let's say for the sake of argument that I'm either armed or enough of a threat physically that Scott isn't prepared to fight for it. Plus, it's unlikely that I ran inside yelling 'I'm gonna kill you,' so you don't know what my intentions are."

Nguyen picked up on Nick's line of thinking. "True. It could just be a robbery. Maybe I figure my best chance is to cooperate."

"You work for Ernst and Young. Remember, you've spent your whole life maneuvering, negotiating, gambling. And you've been pretty damn successful. It's what you know."

"So, I try to buy my way out of it? Tell you I can make you rich?"

"Exactly. If you can get me to bite on the safe…"

"Then worst case, I lose some serious bucks from the safe which I probably have insured anyway. Best case, I trick you into opening the safe with a panic code and the cavalry comes."

Nick nodded. "That's how I'd do it. Losing isn't an option for a guy like Wainwright. He has a plan for everything. He thinks he can manipulate any situation. If I'm him, I'm betting I can outsmart the guy. So I offer up my safe and the panic code."

"Okay. That fits. I'm with you. Then what?"

"That's the easy part, I let you think you've got control and tell you to lead on." Nick motioned for Nguyen to face away from him. "When you turn around," He poked Nguyen in the back of the arm with a finger. "I stick you."

"With what? A sedative?"

"Paralytic," Nick said. "He's used it before. Pancuronium Bromide. Onset in less than two minutes. Keeps them awake and aware but unable to move."

"Oh, *hell* no," Nguyen said looking back at Nick, his face twisted into a grimace of horror.

Nick nodded and led the conversation into the next room. He crouched next to the primary bloodstain. "Here's something I don't get. Why here at the back of the table? Facing *away* from the entry. Any thoughts? Why hide my work?"

Nguyen shrugged. "Weird for an…" he made quotes in the air, "artist."

Nick heard Xavier's words like a mantra in his mind. *Everything is deliberate—especially that which seems random.* The thought that had been at the edges of Nick's mind for the last few days felt extremely close here. He shivered. What the hell was it?

"What?" Nguyen asked.

Whatever it was, it still hovered just out of Nick's reach. He frowned and shook his head. "Dunno yet. Let's keep going. The M.E. concluded this blood pool was prior to TOD?"

"Yes. Gravitational, but too much if his heart wasn't beating. Doc said he was most likely alive for twenty minutes, at least."

"So I take your thumb with me and head upstairs to check out the safe. Come on."

The two men followed the blood trail leading away from where the body was found and went to the stairs. The diminishing size of the droplets showed directionality and became further apart as they climbed.

Nick commented. "Interesting that these drops are fairly centered in the stairwell. If they were further to the right or the left, we might have an idea of his dominant hand."

"Think that's intentional?"

"Oh, yes. As a colleague pointed out to me the other day, everything he does is intentional. He's trying to limit the information we have to work with. Did you get a chance to review the other case files?"

Nguyen's eyes flashed again like he thought Nick was challenging his competence. He opened his mouth to say something then closed it again as if he'd thought better of it. Instead he steeled his jaw and nodded.

Nick decided to leave it alone. "The Bakersfield case indicates a right-to-left cut across the victim's throat. Left-handed. In the Detroit case, the wound depths and directions indicate both hands were used. No hesitation or shallowing of the wounds like you might expect if he were using his weak hand."

"So he's ambidextrous," Nguyen concluded. He made another note in his tablet.

"Could be. But whether it's learned ambidexterity or innate is a question. Usually, lefties learn to be righties because they are taught by righties, and because most objects are designed for right-handers. One way or another, people still tend to have a dominant hand for certain activities. True ambidexters are a unique breed and can be extremely intelligent, but are somewhat more likely to have mental health issues."

With Nguyen at his side, Nick followed the blood droplets into the office. He had a sense of déjà-vu as he recalled the panoramic video he'd watched on the plane. By now the drops were much further apart and smaller, but there was a cluster of tiny drops behind the desk.

"He obviously came back here with the thumb," Nguyen said, pointing them out.

"He lingered for a bit, too," Nick noted. "Do me a favor, and swing that bookcase panel closed, would you?"

Nguyen made his way over, closed the safe door, and then rolled the shelf unit back into place. Nick looked around from his unsub's vantage point.

"Why would I come here?" Nick asked.

"Full view of the room?"

"Sure. Maybe I didn't know where exactly the safe was. Makes sense. But when you took that panorama, you shot it from the center of the room, right? He'd be just as likely to find the safe there as anywhere."

"You think he wanted access to the computer? We checked the history and the cache. There wasn't any indication that it was used during our window. And we dusted everything in here including the mouse and monitor, but there were no foreign prints. None anywhere in the house, actually."

"No surprise. He's never left any forensic trace." Nick looked at the top of the desk. His frown turned to a smile as the realization dawned. "Tell me about the safe, Detective."

"It's a high-end biometric model that requires both a thumbprint scan and a six digit passcode. If the wrong print or code is entered, it triggers the in-house klaxons and alerts the monitoring company instantly. If the panic code is entered, it trips a silent alarm, and the police are notified in minutes."

"So if you're not home and someone breaks in, they're scared off by the sirens. If you're home and being coerced, the panic code alerts the PD. The perp walks right out into the waiting arms of the authorities. Very smart."

"So why was this guy behind the desk?"

"I think he was confirming that Scott was left-handed," Nick said. "The position of the mouse in relation to the monitor, the pen cup, the letter opener… They're all on the left."

Nick stayed quiet for the minute it took Nguyen to puzzle through it.

Eventually the detective nodded. "Prints are different on every finger. He was making sure he had the right… the *correct* thumb to open the safe."

"Exactly," Nick said. "Odds are Wainwright would have programmed his safe with his dominant thumb. If the unsub discovered he was wrong, he could have just gone downstairs and removed Scott's right thumb."

"But he wasn't wrong."

"No, he wasn't. And I don't think he often is. He pays very close attention to his surroundings. Wainwright wore his watch on his right arm—that usually gives away a leftie. He probably opened the front door and punched the alarm keypad with his left hand. The unsub would have noticed. Things the average person wouldn't normally pick up on are critical to him."

Nick spent some time wandering the rest of the second level. The master bedroom was enormous, large enough to comfortably house three of his own bedrooms, and that didn't include the walk-in changing room (it was far too big to call a closet) or the master bath, which bordered on ludicrous. Nick shook his head at the opulence. Nothing appeared disturbed with the exception of a giant standing jewelry armoire next to a full-length mirror on the north wall of the changing room. All of the drawers and panels were open and empty.

He looked in on a huge entertainment room replete with a pool table and a full bar that would rival that in many restaurants. Damn near the entirety of the east wall was television screen.

A medium-sized bedroom had been converted into a ballet studio. Wooden barres circled the room at two different heights. Mirrors paneled every wall, and glossy, polished oak covered the floor.

The next room down the hall was a girl's bedroom, all pink and postered with pictures of celebrities and boy bands Nick had never heard of. That tickle was back again—stronger. His subconscious whispered things in his ear—still gibberish.

"You in there?" Nguyen asked him.

"Yeah, sorry." He shook his head to clear it. "Your report said the daughter had some quality pieces in her jewelry box, but it didn't look like it had been touched?"

"Yeah. There's a diamond pendant in there that's several carats. I don't know shit about jewelry, but it's probably worth a few thousand bucks. Diamond earrings, gold, platinum. It's nice stuff. You want to take a look?"

Nick shook his head. "Not yet. Let's go back downstairs for now." He led the way. As they descended he said, "I left your thumb in the office with the intention of coming back to open the safe after I'd killed you. Then I maybe wander the house a bit to get my bearings and make sure I have an escape route planned."

"And to find the hose for the vacuum unit," Nguyen said.

Nick nodded then took a deep breath and closed his eyes.

He plugs the hose into the wall; a low-voltage current turns the unit on automatically. He tests the suction, and then crouches down in front of Wainwright. The man's head hangs limp, his chin pinned to his chest. He reaches out and tilts it back so that it rests on the marble tabletop. With the exception of a slow, faint pulse in his throat and a barely perceptible rise and fall of his chest, he is motionless.

Tear tracks are on Wainwright's cheeks. His mouth is slack and spittle dangles from his chin. He's trying to scream but can only force enough air through his trachea to produce a faint wheezing. His tongue protrudes from his open mouth and lolls to the side.

He shows Wainwright the hose and smiles. His victim can't move his eyes, can't squint, can't voluntarily move a single muscle, but somehow the terror on his face is still plain.

So easy. There's no gag reflex. He can't bite, fight, or flail. The hose slips over his saliva-slicked tongue. The spit pooling at the back of his throat makes wet slurping sounds as the vacuum pulls at it. Then the hose suctions against the back of Wainwright's oropharynx. There's a muted popping sound. Wainwright's eyes change almost imperceptibly—a subtle widening. A hiss comes from his nostrils as air is pulled through his sinuses.

He pinches Wainwright's nose closed, sealing the vacuum. There's another muffled pop from somewhere inside of the man's body. He lets go of the hose but keeps his fingers closed around

Wainwright's nose and leans forward to look into his eyes. Oh yes, there's agony there, paralysis or not.

It doesn't take very long. Unfortunate, but necessary. Scott Wainwright suffocates and something impossible to quantify or define leaves the man's eyes. They dilate suddenly, and a glimmer of life winks out of them. Wainwright is gone.

Nick finished recreating the remaining events from the evening in his mind. He took Wainwright's gold Rolex from his right arm, the wedding ring from his left hand, and emptied his wallet of cash. He positioned the body and placed the statehood quarters over his eyes and in his palms. He returned the vacuum hose to the closet—why make it easy for investigators? He went back upstairs and emptied Sarah Wainwright's jewelry box, then the safe in the office and was out of the exquisite home's back door less than a minute after the panic code had alerted the safe monitoring company. The route of his escape had already been pre-planned, and he was gone before the first wave of response arrived at the residence.

Nick stood with a shiver that was equal parts exhilaration and disgust. For a second he was both hunter and hunted and felt the emotions of each.

"You know that's creepy as shit, right?" Nguyen said. "That little disappearing act your brain does?"

Nick figured it probably was, but ignored the comment. "How long before your boys rolled in after the alarm was sent?"

"Fourteen minutes. One of our guys was on the premises in eleven. He waited for backup per procedure, but saw nothing. They entered, found Wainwright almost immediately and called it in. BCA was here about an hour later. They arrived just before the wife and daughter got home. That was a treat. An officer stopped the wife at the vehicle, but the girl ran past everyone yelling, 'Daddy! Daddy!' I caught her just as she got to the living room. I don't think she saw much since he was facing the back wall. Still, it was pretty awful."

With the speed and force of a lightning strike, Nick realized what it was that had been skirting the periphery of his brain for the last few days.

"Fuck! He was trying to protect them."

Nguyen looked confused again. "Huh?"

Nick shook his head, angry with himself for not seeing it sooner. He looked up at Nguyen. "The son of a bitch has a daughter. Or did."

TWENTY-FIVE

Nick's siren ring tone went off. The Bureau. "Sorry, Detective. I need to take this."

Nguyen shrugged.

Nick went outside. It was hot as blazes, and sweat beaded instantly on his forehead and neck.

"Good afternoon, Nick," Indra said. "We've arrived at your field office. David is here with me. You're on speaker." Nick was again struck by her soothing voice and precise articulation.

"Good flight?" Nick asked. He jumped into the Explorer and cranked the air. Nguyen had followed him outside but diverted to his squad. Nick watched him through the windshield. The detective leaned against the front fender and somehow managed to look put out while he munched on half of a sub sandwich. Nick's stomach grumbled.

"Just fine, thank you. We're getting settled in now. Still looking for possible connections between the victims."

"Anything?"

"I'm afraid not," Indra said. "I was able to obtain our warrant, however. It will be signed and ready to execute by morning."

"Excellent. Thank you. I'm planning to hold a videoconference tomorrow at 2:00. I'm going to ask that our NCAVC liaisons in the affected field offices be on fifteen minutes early so we can fill them in on what we're dealing with. I'd like for both of you to be on the call to lend your thoughts and input."

"Of course," Indra said.

Nick filled them in on his morning with the ME and his afternoon at the Wainwright scene as well as his suspicion that their unsub had a daughter.

"An interesting theory. I take it you're basing that on the fact that neither of the girl's jewelry boxes were stolen from?"

"That's part of it, but there's more to it than that. Both Helen Lyman and Scott Wainwright had daughters. Both had jewelry boxes that were untouched, but everything else was fair game. Neither girl was home at the time of the murders. That may not be so unusual in the Wainwright case, but in Bakersfield, the daughter had snuck out of the house the night the unsub struck. Wainwright was strapped to the coffee table facing away from the entrance almost like he was being hidden. At first I thought it might be a sign of remorse, but he hadn't shown any hint of remorse in the other cases. Those were as in-your-face as you can get. I think it was in case the family arrived home before the police got there. He was trying to shield Tamara Wainwright from seeing her father's dead body. And what was different about the case in California?"

Indra answered without hesitation. "The front areas of the house had been ransacked."

"Exactly. I think our guy was trying to prevent Lindsay from going into the house by making it very obvious that something had happened there. If 'everything is deliberate,' as David said, there has to be a reason he tossed the place. I think he tried to anticipate Lindsay's reaction but underestimated her courage." Nick remembered what Valerie had told him just two days before. "Teenagers can be unpredictable."

Indra laughed. "That's an understatement if I've ever heard one." She paused, as if she were thinking the possibility through. "It's far from definitive, but it does make sense. Excellent reasoning, Nick."

"It wasn't a terribly big leap when it dawned on me that it seemed like he was trying to protect the girls," Nick said. "Psychopaths don't really empathize with anyone, but it's possible that he believes he *should* shield them out of a specious sense of obligation. Sergio Peña was found by his teenage grandson in his garage, so our unsub didn't seem to have the same compunction with a young man. If we go with the theory that he was trying to protect Lindsay Lyman from finding her mother's body and tried to predict her actions in advance…"

Indra finished his thought. "Then you were correct about him profiling the victims. David is nodding. He concurs."

"Good, because I have something else that he might enjoy toying with. I think the pattern of the quarters is a code of some kind. They're different at every scene."

"My, you've had a productive day," Indra said. "I do hate to burst your bubble, but David is way ahead of you. He was looking into that possibility even before you left BAU yesterday. It is precisely the kind of thing his mind latches onto."

Nick was frustrated that Xavier hadn't shared his insight right away, but decided to let it slide. "Does he have any idea what they might mean?"

David's oddly rhythmic voice coming through the speaker surprised him. "We do not possess sufficient parameters at this time. There are sixteen potentialities. Four squared. Presently, we only possess four complete variations, each dissimilar. The numerous chaotic elements of the five cases make it impossible to deduce any existing pattern or rationale for their variations."

"I know you don't like to speculate, David, but if you had to guess?"

There was a long pause. Nick imagined Indra coaxing him. "The sixteen possible variations likely represent either specific characteristics of the victims or the manner of their deaths. Possibly a combination of both. Until there is duplication of a pattern, anything beyond that is pure conjecture."

"Thank you. That gives me something to think about, at least."

"There is something else you should consider, Nick," Indra said. "David has been applying the principles of game theory to our unsub's motives."

"Some game."

"I agree. But if he is indeed leaving cryptic messages for us to decipher, then it is reasonable to assume that this is a kind of contest to him."

"All right. I'm on board with that."

She continued. "Most of this is over my head, but David calls it 'complete information,' wherein the moves we will make are not known to him—nor his to us—but the rules, objectives, motives, and strategies of the game *are* known to some degree. We have investigative procedures, and he has an established signature. His goal is to kill, ours is to prevent him from doing so. We can, therefore, try to anticipate one another's moves within the structure of that conflict."

David interjected, his voice excited. "As in chess, one must not only plan their next several moves, but their opponent's theoretical responses to them. We must not only think about his actions but also what he expects us to do about them."

"So he's not just profiling his victims, but us as well," Nick said. "That's not going to make things any easier."

"There is another variable to any prevailing strategy," David said. "We must consider the moves he chooses *not* to make. And why."

TWENTY-SIX

Minnetonka, Minnesota
Wednesday, August 3 2016 4:37 PM

"The fuck is going on in my crime scene?" The voice boomed through the house as if it came from the very walls.

"Oh goodie. Chief's here," Nguyen said. His eyes had widened, but a small smirk had formed at the corner of his mouth. Nick could only describe the look as part horror, part amusement.

For his own part, Nick couldn't help but grin. He made his way back to the foyer with Nguyen in tow.

Morgan Bates was a giant—6'4 and 285 pounds of African-American granite. He even looked cut from stone, everything about him squared and chiseled. He was hopelessly crass and appeared intimidating, but Nick knew it was *mostly* bluster. Still, he wouldn't want to be on the receiving end of the man's anger.

When Bates saw him, he scrunched up his face. Deep chasms formed on his massive brow. "Aw, fucking Feds! Nick Keegan, you piece of shit."

Nick laughed and extended a hand that Bates swallowed in his own. "God knows if I left this up to your incompetent ass, we'd never get anywhere. How are you, Chief?"

Nguyen paled and looked queasy as he realized that his boss and Nick had history.

"Ha!" Bates barked. "Finally, someone with some balls around here. I can't even tell you how much of my damn time I spend peeling the lips off my black ass."

"How the hell do you still have a job, Bates?" Nick said. "You still kiss your mother with that mouth?"

"Shit, I kiss the mayor with this mouth. She fucking adores me." He leaned in conspiratorially. "She'd probably slip me the tongue if she could get away with it." He pointed at Nguyen. "This turd keeping you out of trouble?"

Nick laughed again. "Your detective has been very helpful." He paused and flashed Nguyen a sly smile. "For a turd."

Nguyen flushed, and Nick saw him release the breath he'd been holding. Maybe that would earn him a few points.

"What brings you?" Nick asked. "You checking up on me?"

"Nah. You're at least semi-fucking competent. Press conference at 5:00. They're setting up out there now." Bates was a notorious camera whore. He ran a hand over his short-cropped hair. "How do I look?"

"Like a mountain, Chief," Nick said.

"Goddamn right. Got anything new for me to tell 'em?"

"Nothing you're going to want to make public yet," Nick said. "Robbery was a secondary motive to the murder. Serial. At least five vics, probably a lot more. Statehood quarter signature. It's big. Task force will be up and running by tomorrow. Your guys got anything?"

"Not a damn thing. Door to doors have been a waste of time. Nobody saw shit."

"Not a total waste. It tells me he's good at this. Practiced. He knows how to not be seen. How to blend in. Sometimes what we don't see tells us just as much as what we do."

"Doesn't get us any closer to the sick fuck," Bates said.

"Everything helps."

Bates grunted. It sounded like a rumble of thunder. "Tell that to Wainwright's little girl."

Nick acknowledged the sentiment with a nod. "I know. How are they holding up?"

"Daughter's having a hard time. Wife doesn't seem all that broken up about it. She's a total MILF, by the way."

Nguyen coughed and looked at the floor. Nick had learned long ago not to be shocked by what came out of the chief's mouth and bit down a smile.

"Keegan doesn't think she was involved," Nguyen said. "Despite the motive." His tone made it clear he still wasn't convinced.

"I coulda' told you that, brainiac." Bates said. "There was no love lost between them, but she knew where her buns were buttered."

"Yeah, well it sounds like she was getting them buttered elsewhere too," Nguyen said.

Bates snorted. "So was he, apparently. She's a fine piece of trophy ass, but she's not the brightest bulb, either. Hacking off her hubby's thumb and leaving a fake signature to throw us off would take a criminal mastermind. She can barely tie her kid's shoes."

Nick only just registered the argument. He was thinking about his unsub's daughter and David's words. *We must consider the moves he chooses not to make. Everything is deliberate.*

"Keegan?" Bates said.

"Excuse me, Chief." He pivoted and ran up the staircase.

"The fuck?" Bates rumbling baritone chased him up the steps.

Nick went straight to Tamara Wainwright's room and stopped in front of the dresser and the jewelry box that sat atop it. He took a pair of latex gloves from his back pocket, slipped them on and lifted the lid. The top tray held a handful of loose rings and several empty boxes. He slid out four ornately decorated drawers and set them on top of the dresser, not at all sure what he was looking for. Still nothing stood out.

"What the hell are you doing?" Nguyen asked from the doorway.

"Did the BCA check this?" Nick asked.

"They printed it, but I doubt they gave it more than a cursory look. The mother confirmed nothing was missing."

Nick stood up and blew out a sigh. It was only then that he saw the tiny gap between the top tray and the wood of the box. It was a separate piece. Blood crashed in his ears, and a shiver ran down his back. He gripped one of the dividers and lifted the tray.

Beneath lay a shiny quarter, eagle side up.

TWENTY-SEVEN

Nick sat on the girl's bed examining the coin between his gloved fingers. He held it carefully by its edges. The quarter was a 1993D and still held its original luster. When the light hit it just right, he could make out hints of tiny grooves on the surface—broken arches and a fraction of a whorl. A partial print. Probably not enough to manage even six points of comparison, much less the twelve needed for a firm ID. Maybe the lab could raise more.

He took out his Blackberry and snapped several close up pictures of the quarter, with and without flash, trying to get a reasonably decent shot of the barely-visible friction ridges.

Nick felt lightheaded as he turned the quarter over and over again, willing the date on the obverse to change. It was a coincidence, of course, but that didn't make the significance any less powerful to him. He didn't have time to think about his father, or his murder in the year pressed into the cupronickel.

He blew out a breath and fought to get his head back in the game—back to the present. There was a chance that it hadn't been left by his unsub at all; it was possible that it belonged to Tamara Wainwright. Nguyen had gone out to phone Sarah Wainwright and the girl to see if she had kept the quarter hidden inside the jewelry box, but Nick already knew the answer. He was sure that Nguyen would return with an evidence baggie any minute.

The good news, if there could be any, was that he had made a connection with his unsub. He'd slipped enough into his darkness that he'd identified an action that might easily have been overlooked. A day into the case, he'd discovered new evidence. It was a promising start.

Nick doubted this was the only thing the unsub had left behind. He put in a call to Jim in Bakersfield and left a message asking him to send someone to the Lyman scene to tear Lindsay's jewelry cabinet apart.

As he was hanging up, Nguyen returned waving a small baggie. "That was a goddamn good find. It's not the girl's."

Nick nodded as he slipped the quarter inside, feeling a tiny bit like he was losing his father all over again.

Nguyen jotted down some information on the plastic surface. "You all right? You don't look so hot."

Nick forced a smile and rose from the bed. "Fine." He spent a minute putting the jewelry box back together.

"Chief just finished up out there. I filled him in."

"Good."

Bates met them at the foot of the stairs. "All right, that was some wicked fuckin' voodoo shit right there, Keegan."

It wasn't the first time what he did had been described that way.

"Lucky guess," Nick said.

"Lucky, my ass," Bates scoffed.

Nick changed the subject. "Anything from the BCA?"

Nguyen shook his head. "Nothing. No prints. No fibers or hairs. No DNA. Zip ties were pretty standard—you can buy them at any hardware store. Nothing specific about the knife except that it was serrated and sharp as hell. We may get something from the vacuum hose and canister they collected, but I'm not holding my breath." He patted his pocket. "Maybe the quarter."

"It looks like there's a partial latent on the obverse," Nick said, "but I doubt it'll amount to anything. This guy is too careful." He turned to Bates. "I'm going to need to assemble a multi-state task force. Do you think you can spare two or three for me, Chief?" He gave Nguyen a quick look. Nguyen returned it with a barely perceptible nod. "I'd like Detective Nguyen to be the lead here, if you can spare him."

"No sweat off my balls. It's your case—you can fuck it up with whoever you want," Bates said. He gave Nguyen a toothy grin and shot him a wink to show he was kidding. "We'll make it work."

Nick chuckled and turned his attention to Nguyen. "Videoconference tomorrow at the Bureau field office in Brooklyn Center. 2:00. In the meantime, check with Mrs. Wainwright to see if she can provide you with descriptions of the missing jewelry. If we're really lucky, they'll have taken pictures for insurance. Get everything you can to local pawnshops. Maybe we'll catch a break."

Nguyen nodded and typed furiously into his tablet. After a minute, he looked up.

"What the fuck you waiting for, Detective? An invitation?" Bates growled. "Get on it."

Nguyen flushed. "Yes, Chief." He headed outside.

When they were alone, Bates cocked a thumb and threw it toward the door. "He can be a prick, but he ain't half bad at his job."

Nick nodded. "I got that impression."

"I told him to play nice or I'd break him in half."

"Aww, that was sweet of you, Bates. See, you're just an overstuffed teddy bear with the mouth of a drunken sailor."

Bates grinned. "Tell anyone that and this teddy bear will break *you* in half."

Nick laughed and held up his hands in surrender. "Your secret's safe."

"This is some bad shit, Keegan. I don't like when these fuckers play with us."

"Me neither, Chief. Me neither."

TWENTY-EIGHT

Nick sat in the recliner typing notes into his laptop. Connie made a short high-pitched moan in her sleep that momentarily stole his attention. It was dark, but he could make out her silhouette sprawled on the bed cast in the pale blue glow of his monitor and the streetlights seeping in through the curtains.

Looking at her now, he felt a piercing ache in his jaw, and tears stung his eyes. After his dad died, Nick never expected it would be possible for him to care for someone quite so much again—to feel that his entire existence was bound to another in such a critical, imperative way. His relationship with his mother had imploded after his father was killed, and he'd spent the bulk of his free time at the Jacksonville precinct with Burt and "the boys" to avoid her frequent outbursts and overprotectiveness. He knew now that she'd suffered with depression and anxiety disorders triggered by his dad's death, but he also knew they'd never be the same as they'd been before.

Nick's bond with Burt was the closest thing he had to a normal familial relationship during his teen years, but there was always a subtle distance between them. He assumed some of it was Burt's wariness of overstepping his bounds, coupled with the automatic cautionary distance that cops put between themselves and everyone else. LEOs tended to know better than most how easily and quickly things could come to a crashing halt—for Burt, Nick was that fear personified.

Nick had his own problems getting close to people. A few short-lived and tumultuous relationships in high school and one semi-serious relationship in college taught him that he'd never been able to put down the defensive mechanism that had been in place since that fateful night on a dark Florida highway. He'd once thought that distance would always be there and had come to terms with it. He'd even embraced it, believing that less vulnerability would make him a better cop—like Superman sans Lois Lane and kryptonite.

Self-therapy in the form of fifty-seven credits of psych classes gave him enough insight to understand how his father's sudden exit from his life had shaped him. He'd become callous, self-reliant, difficult, and virtually impenetrable. If he was really honest with himself, he realized too that he'd become a selfish prick. Even as he tried to work through his emotional deficiencies, he was promiscuous and often partied to blackout. It wasn't until he realized his behavior could jeopardize his ambitions that he started to settle down.

Virtually all of his remaining walls had been utterly obliterated by the tiny hurricane now wrapped loosely in a wispy sheet, half-sprawled over his side of the bed. She'd been contracted to assist the Bureau with a fraud case he was working on in D.C. in 2011. After a few weeks of vigorous flirting, she asked him out. He surprised himself by telling her about his father on their first date. She cried. Twenty minutes later, they were giggling like fools on the dance floor of a downtown club. An hour after that, they were back at his apartment talking (mostly) all night long about things they'd never told anyone else.

He caught himself smiling at the memory. He sighed. *What am I doing?* Why was he spending almost every waking minute obsessed with the darkness in people when he had something right in front of him worth so much more? Nick closed his laptop, got up and slipped into bed next to her. She settled into him with a contented groan, and pulled his arm over her so that it lay on her belly.

There. There was the fear that he couldn't shake, sitting like a lead weight in his gut.

What if someday he too stopped coming home? What if he left a little life to fend for itself in a world where people did the unimaginable to one another?

Eventually, hypnotized by her peaceful, rhythmic breathing, Nick fell asleep.

There's a knock on the door—three heavy raps. There's menace in them. Nick can hear it in the slight bit of hesitation between the first and second knocks. He's not yet twelve, but his chest tightens in something that he can only compare to the nervousness he feels when Melanie Anderson smiles at him in physical science class. Mom's already worried (but she always is a little) because Dad's late. His shift ended at 6:00 AM and it's already 8:30. He usually calls if he's running late, but the phone hasn't rung at all this morning. Mom jumps at the sound of the raps on the door instead of the familiar sound of Dad's car pulling into the driveway. She gets up slowly, her steps heavy and hesitant, like the knocks on the door. There's something pulsing off of her in waves—Nick can feel it, and it's making that tightness in his chest worse. He's not sure why, but his eyes sting a little.

She freezes with her hand on the knob. She looks over at Nick, and he sees her jaw and arm quiver before she opens the door.

Nick recognizes Burt right away. He's been over a bunch of times for barbecues and football games and stuff. He's a good friend of Dad's, and he always has a candy bar in his pocket. Nick senses there won't be any Snickers, Baby Ruth's, or (his favorite) Reese's peanut butter cups today.

There's some other guy in front of Burt that he vaguely recognizes from the few times Dad's taken him to the station. He's got his cop hat in his hands, and he's turning it nervously around and around in front of his chest. A third guy is standing to the left, wearing all black and holding a well-worn black book in both hands.

Mom starts wailing and falls to her knees. Tears well up in Nick's eyes too. Some of it is from Mom's distress, but maybe he knows what this means too. She's sobbing on the floor, and Nick's sitting on Dad's big La-Z Boy, half-in and half-out of his second sock, frozen in place. The men are just standing there, speaking in quiet voices that he can't make out, until Burt pushes his way into the house, kneels down and embraces Mom. He's saying, "I'm sorry" over and over again and something about trying to save him, but it had just been too late.

Mom cries for a long time on Burt's shoulder, and the two other guys just stand there in silence looking at Nick solemnly from the doorway. Mom finally stands and with shiny, wet cheeks screams at the man in the black collared shirt to "get the fuck away from our house," and to "shove his bible and his God up his ass." He's never heard Mom talk like that. Nick sees Burt give the guy a look and shake his head. The man looks kind of relieved and walks away with his shoulders hunched.

Nick finally recognizes the other guy—the one with the hat. It's the Chief of his dad's patrol division. He's talking now, and his voice is loud enough for Nick to hear from his spot on the chair. He hears something about Dad being a hero, and how Mom doesn't have to worry about anything—the Sheriff's Department will take care of all of the arrangements, and if there's anything at all...

Nick feels the warmth of tears slipping down his cheeks and pooling around his chin. His vision is blurry, his lips are salty, and he can still hear Mom's choked sobs coming from the doorway. He sees Burt walking toward him. He doesn't want Dad's friend to see him crying, so he draws an arm across his eyes and face to clear them, but then he see that Burt's crying too, and that scares him a lot.

"I'm sorry, Nick. So sorry, bud." Burt says to him.

He's old enough to get it, but still young enough to pretend he doesn't. He has to think for a minute about what he's going to do. In the end he decides to be grown up about it and, in that moment, he lets go of his childhood forever. He's twelve, but he somehow understands that he'll never be the kid he was just fifteen minutes before.

In a steady and deliberate voice, Nick says, "He isn't coming home again. Ever. Is he?"

Burt sobs once—a choked sound that he struggles against, and he shakes his head as new tears fall down his face. "No, champ. I'm afraid not."

Burt reaches into his pocket, and for a second, Nick's pretty sure he's going to pull out a candy bar. He can feel something happening inside of him, there's some emotional edge that he's teetering on. Something dark and empty is on one side, purpose on the other. And as much as he can't understand why, he knows everything depends on what Burt is holding out to him right this second. He can't see it clearly at first through his bleary vision, but it glints gold—like a Twix wrapper, maybe. He feels a pressure inside of him building. He's tipping, slipping—rage threatening to tear him to shreds. But as a tear falls away, Nick gets a clear look at what Dad's friend is holding. Burt pushes the cold metal into his hand. Nick's rage slips away, and he nods at Burt, who somehow seems to know exactly what just happened inside of him because he nods back once and pulls him into a big hug where it's safe for him to cry. And he does.

He squeezes Dad's badge so tightly that the sharp corners cut into his hand.

TWENTY-NINE

Shoreview, Minnesota
Thursday, August 4 2016 6:22 AM

Nick was rescued from the dream by the sound of his cell phone vibrating on his nightstand. He checked the clock. Getting messages at this hour was never a good sign. The message was from Valerie. *+3. Files are on the way. Brace yourself.*

"Everything okay?" Connie asked him through a squint. She untangled her beautiful nakedness from the sheets and rolled herself to a sitting position on the edge of the bed. She fumbled to turn off her alarm, which was still at least twenty minutes from going off.

"Sorry, hon. Quantico." He swung out of bed and ran over to grab his laptop from the recliner.

She shrugged. "It's okay. I'll go in a little early and maybe sneak out of there before five. I'll just jump in the shower." Instead she sat there and stared at the wall for another minute or so in a sluggish daze. Nick watched her quietly in admiration and amusement until she shook her head a little and finally lurched across the room, dragging her bare feet along the carpet. At the door she turned back to him. "It was nice to wake up next to you for a change. Thanks." She yawned and disappeared into the bathroom.

He knew she meant well, but it stung just as much as it made him feel better. He swallowed down his guilt and opened his laptop.

Gruesome is in the eye of the beholder. While blood and gore might get to one person, sometimes identifying with the agony of another might be worse for another. More than once, Nick had been deeply shaken by scenes without a single drop of blood present, and he was sometimes hardly moved at all by the most brutal of massacres. It was the eyes and facial expressions of the dead that he often found most disturþing. Though muscles relax upon death, it was sometimes still possible to distinguish looks of fear, shock, confusion, and pain on a vic's face.

For some reason, the look of confusion was particularly bad for Nick. Maybe it was knowing that those lives ended with a question—"why?"—that often had no logical or reasonable answer, even after their killers were brought to justice.

This most recent batch of case files had a little something for everyone. After what he'd already seen from this unsub, Nick didn't think he could be shocked by much of anything. He was wrong.

A fit, twenty-eight-year-old white male from Pennsylvania had been scalded to death in his bathtub. Where he still had skin, it was badly blistered and nearly as red as the flesh beneath. Most of the water had drained out of the tub, leaving a thick milky substance speckled with clotted, brown drippings and flayed skin. Pancuronium Bromide had been found in his system.

Another: a body discovered in a seedy motel in Pershing County, Nevada. This time, the victim was a thirty-six-year-old prostitute with dark hair and pale skin. Track marks on her arms and behind her knees along with subsequent toxicology screens suggested a long-term heroin addiction. Though she might have been pretty once, after years of drug abuse, she certainly wasn't anymore. She was found nude, lying on her back in the middle of the bed with her arms to her side, palms up. She looked almost serene, as if she'd died in her sleep, but a broken hyoid bone and petechial hemorrhaging indicated strangulation. The scene and M.O. were in such stark contrast to the other case files, Nick almost didn't believe that his unsub was responsible. But the statehood quarters were there—as obvious and identifiable as a signed piece of artwork—Nevada this time, suggesting a second, subsequent kill there.

A little more than three weeks later, a twenty-five year old stripper had been found in the bathroom of her posh Vegas home. She'd been secured next to a tub that had been used as a basin for a bleach and ammonia mixture. The combination had resulted in the release of chlorine gas into the air, which had proven fatal.

Nick looked at a small digital image of the woman from before the incident. She had short blonde hair, high cheekbones, and full, pouty lips. Her colored contacts turned her eyes a striking shade of violet. She'd been stunning. In stark contrast, the most graphic of the crime scene photos looked like something straight out of a horror movie. Her head was tilted backward onto the toilet seat lid, and her palms were lying on the floor face up, much like Scott Wainwright had been found. Mascara and tears had traced dark tracks down her face, neck, and chest in a manner that made it appear as if she were melting. Dried vomit, bile, mucous and vast amounts of frothy spittle mixed with blood pooled on the floor in front of her and spattered her bare thighs. She was utterly unrecognizable as the woman from the other photo.

California statehoods had been left on her body. The timing of this murder was about five weeks prior to Helen Lyman's death in

Bakersfield. It couldn't possibly be a coincidence—the statehood quarters were left to identify the *"where"* of his unsub's next kill. Nick could almost hear the challenge the coins represented: *catch me if you can.*

Nick grabbed his notebook and flipped it open to compare the quarter patterns left at these scenes against those he'd jotted down while on the flight home. If his theory was right, the patterns should have matched for the Vegas stripper and Amanda Roberts in Georgia, both poisoned.

They didn't.

"Shit," Nick said aloud. He'd been certain that would turn out to be the connection to his unsub's *"how?"* He gnawed at the inside of his lower lip and watched the steam from Connie's shower roll out of the bathroom while he wondered what it was that he was missing.

He hoped he could figure it out before someone else died.

THIRTY

Nick hadn't even made it as far as his desk before his phone rang. He didn't bother to check the caller ID.

"Keegan."

"It's me," Jim Harris said.

"You find anything?"

"Maybe. There was a quarter, standard eagle, hidden inside the jewelry box. I thought that was a little much to be coincidence, so I had it bagged. Lindsay's still non-responsive so I can't ask if it's hers."

Nick wasn't sure what he'd been expecting, but it didn't get much more obvious than that. "It's not. And it's no coincidence either. I found one here in exactly the same place."

"What the hell?" Jim asked.

"Not sure, but it looks like it's another piece of his signature. Prints?"

"Hard to say. Maybe a partial. Could just be smudges."

"Do you still have it, or did you give it to CSU already?"

"No, I've got it. Like I said, I wasn't sure if it was evidence or not."

"Good. Can you snap some macros of it and send them to me before you hand it off?"

"Sure."

"How're you holding up?"

Jim blew out a sigh. "I'm all right. Wish she'd come out of this. Lindsay, I mean. You don't think she's in danger, do you? Should I put people on her at the hospital?"

"I don't think so. I actually think he was trying to protect her."

"How the fuck do you figure that?"

Nick explained his theory.

"Hmm," Jim grunted. He didn't sound convinced.

"He doesn't care about loose ends, Jim. I think she's okay. Really."

"All right. I trust you."

"Profile and tactics video conference at noon your time. We'll be in touch with the details a little later."

"I'll pull a team together."

"Thanks. Hang in there, bro."

Nick found Indra and David holed up in the conference room. A box of donuts was open on the table. David had evidence in the form of powdered sugar on his face and the front of his shirt. A can of Mello Yello was in front of him. A yogurt cup with a plastic spoon sticking from it and a cup of steaming coffee sat beside Indra's laptop. The two were a study in contrast.

"Good morning," Nick said. "I take it you've both heard?"

Indra acknowledged him with a nod. "Yes, Valerie sent the files right away this morning. The scalding is particularly awful."

Nick pulled out a chair next to Indra. "I thought so too. It looks like we were wrong about the heads-tails patterns signifying the M.O."

David peeked up from his monitor and cocked his head.

Indra took his cue. "What makes you say that?"

"Both Amanda Roberts and Jenna Jordan, the stripper from Vegas, were poisoned. The coin patterns didn't match."

David pursed his lips and wrinkled his nose. He looked somewhere over Nick's shoulder as he addressed him. "Why would they?"

"Why wouldn't they?" Nick countered and resisted the urge to look behind him at the spot on the wall that David was staring at.

"We've established that the statehoods indicate where his *next* victim will be geographically. It therefore stands to reason that the pattern would indicate something related to his next victim as opposed to the last."

Nick cupped a hand over his mouth, sighed, and nodded slowly. "Shit. You're right."

"Yes," David said matter-of-factly. He returned his attention to his computer.

"Do we have enough consecutive cases to confirm that?" Nick asked. He flipped open his own laptop.

"Not at this time," David said.

"Dammit," Nick said, frowning. "Any ideas on the Washington quarters found at the Lyman and Wainwright scenes? Thanks for that David, by the way. We wouldn't have found them without your insight."

David gave him a quick little salute of acknowledgement without looking up.

Indra pulled up the images of the two coins and split screen them on her monitor. "They're both in extraordinarily good condition for coins that of that age. It's possible that the dates may be important to him. 1988 would be within our profiled age range. His year of birth, perhaps?"

"I wondered that too. That would make him twenty-one at the time of the Sergio Peña murder. It could work. It's also possible there are more coins that were never discovered. Or maybe the dates don't matter at all."

David shook his head.

Nick held up his hands. "I know. Nothing is unintentional."

"There is no purpose to leaving evidence for us to find unless it bears significance," David said.

Indra daintily spooned some pink yogurt into her mouth and chased it with a silent sip of coffee. "So let's say, for the sake of argument, that the fifth quarters are significant to him and the statehoods dictate where and how he's killing his next victim. Might they also be responsible for the who? Possibly even the when?"

That was an interesting consideration. "What are you thinking?" Nick asked.

"Coin flips, perhaps?"

"God, I hope not," Nick said. "That would mean his actions are completely random."

David chimed in again. He was positively chatty. "From a strictly scientific perspective, no factors are ever completely random."

"How so?"

"Randomness supposes equal probability in every potential factor, which, statistically, is impossible. Pseudo-randomness or chaos more precisely characterizes what you are suggesting. Even random number generators are not entirely arbitrary because factors exist which limit their outcomes. For example, the number of digits or 'keys' required is a parameter. Say that number is ten. That means that the number can only be truly *random* to ten billion. Further, in a strictly random scenario, no one number has any greater probability of being selected than another, so the odds are equally likely that a ten digit number consisting of all ones would be generated as any other of the ten billion less one combinations remaining."

Nick's head swam, but he was pretty sure he followed.

"But assume that same ten digit key is intended to serve as a code to protect something valuable. A password consisting of all ones, or a sequential series of numbers would not be effective. Therefore, more parameters are added. Perhaps any combination of numbers that contain more than five of the same digit would be rejected. Perhaps any sequential series of numbers longer than four digits would be abandoned. Perhaps repetitions of three digits or more, such as 'five-five-five' would be disregarded. Or perhaps the integer zero cannot start a sequence. Each of these constraints dramatically reduces the total number of possibilities and therefore does not allow for true randomness."

"I think I follow," Nick said. "Basically, you're telling me that even what we describe as 'random' is still somewhat predictable based on any number of assigned parameters which define or limit the result."

"Correct. Chaos follows somewhat predictable patterns of behavior and suggests that if one could accurately ascribe the effect of every variable that impacts a given scenario, they could also accurately predict the outcome."

Nick's brain hurt. "Okay, so what does that tell us about our case?"

"Many things. Let's look at an element that is absolutely *not* random. Geography. Even if the unsub put 50 quarters into a bag, shook them up and selected one coin to determine where he intends to go next, the odds that he'd stay in the same place for two consecutive kills would be one in fifty. The odds that would occur twice—in Nevada and here in Minnesota—are approximately one in 2500. We have only eight cases so far. It is near impossible that repetition would occur randomly in so few instances. So how is he determining where to linger?"

"Maybe a single coin flip? Heads he stays, tails he goes?"

"That also adds a parameter and thus reduces the scenario's chance elements. Anything that deviates from a singular pattern is a limitation. And those are many. Why four quarters instead of two? Why a single coin flip, instead of four? If the coin pattern is indicative of his M.O., how did he determine which pattern corresponded to manner of death? Even the coin flips themselves are almost certainly not random. Golfers swing the club in precisely the same manner many thousands of times so they can repeatedly duplicate a desired result. What is the probability that they will put the ball precisely where they want it, in comparison to someone who has never held a golf club?"

"Point taken, but there are still a gazillion factors that impact that swing. Wind speed and direction, contact point with the ball, position of the body, even barometric pressure."

"Exactly."

It took Nick a minute to realize that he'd made Xavier's point for him. If one could learn how each of those factors impacted their swing, they could minimize their negative effects and even use them to their advantage.

"So you think he may be manipulating the variables to get the results he wants?" Nick asked quietly, chewing on the idea.

"It's simple logic to assume that someone with abundant practice will be more adept at ensuring a desirable outcome. This, of course, does not take into account the potential for mulligans."

Nick found himself amused by David's grasp of golf fundamentals, but he was absolutely right. Who was to say whether or not their unsub didn't simply *cheat* once in a while? The coins would provide an effective chaotic element that would make his actions largely unpredictable, but not completely random.

"So, in theory, with enough vics we might be able to establish a type. A preference."

David raised one shoulder in a quick shrug.

"More great insight, David. Thanks." Nick was just beginning to grasp how helpful David's beautiful mind could be in a case like this.

Indra gave him a smile and a stealthy wink. He could tell she knew exactly what he was thinking.

The three outlined plans for their conference call, and Nick went to brief Quentin.

Later, Nick pulled a quarter from his pocket and flipped it into the air. He found if he really focused, he could generate almost any sequence of heads or tails that he chose. It didn't work every time, but it worked often enough that he could see Xavier's point. If he concentrated on the positions of his hand, the height of the toss, the force exerted on the coin itself and the number of revolutions in the air, he could flip four consecutive heads with relative ease. How much easier for the unsub then? With enough repetition and practice, one could almost manage some measure of consistency.

Shit, he thought. It was almost easier assuming that everything *was* random as opposed to not. Introducing a whole set of unknown parameters to an already muddled mess just made the whole thing even more incomprehensible. The only thing Nick was sure of—the word "chaos" was extremely fitting.

THIRTY-ONE

Nick stood, his heart slamming in his chest. Somewhere in the neighborhood of fifty cops and Bureau personnel from the impacted cities and field offices had eyes on him. Every one of them expected him to lead them to their suspect. He looked to his right at Indra. She gave him a slight smile and nod that told him she had every confidence in him. He could have kissed her.

"Good afternoon. For those of you that just joined, I'm Special Agent Nicholas Keegan with the FBI's Minneapolis division. We've asked you all to join us today because the files we contacted you about are almost certainly tied to a mobile serial killer. Everyone on this call has a stake in this.

"This unsub has killed in every one of your jurisdictions at least once. To date, we've confirmed eight kills, and more are being discovered every day as your ViCADETs are keying in new case files. He's an equal opportunity killer. The victimology, M.O.s and obviously the geography have been different in almost every situation so far, but his signature is distinctive and unmistakable.

"If you'll all take a quick look at the primary photos of your vics, almost all of you will notice a set of four quarters, placed over the eyes and in each hand. In every case but one, these are statehood quarters. The lone exception is a case that occurred in Texas in 2009, in which standard eagles were used. We believe this was before he perfected his current signature. These quarters appear to be the unsub's way of communicating and possibly even determining his actions, which I will get into in a few moments. Before I do, however, I'd like to turn the call over to Supervisory Analyst Valerie Shianco so she can review the chronology, victim list, and scope of what we are dealing with."

Nick felt like an invisible weight was lifted from him as everyone's eyes shifted to Valerie in their monitors.

"Good afternoon, y'all. As Special Agent Keegan mentioned, as of this morning we have eight victims attributed to this serial." She listed the cases in reverse chronology, and included the particulars of each.

Nick watched the LEOs scribble furiously onto yellow legal pads, type into their laptops, or flip through files as they followed along. Quentin caught his eye and gave him a nod of encouragement. Across from him, Chief Bates snuck Nick a thumbs-up when no one was looking.

Valerie continued. "Based on his unique signature, we know this unsub has been active for at least seven years. In those cases where we believe we've identified sequential kills, his timeline is anywhere between two and five weeks. If that remains consistent, we're looking at a highly prolific killer. This case is a top priority for the analyst team here, and we are running queries and reviewing potential positives as soon as they come in from your ViCADETs. That's all I've got for now."

Nick took a swig from a bottle of water and cleared his throat. "Thanks, Valerie. So far, there are no known links between the victims, but we're still looking into potential connections. As you heard, the kills are literally all over the map and also the age, gender, and race spectrums. The only obvious link right now is the quarter signature. We've been discussing the purpose of the coins in this unsub's psychopathy, and we think they may have multiple meanings." He went on to explain their impressions, and then recounted the finding of the fifth quarters in Bakersfield and Minnetonka. "Where possible, you'll need to revisit your crime scenes to check for this. We know in some cases it's been years, and it may not be obvious where to look. We don't even know how long this component has been part of his signature. It's a long shot, but everything new that we find tells us a little bit more about this guy."

"We also think that this unsub is using the quarters to add an element of unpredictability to his actions, making it all but impossible to figure out what he's going to do next."

A female officer from Baltimore looked up from her notes, a pen hovering over the pad. "So it's random?" she asked. Nick heard a hint of defeat in the slight stress she put on the word.

Nick saw David tense behind his monitor, and his perpetually flying fingers stopped over the keyboard.

For his benefit, Nick said, "As a colleague has pointed out to me, it's more chaotic than random. For us, it means about the same thing. We're probably not going to get ahead of him. But," he emphasized, "we *will* catch him."

"Do we have any idea *why* he's killing people?" one of the Vegas cops asked.

"I'm going to steal some of the thunder from the profile to answer that," Nick said. "This unsub has an antisocial personality disorder. He's a psychopath and a narcissist. Not all psychopaths become killers, but they do all have a profound lack of emotion and empathy and have a tendency to believe those traits are weaknesses in the rest of us. The ones that do become violent often see their victims as prey and themselves predators. Many think they are evolutionarily superior to the rest of us. Ironically, it's the thrill and exhilaration of killing that drives them. It makes them feel something in an otherwise empty existence.

"There has been no outward evidence of it, but the sadistic quality of his kills also suggests a sexual element. A paraphilia. He gets off on the suffering of his victims. He has a fundamentally different view of the world, but he also has a purpose. There's something beyond the sexual gratification that is motivating him. He *wants* us to know he's out there—that's why he's leaving the quarters. He's telling us a story, but it's in a language we can't interpret yet."

"Anyone here fluent in nutbag?" Bates said in his booming baritone.

There was an eruption of laughter. Even Nick was caught up in it. Humor was just one of the ways that LEOs bled the pressure and stress of these kinds of cases. No one was better than Bates at keeping things light.

Nick gave everyone a minute to bask in it before continuing. "The problem is, psychopaths are exceptionally good at blending in. They learn to mimic behavior they can't comprehend so as not to appear different. They fake what they don't feel. You're not going to find our unsub talking to himself, flinging his shit at the moon, or otherwise acting unusual. He'll seem as normal as anyone else at first.

"I'll let Special Agent Tandon from the BAU share the rest of the profile with you. Indra?"

"Thank you, Nick." Her accented voice was calm and melodic. If she was nervous, Nick couldn't sense it in the slightest. "Our profile is still incomplete, but there are some things we can be reasonably certain about that might help with the investigation. We're dealing with a highly organized and very intelligent white male, most likely in his late twenties to early thirties. He is of at least medium build, but likely larger, and he will be in exceptional shape. His narcissism won't allow for anything less.

"On more than one occasion, he's demonstrated an astute understanding of human physiology and therefore may have a medical background of some kind. He's been known to use a paralytic called Pancuronium Bromide to subdue and control his targets. This is significant because it would typically paralyze the diaphragm and usually requires assisted breathing. The dosage must be incredibly precise in order to assure his victims are kept alive but incapable of moving without mechanical ventilation."

"How's he getting this stuff?" a cop from Texas asked. He looked ancient, but had the sharp, watchful eyes of a hawk.

"An excellent question. There are many dark Internet and international sellers that are difficult to track. Thus far we've had no luck, but it's an avenue of investigation we should continue to pursue." Indra paused for a second before resuming the profile.

"He's exceptionally confident and driven in part by the challenge of the kill. He's constantly adapting and evolving. If he is indeed using the quarters to choose his M.O., there are presumably sixteen methods that he is fully prepared to enact. Like many psychopaths, he'll be charming and engaging. Chances are you will like him when you first speak with him."

Nick noted her clever choice of words—not *if*, but *when*.

She went on. "He is an opportunist. He steals from his victims, be it money, jewelry or other valuables. There are indications that he was able to acquire nearly a quarter of a million dollars from his latest victim's safe."

There were whistles and several profanity-laced exclamations at the revelation.

Indra waited for the commotion to calm before she continued. "There are strong indications that this unsub is, or perhaps was, a father to a daughter of unknown age. He is a perfectionist, and exceptionally cautious. He stalks his victims until he is confident of their routine. He likely has knowledge of police procedure, as he's never left behind any physical evidence. Special Agent Keegan has even theorized that he may be profiling his victims, which would indicate a significant understanding of human nature and psychology."

"Sounds like a LEO." Nick couldn't place the speaker on the video feed, but his accent suggested it was one of the Georgia cops. "Could he be one of us?"

Nick had entertained that notion more than once.

"It is a possibility," Indra said. "As Agent Keegan mentioned, psychopaths are fearless and sometimes take high-risk positions in military and law enforcement just for the thrill of it. We should keep an open mind.

"When we do come up with a suspect, the interrogation tactics are very specific. Special Agent Keegan or someone else from the BAU should conduct the interview, if at all possible. This isn't someone who is going to respond to the usual techniques. I believe that is all for the moment. Nick?"

"Excellent profile, Indra, thank you. So, we've established that we're probably not going to predict this unsub's next move, so we're going to have to follow his back-trail. Review your case files for anything that might have been overlooked the first time—especially in light of all we now know. Check airline, hotel and car rental records that correspond to the timelines. Check pawnshops—see if any jewelry or other property from your victim's scenes or those prior to yours showed up. We've already secured a blanket warrant for all of those avenues of inquiry so you shouldn't have any problems."

"That's a metric shit ton of data," someone said.

"It is," Nick agreed. "And there are a lot of us involved and probably more to come. We're activating ORION for that reason. With it, we'll be able to maintain constant two-way communication, and all of our available resources in Quantico will assist in collating, filtering, and distributing data. As new cases pop we'll be able to onboard new task forces and get them up to speed right away. All of you will see what we see, when we see it. This isn't a contest or a race. We're all working toward the same goal—to bring this son of a bitch down. I really don't care who gets the collar as long as it's done right. For purposes of this case, we are a single unit. One team. Are we all clear on that?"

He was answered with silence. He took it as an unspoken "yes."

"Good. Under no circumstances should anyone talk to the media about the case until cleared through the Bureau's National Press Office. They will make sure that everyone is presenting a unified message, and that we're disseminating the right information. There are some things we will want to withhold to weed out the crazies. No camera whoring." Nick raised an eyebrow at Chief Bates across the table.

Bates held up his hands and tried to look innocent. "Who me?" he mouthed.

Nick stifled a laugh. "Until things calm down, I'd recommend checking in on ORION and ViCAD several times daily. We'll update it as quickly as we can, but our resources aren't unlimited. There may be some minor delays in the data entry.

"How do we access it?" Detective Nguyen asked.

"Through your secure intranet link to the FBI.gov page. Same place you access ViCAD. The first time you login, you will be asked to enter the case file ID that you wish to view. The case file ID is: C-H-A-0-5. That's Charlie, Hulu, Alpha, Zero, Five."

EAD O'Neill took over. "The database for this case is being uploaded to ORION as we speak. It should be live with everything we have by tomorrow. In the meantime, you can pull all of the relevant case files from ViCAD and get to work on the airlines, hotels, and car rental places. The quicker we get those lists, the quicker we can start cross-referencing them and looking for recurring names. Start with departing flights, hotel-check outs, and car rental returns from the day of, and up to three days following your murder. That should keep our results somewhat manageable. If we have to widen the net from there, we can, but I think we'll have better luck anticipating when he left an area after a murder than when he first arrived. Especially in those situations where there wasn't a lot of time between kills."

"Thanks, Director," Nick said. "If any of you have questions, contact the NCAVC coordinators at your local FBI field offices. If they can't assist you, they'll know who can. And, you can get messages to all of us through ORION or our Bureau email addresses. I appreciate you all being on the call today. Now, let's go find this asshole."

As the feeds went dark, Nick suddenly felt lightheaded and nauseous. He sat and took a long slug from his water, then hid his trembling hands beneath the table.

As everyone filtered out of the room, Indra put a gentle hand on his elbow. "Nicely done. You're a natural," she whispered.

Nick was just glad he didn't puke in her lap.

THIRTY-TWO

Zorin strolled through the campus, protected from a fine drizzle by a baggy black and crimson St. Cloud State hooded sweatshirt. It was the last day of summer classes, and there were plenty of euphoric potential victims celebrating the end of finals week. College campuses were a favorite hunting ground. He blended in effortlessly. No one gave him a second look. Over many years, he'd become a masterful chameleon and was able to go just about anywhere without drawing the slightest bit of attention. Until, of course, he became some lucky Non's last (and only) focus.

The quarter turned in the air, the same bleak silver as the clouds behind it.

For years, Zorin had operated silently, under the plentiful ineptitude of law enforcement and a virtually worthless FBI database. He'd played their own system against them, targeting the geographic regions least likely to utilize ViCAP—both large urban areas that were overburdened with cases and extremely small rural areas with limited manpower and resources.

Then the invitation came—a letter from the FBI, asking discharged combat veterans to join a program to greatly expand their database. Of course, he had no intention of enlisting—that would be a fool's errand—but it did, at least, tell him that his carefully created cover was now at an end, and gave him time to formulate a new plan. A coming out party of sorts. After so long in the shadows, it was exhilarating to know he was now in the open—visible and hunted. He knew they were searching for him, and that too was just as he'd intended. It had always been part of his plan to emerge with the unstoppable force and fury of a raging cataclysm. This new strategy of the FBI's would enable just that.

Of course, there were rules. But none were more paramount than his survival. If the coins dictated something that he felt was too risky, well, perhaps fate needed a little nudge. And that was within his power. He would adapt, learn, develop and do whatever was necessary to sustain his existence. And like everything he did, whether by coin or by design, there was always purpose. He hunted by the call of chaos, but he heard other calls as well. Nothing was forbidden to him except that which might end him. He took as he desired, and he desired much.

Now what he desired *most* was within reach.

He was flawless. Absolute. The Non believed that they were the pinnacle of evolution, but they were oblivious to the predator in their midst. He was a hunter. A gatherer of souls. He was far more than they could ever hope to be. And he would make them ready for the gaping, waiting maw of the Else.

Raucous, high-pitched, and overly exuberant laughter came from up ahead. An ostentatious young black man in his early twenties said goodbye to a female friend and waved at her as she pulled out of the parking lot.

Zorin grinned. The fourth consecutive tails was in his palm.

THIRTY-THREE

Nick leaned over the railing with a beer in hand and looked out over the wooded lot adjacent to his house. He was exhausted. His restless sleep in the crushing grip of his nightmare and the intense stress of his day left him spent, and he was glad for a few minutes to himself to decompress and think.

After his father died, Nick became an honorary "sheriff" of the department. He came and went as he pleased, always welcomed by everyone from the chief on down. If anyone ever had a problem with Nick being in the precinct, it was never spoken of aloud. Looking back, Nick realized that, in a way, he'd become a surrogate for his dead father and a way for all of them to cope with Richard's death. But none of them looked after him, or *groomed* him quite like Burt had.

During summer breaks and evenings when there was no school the next day, Nick would sometimes ride along with Burt on patrols. When he turned fourteen, Burt taught him to shoot at the officers' range. A few years later, Nick learned to drive in a squad car on a closed course behind the precinct with Burt coaching him from the passenger seat while he held on to the 'oh shit' bar with white knuckles. Though it was obviously against regs, Burt would sometimes sneak Nick cold case files, which both inured him to the horrible reality of violence and taught him how to work through cases and think like both a cop and a criminal. Over the years, he watched countless interviews from behind the one-way mirrors as Burt and some of the other cops questioned suspects in Interrogation.

Nick was a natural. He was athletic, inquisitive, and an analytical problem solver, yet he also possessed an almost unnatural empathy and insight into criminal behavior. On more than one occasion, he identified the critical pieces necessary to close those cold cases. He eventually became so good at reading people's body language, tells, and microexpressions, the guys started calling him the Human Lie Detector and often requested him to observe and give his insight into their interrogations. It was probably a damn good thing that the DA had never figured out what was going on in the small dark room behind the glass. Thanks to Burt's coaching, Nick was the virtual equal of many on the force before he'd even finished high school.

The summer before his senior year, Burt presented him with a gift. For the more than six years that Nick had been an honorary junior sheriff, every officer that had known or worked with his father had been putting at least a few bucks from every paycheck into an account for Nick's college. Coupled with a scholarship or two secured by glowing recommendation letters from the Division Chief and Burt, it was enough to cover a full-ride to the University of Maryland's esteemed Criminal Justice program. Nick was astounded by their generosity and struggled with the idea of taking so much from those he'd come to think of as extended family.

Ultimately, Burt explained that Nick really didn't have a choice. The gift was as much a tribute to his father and the bond of brotherhood they all shared as it was based on Nick's ability and desire to follow in his father's footsteps. Cops took care of their own, Burt had told him, and the loss of a fellow officer was a weight they all took personally and carried forever. The best way to repay them was to live up to his fullest potential and all of their hopes for him.

Nick had been trying to meet those expectations (and those he'd invented for his father) ever since. And though he'd already helped put away dozens of criminals, he knew it was an impossibly high and probably unattainable bar.

But this unsub would be a pretty excellent addition, he thought.

Nick took a long drink and relished the cold burn on the back of his throat.

"Who are you, damn it?" he muttered, dangling the bottle from his fingertips. Nick could see him out there, but barely. It was a bit like looking at someone at a great distance standing in a swirling fog. At first you could only see shapes and shadows in the haze. But with every new insight, a tiny bit of that fog would lift and the figure would become just a little less vague—a little more *there*.

Every once in a while, Nick felt like his dad was whispering in his ear, trying to help him make sense of the forms in the mist. This was one of those times. As much as it hurt, he let the memory of that moment just before Burt handed him his father's badge spill over him again. A searing, white-hot rage bloomed in his chest and pushed its way up into his throat—Nick wanted to scream until it bled. His cheeks burned. He clenched his fists so tight his arms shook. Blood crashed in his ears. All he wanted in that instant was to destroy. To devastate. To inflict his agony upon the world.

Nick came back to the present, trembling. His left hand ached from squeezing the neck of the bottle. He blew out a breath and loosened his grip and watched as his fingers pinked back up. He set the bottle down on the railing and shook out the pins and needles.

Nick remembered one of his abnormal psych professors talking about a theory known as "resilience." She described it as the tipping point between one's level of stress and adversity versus their coping abilities and available support systems. It was particularly critical between the ages of eight and twelve, the most formative years of the brain's emotional development. Nick recognized that he had teetered precariously on the point of that fulcrum.

He felt a kind of kinship with his unsub at that moment—an understanding of just how close he himself may have come to being precisely who he was now hunting. Suddenly, Nick felt very strongly that the unsub had also lost a parent at some point prior to his teenage years, during that time of malleable youth where everything is so critical. They'd both tottered on the brink of an abyss. But instead of being pulled back from the edge as Nick had, the unsub had been forced over it—his already anomalous mind pushed beyond all hope of redemption.

His unsub didn't have a Burt. He didn't have an entire Sheriff's Department supporting him. He didn't have the convictions of a father who'd been like a hero to him.

For a brief moment, the fog lifted.

"I see you, you son of a bitch." Nick said to the nebulous form in his mind. "And I'm coming."

Nick thought he heard laughter emanating from the mist.

THIRTY-FOUR

It was a breezy and overcast morning, the sky the color of slate. A fine, misty drizzle helped to keep Nick cool as he ran and had the added effect of clearing his head. So much had happened in the last week, it hardly seemed possible. He felt wholly overwhelmed. And terrified.

It wasn't the first time he'd been involved in a serial case, but this was a different beast altogether. Under normal circumstances, a review of a handful of potentially linked cases would be sent to BAU, which would lead to a profile, which would be provided to a police task force. Detectives investigating the cases would do the majority of the legwork, and the Bureau would assume a supporting role.

In this case, Nick was far more directly involved than he'd usually be. And if that weren't pressure enough, the magnitude of the case was growing by the day. He hadn't yet heard from Valerie this morning, but he wasn't anticipating good news.

The rhythm of his footfalls against the pavement and the slowly roiling clouds were hypnotic. His stride fell in with the beat of the music in his headphones, and for a few minutes he slipped into an almost meditative state. His mind relaxed and briefly existed in a place outside of the Chaos murders. It was blissfully peaceful there. So much so that Nick nearly stumbled when a tone interrupted the driving Dragonforce track that he was using to pace himself.

He slowed to catch his breath for a minute, walking off the pins and needles in his legs. He fished his cell out and checked the screen. Valerie. He said a silent prayer as he opened her text, but his stomach was doing furious internal gymnastics. He was convinced that there was some kind of prescient nerve bundle in the there that sensed bad news.

Nine more, God help us. Tenth possible—haven't reviewed it yet. Six statehoods in larger metros—all within the last eighteen months, three eagles in smaller towns from as far back as '07. It's insane here. Files are on the way.

"Jesus fuck. No way," Nick muttered, pulling the headphones from his ears. He'd pitched headlong into a damn nightmare. At this rate, they could be looking at the largest serial murder case in Bureau history by next week. Bile crept up his esophagus and pooled in the back of his throat. He felt sick. Thank God he'd not eaten before he left or he'd have surely puked on the trail.

Nick bent over and put his hands on his knees, sucking air.

He trusted his instincts. He knew there was no one more capable of getting inside this bastard's head. No one was better prepared to catch him. None of that stopped a tendril of doubt from snaking its way in and constricting around his heart.

Footsteps neared from behind. Nick heard them slow. He pushed himself back up to standing and moved to the side of the trail.

"You okay, buddy?" the jogger asked, turning to run backwards as he passed.

Nick lifted a hand. "Good, thanks."

The man nodded once then turned and found his rhythm again.

"Solid pace," Nick called. The man waved over his shoulder and soon disappeared into the woods.

Nick checked his watch. He had time for another mile. He was less than a minute into it when another text came through. He grabbed his Blackberry, expecting it to be Valerie confirming the tenth file, but it was Connie. His stomach did another flip. She never texted him this early.

There was only one word on the screen: *help*

He listened to the unanswered rings over speakerphone for the fifth time. He willed himself to run faster, but he had no more speed to give.

He hit redial again.

"C'mon, Con. Pick up." It was then Nick heard the sound of a distant siren approaching. "No, no!" He abandoned his attempts to call, and somehow found a little more. He burst out of the woods and immediately cut left angling himself toward the house. The siren was much closer now. An ambulance, he was certain.

"Connie!" he started shouting for her long before she could have heard him. He was in a full-blown panic. His throat was raw and felt like shredded parchment. He kept yelling. He sensed muted cramps in his calves, the pain held at bay by adrenalin and fear, but he knew he'd pay a brutal price later. He kept running. As he neared the house, he saw the ambulance turn onto his street. "Shit!"

He wasn't about to wait to meet them. He tore open the basement level sliding rear door, still calling out to her.

The silence that answered was terrifying and nearly debilitating, but Nick shot up the stairs to the main level three at a time. He had a split-second of clarity as he reached the landing and detoured quickly to the front door, flipped the deadbolt and flung the door open before tearing back to the staircase.

"I'm coming, Con!" he called, oblivious to any danger that might be waiting for him upstairs. He tore down the hallway and flew into their bedroom. She wasn't there. He checked their bathroom. Empty.

His terror threatened to choke him. His chest was on fire. He realized he wasn't breathing and allowed himself a gulp of air. *Where was she?*

"Con?" he begged the room.

She texted you. He looked over at her nightstand. Her phone wasn't there, but he could see a smear on the white wood.

"Con!" he cleared the room in three bounding steps and leapt onto the bed. She was lying on the other side. *Oh God, she's pale.* "Babe?" he asked. He scrambled over the rest of the bed to get to her. Something warm and wet squelched under his hand. He lifted it up in front of him. Blood so dark it was almost black covered his fingers and palm. A trickle of red ran down his wrist. He stared at it dumbly for a half second every bit as long as any eternity.

Nick the husband withdrew and was instantly supplanted by Nick the cop.

He leapt down to the floor beside Connie. Her lips were blue. He put an ear to her mouth and bloody fingers to her throat. She was alive and breathing shallowly, but her pulse was weak. Her eyelids fluttered as she fought unconsciousness. He couldn't see any obvious wounds on her body, but there was mottled blood all along the inside of her bare legs and on the floor around her.

Nick heard distant voices and a loud knock. "Upstairs!" he yelled. "Bring the stretcher!"

An iPhone lay on the floor by her hand, the screen stained with dark fingerprints. He used the light on his own phone to check her pupils. Thudding came from the stairs as paramedics made their way up to them. Nick yanked the bed sheet and draped it over Connie's naked body and scooped her up off the floor. He carried her as far as the door when two paramedics reached him.

"Uh, sir you can't—"

Nick cut him off. "Twenty-eight-year-old female. Seventeen weeks pregnant." He lay her body down gently on the stretcher. "Respiration shallow, pulse thready and rapid, pupils reactive. Severe blood loss from the pelvic region." He looked at his hand. "More than a pint. She needs a transfusion."

The second EMT, much bigger than the first, held out a hand to Nick. "Sir, you need to step away. Let us do our jobs." He stepped in front of Nick and drew the bloodstained sheet off of Connie and wasted precious seconds trying to confirm all of the things Nick just told him.

"Get her in the bus." Nick said, his voice frantic. "I'm her husband and a Special Agent with the FBI. I have first-responder training. If you don't get her to the hospital right now, she's going to die."

"We'll do everything we can to keep that from happening," the smaller paramedic said as he wrapped a blood pressure cuff around Connie's arm. "For now you need to step away or it's going to take us longer to get her there. Understand?"

Nick clenched his teeth but stepped back with his hands in the air. He knew they were better equipped to handle this than he was, but giving up control went against his every instinct. After an agonizingly long minute, the big EMT gave a quick nod to his partner. The two men took positions at either end of the stretcher and carried Connie downstairs and outside without another word. Nick followed and piled into the back of the ambulance with his wife and the smaller of the two men who stayed busy treating Connie. Nick swung the ambulance doors shut and scooted onto the seat at Connie's side as the paramedic grabbed a bag of saline and a large bore needle and prepped her for an IV.

"HCMC." Nick called to the driver. "Go!" He grabbed his phone and dialed Quentin while trying desperately to ignore the charley horses tearing into the muscles of his calves like searing hot blades.

THIRTY-FIVE

Connie's OB/GYN doctor came out of the operating room. As she came over to him she pulled her mask down beneath her chin. Nick couldn't read her face. That was a rarity, and it scared the shit out of him.

"Is she okay? The baby—? Are they…?"

"Connie's stable at the moment. I'm afraid the baby was gone long before you got here. There was nothing we could do. I'm sorry, Nick."

Nick wasn't sure where the relief ended and the sadness began. "Okay. That's um—" He trailed off, not knowing what it was.

The doctor pointed him to a small bank of seats. Nick sat and stared at his hands. They were shaking and raw. He'd washed them at least a dozen times, but there were still dark crescents of Connie's blood under his nails.

"I'm afraid Connie's not out of the woods just yet."

Nick felt the blood drain from his face as his eyes darted back to her. "What do you mean?"

"Your wife had a number of uterine fibroids—benign tumors, essentially. They're not life threatening in and of themselves, but they can force the placenta to become detached from the uterine wall, which can cause severe hemorrhaging. That was the case here."

"Wouldn't we have seen that on the ultrasounds?"

"Not necessarily. They can grow very quickly during pregnancy. Sometimes there's little or no warning at all."

"So you have to remove them? More surgery?"

Her poker face slipped slightly. "It was a bit more serious than that. The damage to the uterine wall from the tear and the fibroids is extensive. The surgeon wasn't able to get the bleeding under control. We need to remove her uterus altogether."

"A hysterectomy," Nick said to the floor. *Oh God.*

She nodded slowly and put a hand on his shoulder. "Yes. I'm so sorry, Nick. If there were any other way—"

Nick stood, suddenly unable to sit still. "Just save my wife, doc. Please."

THIRTY-SIX

"But sir—"

"No 'buts.' You're on leave effective immediately. It's not a reflection of your work, Keegan, but your wife needs you more than I do right now," O'Neill said. "We can handle things on our end. Be there for her. That's your only assignment right now. Is she conscious yet?"

"No. They're keeping her under for a few more hours to make sure there are no complications. They don't want her moving around."

"Damn." On the other end of the line, Nick heard O'Neill sigh. "You have my most sincere condolences."

Nick appreciated it.

"How are *you* holding up?"

Nick swallowed down a bitter lump of sorrow and guilt. "There's not really much I can do. To be completely honest, I feel pretty helpless."

"I can imagine. When the time is right, I want you to make sure you talk to someone."

"Yes, sir. I understand the protocol."

"Screw protocol. I'm not telling you this as your boss. I'm worried about *you*. This is a big loss. It will affect you."

"I know," Nick said.

"I know you know. Take as much time as you need. I've been in touch with Special Agent in Charge Ripley and ASAC Quentin already. They know you are on leave indefinitely. Forget about this case, you hear me? At this rate, it will still be here for you when you get back."

"That's what worries me."

"Let it go, Keegan, and that's an order. Be with your wife. Nothing else is more important right now."

Nick suppressed a sigh. "Yes, sir."

"How much do you want me to share with your team?" O'Neill asked.

"Standard story, I guess. Family emergency. You can let Valerie know, though. She and I are close."

"All right. Take care of yourself, son. We'll wait for word."

"Thank you, sir."

Nick disconnected and paced the waiting room, frowning. He stared at his Blackberry and chewed the inside of his cheek. After a minute, he opened the email program on his phone and pulled up the message Valerie had sent him earlier in the morning. It had not yet been recalled. He opened it and looked at the ten .doc files. The icons swam in the unshed tears in his eyes.

He downloaded them.

Nick ran through the options in his mind. Those closest to him would think they were protecting him from himself and were least likely to help. Indra was also out. She'd know that emotionally charged situations could be a liability, and she didn't know him well enough yet to know how he might respond. He briefly considered Xavier. His emotional detachment would play to Nick's advantage, but he was also probably the least likely to knowingly break the rules. Eventually it hit him. He picked up his cell phone and called Valerie's desk.

"Shianco."

"It's me, Val."

"Oh, Nicky. Honey, I'm so, so sorry."

"Jesus Christ, it hasn't been ten minutes since I got off the phone with O'Neill."

"I know. He pulled me in right away and strictly forbade me from sharing anything about Chaos with you until further notice. Are you all right? How's Connie?"

"They've got her under close observation right now. I can't see her yet, but she's stable. We're both stable, I guess. It's hard, but I don't think it's really even hit me yet, you know?"

"I know, sugar. We all grieve differently and in our own time. You know that."

Nick's eyes stung and his throat hurt again. "I think, uh, Connie is going to have the hardest time with it. I'm still sort of… dazed."

"No one can prepare for something like this. Do they know what happened?"

His voice was strained. "Her doctor said uterine fibroids. She lost a lot of blood. When we got here it wasn't looking good, so they did a hysterectomy. They said they didn't have any other options."

"Oh, sweetie... I don't even know what to say. Is she going to be okay?"

"They think so. Kids are obviously out. I mean..." he swallowed the lump in his throat. "I can live with that, you know? For me, it's all about her." His voice trembled. "But for her, Val... God damn it. She felt like being a mother was part of her purpose in life. She's going to be devastated."

"Nicky, you know I love you, sugar, and I'm here for you, but O'Neill's right. You need to be there for *her*. Connie needs you. She needs to know its okay. Even if it isn't, you know? She needs to believe it. And you need to convince her."

He was silent as he bit back tears. After a moment he said, "Yeah, I know."

"Is there anything I can do?"

"I do need one favor."

"Name it, darlin'," she said.

"There's a recruit in Cyber that I need to speak with. Name's Lange. Addison. Can you have her call my cell as soon as she is able?"

Valerie's voice took on a noticeable edge. "What's this about, Nicholas? You need to focus on Connie, remember?"

"And I am. I just need help moving some files from my laptop and cell phone to ORION."

"Right. Didn't you minor in Computer Science? Don't try to bullshit me."

He sighed. "Please, Val. Just get her the message?"

"Goddamn it, Nick. Haven't you learned anything at all from me? You don't want your work here to destroy all the things that really matter in life."

"I know that. But this case matters too. Saving lives matters. You know it does. It's part of who I am."

"So's your wife."

"I can do both."

"No, you really can't, and you're a damn fool if you think so." The disappointment in her voice stung him far worse than anything his own mother could ever say or do.

"Will you please just pass on the message? Addison Lange." There was a long silence on the other end of the line. "Seventeen, Val," he added. "Or is it eighteen now?"

"Fuck you, Nick," she said, but she sounded more sad than angry. "You think I don't know the count? Those people are already dead. Connie isn't."

"I'm in his head, Valerie."

"It sounds more like he's in yours. Give Connie my best. And call your mother."

She hung up on him.

THIRTY-SEVEN

Nick watched Connie fight the weight of her eyelids. She managed to open them for a fraction of a second, but they slipped closed again. Her mouth worked against a small wet sponge that Nick pressed to her lips.

Anxiety shot through him. He wasn't ready for her anguish.

"I'm here, babe. Take your time. It's okay," he told her quietly.

He felt her muscles relax under his hand, and the chirping of her monitors slowed. Then she opened her eyes. After a second or two they found him, and she turned her head slightly in his direction. She squinted in confusion.

Nick tried to smile but knew it was a shitty attempt.

A wheeze escaped her lips as she tried to talk. She pursed her lips into a loose 'O' and tried again. "Wh—?"

"Shh," he whispered. "Don't try to talk right now. You need to rest."

She tried again, stubborn as always. "Whhh—?" She could have been trying to ask damn near anything: *Where am I? What happened? Who the fuck are you?*

Nick took a shot at it. "You're in the hospital."

Her eyes widened and slogged slowly around at her surroundings. When they settled back on him, she squinted again in place of the question she couldn't yet articulate any other way.

"You're fine, Con. Don't try to talk yet." He pressed the nurse call button on the remote hanging from the railing of her bed. "I love you. Thank God you're okay." He pulled her hand to his lips and kissed the back of it.

Connie's eyelids faltered, and the drugs sucked her back down into unconsciousness.

A male nurse that Nick recognized from earlier entered the room.

"She's starting to come around," Nick told him.

"That's a good sign," he said, checking her vitals. He apparently didn't trust the monitor because he also checked her pulse via her wrist. "She looks fine, all things considered. The worst should be over. Her heart rate and BP are excellent, and her O2 levels look good. According to the blood work, her iron levels are almost back to normal after the transfusion. I don't see any reason for concern at the moment. I'll grab the surgeon to check her dressings and meds. Unless you'd prefer to tell her what happened, he can probably best explain it to her."

"I think that might be best," Nick said, feeling like a despicable coward.

The nurse nodded and headed for the door. "The doctor should be in shortly. Can I get you anything?"

Nick shook his head. "No, but thank you."

"Of course."

After a few minutes, the doctor came in and checked Connie's bandages and incision site. During the examination she regained consciousness again, and seemed a bit more in control of her faculties.

"Are you feeling any pain, Connie?" the surgeon asked.

She sluggishly shook her head.

"Good. I imagine you'd like to know what happened."

"Yeah," she whispered.

He nodded slowly with a grim expression and explained how she'd lost the baby.

Nick wasn't sure which response he was dreading more—wailing and shrieking, or silent tears. Perhaps because she was still heavily sedated, he got the latter. He watched, heartbroken, as her eyes filled. Her lower jaw trembled, and then two impossibly large teardrops rolled down her temples into her hair. Nick held her hand in one of his and used the other to try to catch her falling tears with his thumb.

With the help of a few ice chips, she'd regained a little bit of her voice. "We can try again though, right?" she asked.

The doctor sat on the corner of her bed and looked at her somberly. "The complications you experienced were very rare, Connie. And life-threatening. Those masses caused a placental abruption—the placenta tore away from the uterus. The damage was catastrophic. A hysterectomy was the only way to save your life." He put a consoling hand on her foot through the blanket. "We didn't have any alternative. I'm truly very sorry."

Then the tears came in force, her little body wracked with sobs.

Nick held her hand as she cried and ignored the vibrations of his phone against his hip.

There was a light knock on the door. It slid open, and Mindy's head peeked in. Her eyes were red and swollen. "May I?" she asked.

Nick felt Connie's shoulder tense at the sound of her sister's voice, but she didn't turn her head away from the wall. Nick wasn't surprised. She hadn't looked at him once in more than an hour, instead keeping her head turned toward the wall while she wept.

He gave Mindy a tight smile and nodded.

She came inside tentatively, holding a small arrangement of flowers from the gift shop. She set it down on a counter.

Nick stood. "Thanks, Min."

She wrapped him in a huge hug. "I'm sorry," she whispered and kissed his cheek. "Your mom's out there."

Nick groaned quietly, but nodded his thanks.

When she let him go, he motioned her to the chair at Connie's bedside and gave her a slight shake of his head.

Mindy sat down beside her sister and said, "Hey, Midget."

Connie didn't turn, but Nick saw her chest hitching again.

Mindy took her hand. "I'm sorry, sis. God, this sucks."

Nick's throat closed tight.

"Mom and dad want to come."

That got a reaction. Connie gave an adamant shake of the head.

"Mom's freaking. You know how she is…"

"*No,*" Connie whispered.

"Okay. I'll tell them to hold off for a while." Mindy looked Nick's way, desperation in her eyes.

He pointed toward the hall. Mindy nodded. He wasn't sure whether he'd rather endure Connie's grief or his mother—neither was preferable to the other—but sooner or later it would have to happen. Nick set his jaw and made his way out to the Intensive Care waiting area.

She stood when she saw him, clutching her hands in front of her. She took a hesitant step forward like she wasn't sure if she should embrace him or not.

Nick saved her the trouble and sat down, keeping an empty seat between them. After an awkward second, she took her chair again.

"How is she?" his mother asked without any of the compassion that a normal human being would convey.

Nick took a deep breath. "She'll be okay."

She shook her head. "What a shame."

Her choice of words set his teeth on edge. He looked at the floor and bit his tongue. "Yes. A *shame*." He wasn't the least bit surprised that she didn't ask how *he* was.

After a quiet moment she looked over at him and said, "I was hoping that the baby might bring us closer together."

As if their baby was nothing more than a means to her end. Anger welled in Nick's chest. His jaw trembled with the effort of holding it in. He turned his face to hers. "I know what you hoped."

Her eyes widened when she saw the hardness in his. "I just meant...I...I'm sorry." It was her turn to look down at the floor. "I guess I don't do grief very well."

"Yeah? You think?" Nick said. She looked back at him. Perhaps for the first time since his father died, he saw a glimmer of real hurt in her eyes. He was both satisfied and ashamed at the same time. He sighed. "Look, you don't need to be here." In fact, he rather wished she weren't.

She regained her usual sharp, sarcastic edge. "Where else should I be, Nicholas? I did just lose my grandchild."

It was always about her. Anger reared in Nick again, irrational and ferocious. "*Anywhere* else, *Mother*."

She drew a sharp breath. "I—"

"We just lost *our* child. There will be no others. No more chances for you to *fix* us," he hissed. His face felt like it was afire. He threw up his hands. "You can stop trying now."

A few visitors seated in the waiting area got up and found someplace else to be. His mother sat there, ramrod straight, with her mouth partially open in shock. She blinked at him once.

Nick stood and took his phone from his pocket to give himself an excuse to walk away, but his rage wasn't yet spent. He stood over her, gazing down into her eyes. "You'll never be half the mother you were before Dad died."

She recoiled as if he'd slapped her.

Nick walked away.

THIRTY-EIGHT

Mindy left to feed and let Mork outside with another long, tearful hug and a promise to return later to run Nick home for his car, clothes, and other necessities.

Thanks to an IV bolus of Valium, Connie was finally asleep after nearly three nonstop hours of crying. The hollows under her eyes were still puffy and purple, but Nick was grateful she was getting some relief after the physical and emotional traumas of her day.

He, however, dangled in the uncomfortable space between self-righteous anger and a guilty conscience. Since his mother had gone, he'd cooled off enough to feel like an asshole, but not so much as to feel like he owed her an apology. He felt far worse about the constant, nagging desire to get back to his unsub when Connie needed and deserved his attention most. Nick knew it was, in part, a way to avoid his own grief, but that didn't make him feel any better about it. Why shouldn't he suffer every bit as much as she was?

Though he hated himself for it, he relented and checked his cell phone. There were more than a dozen missed calls and texts from family and friends and one voicemail from a number he didn't recognize with a 703 area code:

"Hi, Nick. This is Addie Lange. Supervisory Analyst Shianco passed along your message. She said it was a matter of some importance for you. I'm not sure how I might be able to help, but you can reach me at this number. Anytime is fine."

Nick fought another internal battle about whether or not to call her back. Doing so would be crossing a line—several of them, in fact. He'd not only be putting his own career at risk, but potentially the future of a new recruit as well. And Valerie's warning still hung over his head like the blade of a guillotine.

There were many things that Nick would need to do over the next several days and weeks, but they wouldn't occupy all of his time. He could sit at Connie's bedside doing crossword puzzles and feeling sorry for himself, or he could do something productive that might save lives. If he came up empty, no one would ever need to know about his insubordination. And if he did find something, there were a handful of people that he trusted enough to hand the information off to.

He tried to ignore how closely his internal justifications sounded like those of an addict. As for Lange, she was a big girl and could refuse to help him if she chose. He'd make sure she understood the risks and she could decide for herself.

Nick bent over and kissed Connie's cool forehead then stepped out into the hall. He added Addie's number to his contacts and returned the call.

She sounded out of breath when she answered. "Hi, Nick. Gimme a sec." In the background he heard the squeaking of tennis shoes, a myriad of voices and the unmistakable *pings* of a basketball impacting the floor. They got more distant with each second that passed.

"Shooting hoops?"

"Yeah. Sorry about the noise, I'm heading outside now."

"You any good?"

"Better than most of these guys, but that's not saying much. I played some in high school and college." Nick heard a door slam. "Okay. I'm all yours. What's up?"

"I need to ask you for a favor."

"I'm not sure why I'd be your first choice for a favor, but I figured this wasn't a social call."

"Before I even get into this, Addie, you need to understand that there's a chance it could come back to bite you in the ass."

"Ah, I get it. So I'm the expendable recruit in this scenario?"

"No, that's not—"

She laughed. "I'm kidding, Nick. How about you let me worry about my own ass?"

He wasn't sure where to begin. "Do you happen to know what I've been working on this week?"

"You mean aside from giving ViCAD seminars? Or are you talking about this new serial case that's got everyone losing their shit?"

"Word still gets around, I see."

"Let's just say it's a good thing we're not CIA or NSA. Nobody can keep their mouths shut around here. What about it?"

"I was assigned the serial before I left Virginia. We're pretty sure the unsub is here in Minnesota. I've been working up a profile with BAU over the last few days and we activated ORION yesterday. It's big."

"So I've heard."

"I was benched today."

"*That* I hadn't heard. Why?"

Nick drew a deep breath and exhaled it loudly. "My wife miscarried this morning." With the admission, he was forced to again swallow down his grief and guilt.

"Oh God, Nick. I'm really sorry."

"Thanks. I appreciate that. I do. But that's not why I called. My access to ORION has been pulled."

"Understandable. You've got more important things to worry about right now."

"Believe me, I'm aware. But it doesn't work that way, Addie. This case is accumulating new bodies every day. Ten more, today alone. The ViCADET program is churning them out so fast the analysts can barely keep up. And this is just one unsub. There will be other links in the coming weeks. I can guarantee it."

"What about your team? You can't be in this alone."

"I'm not. We've got two of BAU's best on it, and SA Shianco is keeping a close eye on things. There are seven local LEA task forces up and running. Several more will need to be added after the weekend."

"So let them run with it. Why does it matter so much that you stay on this? You didn't strike me as the hero-complex type. Is it personal?"

Nick took a minute to really think about the answer. She deserved that much if she was going to stick her neck out for him. "I could care less about the credit, Addie. Even if I blow the case wide open, no one can know I had anything to do with it or you and I will both be burned. This asshole is taking up space in my head—I suppose in that sense it *is* personal. But really that's not even it. For as long as I can remember, my dad was either telling me stories about being a cop, or I've more or less been one. I can't just switch it off. It's all I've ever done."

Addie was quiet for a long moment.

Nick felt obliged to elaborate. "Let me put it another way. Let's say you've been writing music for thirty years and you suddenly suffered a tragic loss. Would you stop composing?"

"I certainly wouldn't bring a frickin' piano into the hospital room."

"Of course not. But you'd still create. You'd still feel it within you. You'd jot down movements and arrangements on napkins, or the damn walls if that was all you had. Just because we're hurting doesn't mean the music stops. The music is *always* in your head. And maybe it helps heal us a little. Does that make any sense at all?"

"The fact that you're comparing music to profiling a psychopath, you mean? No. Not in the slightest." She fell silent again.

Nick let her think it through.

Finally she answered, "I'll see if there's anything I can do."

"Thank you."

"Yeah, well don't thank me yet. And Nick?"

"Yes?"

"Try not to jack up my career, okay?"

THIRTY-NINE

Minneapolis, Minnesota
Friday, August 5 2016 7:04 PM

Nick pinched out on his Blackberry, wishing like hell that he had his laptop. Reading case files on a five-inch screen was a royal pain in the ass.

Their unsub certainly got around. A few gaps in his history looked to have been filled with this latest cluster of links. The small ranch town of Hanna, Wyoming and the even tinier city of Garden Grove, Iowa had been hit in 2014 and 2015 respectively.

In June, coordinates on a geocaching webpage led three adventurous but unfortunate college students to a partially scavenged corpse in Gwynns Falls Park, Maryland. The ex-Secret Service agent's remains suggested he'd died from a savage beating. Four statehoods were found nearby. The subsequent investigation into the web posting led the Maryland State Police Computer Crimes Unit to the IP address of a local Starbucks WiFi hotspot. That trail had dead-ended with the cyber sting of a terrified high-school senior whose laptop's MAC address had been spoofed to make the post. Nick added "tech-savvy" to the growing list of knowns about his unsub. It was also intriguing that he'd gone through the extra time and effort to make sure that the agent's body was found.

New York City had been hit recently, as had Nashville, and there was another double in the suburbs of Chicago. Another murder had taken place in Texas—near Dallas this time—and Nick's home state of Florida had a case in St. John's County. The potential tenth file was from another small town near Roanoke, Virginia.

Causes of death were equally all over the place. A twenty-year-old up-and-coming singer had been found crucified on a small tree in a wooded area near her home in 2013. The tree had been cut down—with the woman still pinned to it—and the coins placed over her eyes and on her palms. One of the earlier cases was a "simple" shooting, though the shot placement was designed to inflict maximum pain and suffering—several joints, including both knees, a hip, and a shoulder had all been obliterated. Another had been drowned in a million-Scoville ghost pepper sauce. The liquid was found in the victim's eyes, sinuses, throat and lungs. Nick winced, recalling how much it burned just to accidentally rub your eyes after handling a jalapeño. There was a third poisoning. One of the victims was eviscerated. Still another had been beheaded—his upturned hands placed in such a way as to prevent the head from rolling. If not for copious amounts of blood and a two-inch gap between neck and torso, he might have looked as if he'd fallen asleep with his fingers laced behind his head.

In two of the cases, the bodies had decomposed to the point where CODs couldn't be determined, but the quarters on scene left little doubt that they were dealing with the same unsub. Nick was quite sure that Xavier had compared the heads/tails patterns against their other M.O.s already, but he made a mental note to check for duplications himself later.

The enormity of the case struck Nick again. There were now eighteen victims, each horribly brutalized. That wasn't counting any files that might have been entered into ViCAD earlier that day or those still deeper in the ViCADETs piles. It wasn't counting any bodies that might never be found, or that the unsub might have killed before he'd conceived of his current signature. Nick really had no way to hypothesize how many total kills this one psychopath might be responsible for, but he suspected they were still just scratching the surface.

Jesus Christ.

He cast a guilty glance in Connie's direction, but she was still sleeping soundly. Nick took a deep breath, closed his eyes and leaned back in the shitty beige recliner. He pulled a set of crime scene photos into his mind and rebuilt the space in three dimensions. He pictured the victim and resurrected her in several more dimensions—not just height, weight and body type, but a set of mannerisms, a smile, a voice—giving her life again. Jolene was in her mid-twenties, unmarried and plain, with long straight hair the color of straw. Her eyes were a dull, caramel shade of brown. Absurd tan lines suggested she often wore short shorts with her shirt tied off above her midriff.

She's utterly uninteresting. Of course, the vast majority of them are. At least until he prepares them, makes them special—sometimes even exceptional.

He straddles Jolene's thighs, pinning her wrists to the floor beneath his knees. She's wailing like a fucking siren. A little thrill runs through him. He doesn't always have the luxury of their screams or pleas or tears. This is a special treat.

He touches the tip of the knife to her stomach about five inches to the left of her navel and watches as her skin dimples in futile resistance. He raises an eyebrow at her in silent inquiry.

She tosses her head from side to side. "No. No. Please. No."

He draws the knife along her belly. The flesh parts easily—like he's pulling open a zipper.

After a minute she stops screaming. She stops thrashing. She looks straight up at the ceiling with tears pooled in her eyes. Her mouth opens and closes soundlessly.

"Listen," he tells her. Her insides squish through his fingers.

He leans back with his eyes closed in ecstasy. The corner of his mouth pulls up into a smile—small, but very real. He plunges both hands deeper into her and yanks out her intestines, slick and shiny with blood. He holds them up. "Do you see?" he asks her.

Her eyes roll down and come to rest on the treasure spilling through his splayed fingers. Her eyes widen, and she starts to shriek again. The look on her face is exquisite. A masterpiece. He groans and ejaculates in his pants. Jolene's scream lasts no more than a few seconds before her eyes lose focus again, and her head lolls to the side.

He can still see the pulse in her neck—faint but quick. Unconscious but alive.

He plays with her viscera for a moment, shifting them between his hands like a Slinky. Then he piles them back inside her abdomen. He climbs off her and drags her into the corner of the foyer, her severed Achilles tendons trailing bright trails of blood behind. He props her body up. Blood cascades from the opening in her belly, spilling down into her pubic hair and splashing onto her thighs. If he keeps very still, he can just hear it dripping into the spreading pools on the tile next to her legs. Musical.

Once he has her in a sitting position, he reaches into her again and pulls out her small intestine. He winds it around her neck several times like so many strands of shiny pink pearls. He sets her hands on her legs and coils her large intestine around them.

He stands back and takes her in. Tilts his head. A worthy creation.

He waits. It doesn't take long. Fortunate, since she doesn't have long left.

Her head twitches. Her eyes flutter open. She makes a mewling sound and raises her head from her shoulder groggily like someone who has been sleeping for a hundred years. It takes a moment for the pain of her wounds to bring her back around. She's weak from blood loss. Too weak to lift her arms. She whimpers and looks down at how he's unmade her.

She begins to scream in the tiniest little voice he's ever heard.

He shudders and comes again.

Then in mid-scream, she dies.

A magnificent end. Not his best, certainly, but more than adequate. She's been made ready.

Nick opened his eyes. He shifted in the chair, the erection in his jeans uncomfortable. He frowned, disgusted by his physiological response. And the descent into his unsub hadn't really coaxed anything new from his subconscious. He gave himself a minute to clear his head, closed his eyes, took another deep breath then did the unthinkable.

Oh, God. Oh, Jesus. Fuck it hurts.

The ache in her ankles is unbearable. Deep. Agonizing. She feels the pain all the way into the pit of her stomach. She knows he cut her, but doesn't feel the sting of opened flesh. There is only the excruciating, intense throb in her ankles. Nothing could be worse.

She's wrong. He snatches her wrists out of the air, forces them down at her sides and plants his knees just above her hands. She briefly forgets all about her ankles as bones snap. The little ones in the base of her wrists grind together. She imagines she can hear them scraping against one another.

She thinks she's screaming, but isn't sure. Her mind is otherwise and utterly occupied.

Fuck. FUCK. Somewhere in there is the knowledge that she's going to die tonight. Soon. God please. FUCK! Let death come soon.

Metal glints in the light.

No. No. Please. No. She's doesn't know if she's thinking it or saying it aloud.

Then her belly is on fire. Oh. Oh. Oh, my God.

He's in her. The room gets eerily quiet, but she barely notices. She can feel his hand moving in there, shifting her insides around. His shadow passes in front of her as he leans forward to brush some hair from her eyes, like a father might. She's not seeing anything but the ceiling anyway.

Look at him, Jolene.

She doesn't want to.

Look at him. LOOK.

He's white. Clean-shaven. Good-looking. Charming. I wouldn't have come here with him, otherwise. Not much older than me. It's too dark to make out the color of his eyes. But they're empty and intense. He's intense. He's strong. In excellent shape. I wanted him to fuck me. Wanted him inside me. Not like this. I wanted to wrap my arms around his neck and press my body against the hard muscles in his chest as he rammed himself into me and made me come again and again. Now his cock pressing against my hip makes me want to puke. My eyes slip back to the ceiling. I wish I could float up there out of his reach.

"Listen."

Pain is my only reality. But I can hear it. Squelching, sucking, squishing.

He leans back and plunges both hands into me. There's a strange tugging, vague and distant. Then he holds something dark up. Out of the corner of my eye, I see it glisten in the light like it's wet.

"Do you see?

Dontlookdontlookdontlookdontlook.

I look.

Nick's eyes snapped open. The room in front of him blurred and fragmented. Both of his hands flew to his belly and he hissed in a sharp breath. *Holy fuck!* After he confirmed his abdomen was intact, he drew a forearm angrily across his eyes and sniffed.

Dammit. He hadn't pulled much of value from Jolene's perspective either.

Only seventeen to go.

He shifted in the chair to check on Connie.

She was staring at him over the railing of her bed.

Nick's face burned with shame. Before he could say a word, she turned away.

FORTY

Shoreview, Minnesota
Friday, August 5 2016 9:04 PM

Nick hesitated outside of their bedroom, a large duffel bag in hand. He felt sick to his stomach. Vertigo made the walls shift and tilt as if they were alive. Breathing. *Eating.*

He put a hand on the doorframe and closed his eyes until things stilled. He didn't want to go inside.

"Get a fucking grip," he told himself and stepped over the threshold into the room. He took a long, steadying breath and flipped the light switch.

He crossed to the bed and put the duffel down on the floor. His eyes kept wandering back to the bloodstain on the fitted sheet on Connie's side about halfway down the length of their mattress. A near perfect handprint painted the wall by the window where he'd steadied himself when he jumped off the bed to get to his dying wife.

He'd seen murder scenes that looked much the same. He made an involuntary choking sound and put his fist to his mouth. He swallowed hard and turned away, focusing instead on the long bureau in front of him. He slid open a drawer and began stuffing clothes into the bag without paying much attention. The mirror atop the dresser refused to grant absolution, reflecting the morning's bloodshed back at him relentlessly.

You wanted this.

"No," Nick said to the empty room. "Not this. Never this."

You didn't want the baby.

"I was scared."

You got exactly what you wanted.

"No, goddamnit. No!" Nick threw a punch without even thinking about it, shattering the reflection of his face into a kaleidoscope of splintered fragments.

He stepped back, startled by his outburst. A band of pressure tightened around his chest and squeezed. He could barely breathe. His hands shook and tingled. A bead of blood traced a path from his knuckles around the base of his thumb.

You only care about the dead.

"Fuck you!" He tripped over the duffel, spilling its contents, and fell backwards onto the bed. "Fuck you. Fuck—" Nick couldn't get the air to finish. He felt lightheaded and dizzy again. Everything *tipped*. He curled his fingers into the mattress to keep steady, feeling himself wobble on the verge of consciousness.

He managed to sit up and drop his head down toward his knees and felt the warmth of blood flow back into his face. The belt around his lungs loosened, and he gulped in air like a drowning man breaching the surface of an ocean.

When he thought he was no longer in danger of passing out, he cautiously raised his head. He put a hand to his chest and felt his thudding heart slow. "Son of a bitch," he whispered. And then he started to laugh. The irony of a guy with a Masters in Psychology having a full-blown panic attack sent him into hysterics. He slipped off the side of the bed to the floor, roaring with laughter. Tears spilled down his cheeks. With his back pressed against the mattress, he pulled himself into a tight ball.

His laughter disintegrated into sobs.

FORTY-ONE

A tiny sliver of moon accompanied Nick on the drive back to HCMC. He had all the windows down and the sunroof open. After the episode at home he still felt more than a little claustrophobic, and the fragrant evening air was a welcome break from the soapy, sterile smell of the ICU floor.

He needed a friendly, familiar voice. He paired his Bluetooth to the car's speaker system and made a call.

It was picked up almost immediately. "Blevins."

"I'd like to report a crotchety old geezer impersonating a Major in the Jacksonville Sheriff's Department."

The bark of laughter on the other end of the line lifted Nick's spirits in a way few other things could. "Yeah? I heard there's some snot-nosed little shit running around the frozen fucking tundra pretending to be some big-shot Fed."

"How are you, Burt?" Nick asked through a laugh that was only half half-hearted.

"I'm good, kid. Getting ready for a glorious retirement filled with marlin fishin' and sailin' and coolers full of beer. But screw all that. How are you and that gorgeous wife of yours?"

Nick hesitated a beat too long.

"Aw, hell. Hang on." Nick heard a door close in the background. When Burt came back on the concern in his voice was unmistakable. "What's going on?"

For all intents and purposes, this man was the only true parent Nick had known since grade school. Tears came again, and his voice was thick. "She lost the baby."

"Shit," Burt whispered. "God *damn* it."

Nick was thankful he didn't say, "I'm sorry." He'd heard it too many times today already. And he heard it plenty in the anguish of Burt's voice.

"I was out running this morning, thinking about this fucking case I'm working on, and I got a text from Con. All it said was 'help.' I think I ran a four-minute mile to get back to her. An ambulance pulled in just as I got there."

Nick tried to pull himself together with a cough and a long gulp of evening air.

Burt let the silence hang without trying to fill it.

Nick loosed a shaky sigh and continued. "There was so much blood. For a second I was sure she was… I thought that she'd…"

"I know, son. Go ahead."

Nick knew Burt understood. "I remember what you told me about when you found Dad."

"Yeah." Burt's voice was soft and thick with emotion. "Worst night of my life."

"Then it was like I threw a switch. The husband in me was gone, and I was all cop. Detached. Distant." He stopped, ashamed. If it were anyone else, he wouldn't have dared speak the words. "I think I gave up on her, Burt. It's like I let go of the love of my life because I thought she… that I'd lost her. Like Dad."

Burt was quiet for a long time. When he spoke next, there was a quaver in his voice too.

"Listen to me, son. You know way more than I do about how the brain works, but I have to assume that's normal. I mean think about it—you're in the doc's office with your wife and find out she's only got a month left to live. Imagine how you'd feel in that moment—the shock, the pain, the sense of loss—even though she's still sitting right there next to you, holding your hand. Above all, your brain is hell-bent on survival and self-preservation, so maybe it prepares you for the worst by distancing you from your feelings for that person just a tiny bit. And how much more for someone in your shoes? For someone who's already lost someone in the worst possible way? It's a damn miracle that you can love Con that deeply at all."

Nick was quiet. He understood the psychology, but he hated himself no less for it. Understanding did nothing to diminish his guilt.

"How is she?"

"She's a mess. Her eyes…they're so empty. Broken."

"She's tough, Nick. She'll need time and help, but she'll come back to you. She just lost something that she'd become attached to in a way that you and I can't understand."

"It's worse than that, though. She can't have kids anymore, Burt. We can't have kids."

There was another long silence on the line.

Burt blew out a long breath. "Jesus." His voice cracked.

"I don't know how to help her."

"All you can do is be there. Go to counseling. Use what you learned in psych class. She may never be quite the same. You know that—look at your mother. Shit, ask Barb. She'll tell you I was never really the same after your dad."

"How do you mean?"

"I was always just a little more withdrawn, no matter how hard I tried not to be. She and I have talked about it. And you're not the same either. You never got a chance to be the man you might have been if Rick hadn't died that night. And who can really say if you're better or worse for it? You still became a great man, a helluva cop, and a terrific husband. You save lives, and your dad would be just as amazed and proud of you as I am."

"I *feel* like a horrible husband. I can't even let go of this damn case I'm working. It's constantly on my mind. This fucker has probably slaughtered more than a hundred people, and I can't get out of his head for the few days that Connie needs me most."

"Of course you can't. For better or worse, we made you this way. You've been inside perp's heads since you were sixteen. You grew up believing that this was your purpose. Your duty. You took an oath to uphold the law to the best of your ability. Do you think that a doctor in your shoes would just ignore a dying patient lying on the floor next to him? How about the defense attorney that's going to try to get your unsub off, even though she knows it may ultimately put others at risk? Sometimes there are things we believe in so much we just can't stop, even if it means we have to sacrifice everything for it. There's no choosing between finding the bad guys and your love for Connie, son. Both are ingrained in you like instinct."

"That doesn't make me feel any better about it."

"Nick, this may sound callous, but you've been a cop a lot longer than you've been a husband. You can only be what you are. And I'm betting even Connie understands that. It's one of the reasons she loves you the way she does."

Nick knew Burt was right, but he still felt like a total asshole.

"Not to mention, if you're thinking about work, you're not thinking about what you've just lost. I'd say there's probably some avoidance going on there."

"Oh, I'm sure of it."

"Sometimes the job is the only thing that gets us through the ugly shit. It's duct tape, obviously, but you do what you've gotta to get by until you can work on a permanent fix."

"Yeah."

"Listen—what happened to you with Connie? I know it's not exactly the same, but it happened to me too. Your dad was my best friend. We were like brothers. When my headlights first fell over his body that night, I let go of him too for a second. Hell, that may have happened as soon as the call went out. I can't say. But for months afterward—*months*, Nick, there were days that my 9mil was loaded with a round meant for my brain. I'll be honest with you, the barrel was in my mouth maybe half a dozen times those first few weeks— and if you ever tell Barb that, I swear to God it will be in yours.

"I had five pounds of pressure on that trigger some nights. If the split-second that I let go of your dad was equal to a half-pound of pressure, then it probably saved my fucking life. Do you understand that?"

Nick did. He again remembered teetering on that precipice of despair where everything might have been totally different for him. "I do, Burt, but I'm glad you didn't give up. I can't imagine where I'd be without you."

"Same goes for you, kid. And just like you needed me then, Connie needs you now. Maybe there's a bit of a miracle in those moments for us, ya know? Without them, who knows if either of us would have had the strength to get past what we lost."

"Yeah," Nick said again.

"You do what you need to do to get through, Nick. But find a way to be there for your wife. Tell her you love her, even if she screams and cries and tells you she hates your fucking guts. And for God's sake, get her some help. Get *both* of you some help. You've lost a lot in this too. Don't lose sight of that."

"Thanks, Burt. I won't." Nick wiped away a stray tear, but he felt like he had a tenuous grip again.

"You want me to come up? Just say the word. I can try to play nice with your mom."

Nick smiled. As much as he'd have liked to see Burt, he hoped for happier circumstances for their reunion. "No, we'll manage. But I appreciate the offer. Besides, I told Mom off today. I doubt she'll be around much."

"Oh, Christ." Burt unleashed an explosive sigh. Nick imagined him slapping a hand to his forehead in exasperation.

"So when's the big day?" Nick asked.

"March 4th. Gave these fuckers thirty-five years. Can you believe it?"

"Actually, yes I can, you old bastard."

Burt laughed softly, much more subdued than earlier. "Got time to tell me about your case?"

Nick gave him the short version, finishing just as he pulled into an empty spot on the roof of the hospital's parking ramp. Before they hung up, Nick promised to make the trip to Jacksonville for the retirement party.

"Can't wait to see you. Keep me in the loop. I love ya, kid."

"Love you too, Burt. Tell Barb I said 'hi.'"

FORTY-TWO

Minnepolis, Minnesota
Saturday, August 6 2016 8:51 AM

Nick changed and brushed his teeth in the tiny bathroom off of Connie's ICU room. His red-eyed reflection was a stark reminder that the hospital recliner was a shitty substitute for his own recliner at home. Sleep had been all but impossible.

Connie had slept on and off most of the night, but hadn't said much. Nick knew she needed time to grieve, but beyond that he wasn't sure what to do for her. More than anything else, Nick hated feeling helpless, and right now, the only thing he had to work with were the ten newest files. He spent most of the overnight hours scouring them for any and everything that he might have missed during the first read through.

He heard a small commotion outside the bathroom door and peeked out to find two nurses helping Connie back into the room after her first walk since the surgery. Connie winced, but looked to be doing most of the work of reclaiming her hospital bed.

"How'd it go?" he asked.

One of the nurses turned to him with a smile while the other reconnected a dozen leads to their monitors. "She did very well. Your wife's a tough cookie. She'll be out of here in no time." They made some entries into the computer and updated the dry erase board by the door. "We'll be back in a few hours. If all goes well, we'll move you out of the ICU this afternoon."

"Thanks," Connie said.

The nurses left them alone.

"Mindy texted," he told her. "Said she convinced your parents to hold off on coming for a few weeks and that we owe her five new boyfriend screenings. She's going to swing by later."

Connie nodded.

"How's your pain?"

She shrugged. "Not bad."

"Can I do anything for you?"

"No. I'm fine." She glanced at him and tried to give him a small smile. She failed miserably. "You should go to work."

"No, babe. I'm staying here with you. Work can manage without me for a few days."

"People are dying. I'm not." She paused then added, "Anymore."

Nick was blown away by her selflessness. "They pulled me from the case anyway. There's a team on it."

Connie frowned at him. She looked dubious, as if she knew no one else was as up to the task as he. Or maybe it was just that she knew there was about as much chance of him giving up the case as winning the Powerball. It was hard to know.

"About last night, I'm—"

She shook her head and held up a hand. "Not now. Okay?"

"Okay. Can I get you anything from the cafeteria or a vending machine? Coffee?"

She shook her head. "I'm good." Her eyes told another story. Nick wondered if he'd ever see joy in them again.

He went to her and took her hand in his. "Listen to me," he said. "I love you, Con. Forever and no matter what."

She tried to smile at him again. Instead her eyes filled with tears and her lips quivered. "I know," she said quietly.

"I'm going to get some breakfast. You sure you don't want anything?"

She adjusted the angle of the bed and settled in. "Not yet."
"All right. I'll be back in a bit," he said, letting go of her hand. He nodded toward her phone on the bedside table. "Let me know if you change your mind."

Nick's Blackberry buzzed as he tried to choke down a swallow of coffee that smelled and tasted like burnt plastic. It was a text from Addie.

We're in. LangeDI@FBI.gov/CA55IOP3IA

Thanks, Addie, he typed. *This means more than you can imagine. How'd you get in? Is it hacked?*

Nothing so devious. I just asked to work on the case—said it would be a good learning experience for me and that my technical "expertise" might come in handy. They gave me access, no questions asked.

Nick wondered what exactly she meant by "expertise." When they'd met at the Wall, she did say she had a "thing" for computers.

Be careful. I don't want to cause problems for you, Nick sent.

I doubt anyone will be watching that closely, but I've got a way to make it appear that I'm the only one accessing the system with my credentials. I'll need the MAC address from your laptop. Do you know where to find it?

Nick did. *I'll send it to you within the hour. Do I even want to know?*

Probably not. A smiley face emoji followed.

Tell me anyway? He wanted to make sure they were both adequately protected.

It's a bot program. It burrows into the syslog, router, host box, firewall—anything and everything that identifies and stores information about a system's usage. It will search the ORION network here and overwrite any instances of your MAC address and the IP address you're using with mine. It will even merge our logins if we happen to be logged on at the same time.

Traceable?

Only if someone VERY good is looking for it. Once it's turned off, though, it's pretty much undetectable.

Sounds...complex, but I'm impressed.

It was a bitch to write the program, but I've used it before on secure servers. Works like a dream.

That I probably shouldn't know about. I owe you one.

I looked at some of the files. Scary. Catch this guy and we'll call it even.

Deal. Thanks again.

No problem. Good luck.

Nick deleted their conversation. He had no doubt that Addie was doing the same in Quantico. If it ever came up, the Bureau could prove they'd been in contact but wouldn't be able to determine what was said.

He was back in the game.

FORTY-THREE

Nick was on his way back to Connie's room when he received another text, this time from Jim in Bakersfield. *Are you benched? WTF? Call me. Lindsay is same, but interesting development. Hope all ok.*

Nick called him right away.

Harris answered immediately and didn't bother with formalities. "There's a bulletin on ORION that says you are temporarily out of contact. What's going on?"

Nick filled in his friend. If he never had to explain again, it would be too soon.

"What can I say, man? 'Sorry' doesn't even begin to cut it."

"There's nothing *to* say, Jim. Shit happens."

"Yeah, but it happens to some of us a lot more than others. You've had way more than your fair share."

"I guess there's no Feces Fairy that divvies it all up equally." That was the most self-pity Nick could allow himself at this point. "We'll get through it. Eventually. What's the deal with Lindsay?"

"I guess I'm not supposed to discuss this stuff with you now, given your mental state and all. But you don't sound like a raving lunatic at the moment. You gonna fall off the crazy cliff if I tell you?"

"And you were doing so well, Jim. Don't fuck up a perfectly good condolence."

"Right," Harris said, instantly serious. "I had a conversation with the Accounts Payable people at the hospital yesterday about Lindsay's medical expenses. She's been paid for. By an *anonymous* source."

Nick felt a tingle start at the base of his neck and writhe its way down his spine. "You're shitting me."

"Nope. Hundred grand. Cash. Arrived Thursday with explicit instructions that it was to go toward Lindsay's care. And before you ask, we're already on the forensics and working with UPS on the sender. We're not going to get much more than the origination point though, if anything. The package was left in a drop box. No cameras in the area. I'll give you one guess where it sourced from."

Nick's answer wasn't a question. "Minnesota."

"Yup. First scan by the driver indicated it was picked up in St. Paul."

"Unbelievable," Nick said.

"Thought you'd like that."

"I'd say this confirms that he has a daughter. That kind of gift suggests a great deal of concern and—whether real or contrived—maybe even some level of guilt. That is totally out of character for him. There must be a reason."

"I thought psychos didn't feel guilt."

"That's a bit of a generalization. In my experience, no one fits into any one kind of stereotypical mold—sane or not. Most sociopaths and psychopaths don't experience emotions and empathy like you and

I do, but they are sometimes capable of living what appears to be normal, productive, even successful lives on the surface. They adapt because they've paid attention to societal norms and act accordingly. He might be acting on what he believes he *should* be feeling, or maybe through his daughter, he identifies with teenage girls and really is experiencing some manifestation of guilt."

"Are you sure he's not Lindsay's father?" Harris asked.

"I don't think so. It doesn't make sense that a deadbeat who's been in the wind for so long would reappear, cut his ex-wife's throat and then, all of a sudden, decide that he had an obligation to take care of his traumatized kid. Why after years of being a selfish prick would he suddenly be so giving? The behavior is contradictory. Have you had any luck tracking him down?"

"Zero. He's completely off the grid. We got his name from Lindsay's birth cert. His mother died four years ago. Father is in a nursing facility with Alzheimer's. No siblings. He's probably getting paid under the table someplace and paying cash for everything so he can avoid child support. We're still working on tracking down extended family, great aunts and uncles. I'm not hopeful."

"And those were his real parents? They never split up?"

"By all accounts, yes, and they were married for 53 years."

"Track him down for Lindsay's sake if you want, but I don't think he's going to factor into the case beyond that. I think the unsub lost a parent young."

"I'd like to find him just to knock his fucking lights out."

"Not to change the subject, but how many cases were added to ORION today?"

"Seven. Is that twenty-five now?"

"It is. If there's any good news at all, it's that we're going to get a break tomorrow and Monday. The ViCADETs are off weekends."

"Thank Christ."

"Tell me about it. We've taken several years worth of information and jammed it into a goddamn week. It's like a serial case on amphetamines."

"Well, you take a break from this, and focus on that beautiful wife of yours. Leave the piece of shit to those of us with bigger brains than yours. You were just slowing the real genius down, anyway."

Nick laughed despite himself.

"How long is Connie gonna be in the hospital? And where is she? We'd like to send flowers."

"HCMC. I should be able to take her home Sunday night or Monday morning if all goes to plan."

"All right. I'd better get moving. Take care and call me if you need anything."

"I will, Jim. Thanks."

"I mean it. *Anything*. And Nick?"

"Yeah, buddy?"

"I really am sorrier than you know."

FORTY-FOUR

Once Connie was settled into a room outside of the ICU, she spent much of the afternoon trying to convince Nick to go back to work. She seemed genuine about it, but Nick flatly refused. It wasn't as if he could just show up at the office, in any case. Other than cafeteria runs and a stop at the gift shop to pick up some puzzle books to keep her mind off of their loss, he stayed at her side all day. He even managed to convince her to eat a Butterfinger despite her continued insistence that she wasn't hungry.

Nick used his laptop to access ORION with Addie Lange's authentication during Connie's frequent analgesic-induced naps. They gave Nick some time to familiarize himself with the seven new cases uploaded to ViCAD that morning.

He opened a document named chaos.master.xls and discovered an ingenious Excel spreadsheet containing all of the vital details from each case. There were a number of columns labeled, "Date," "Location," "Victim Name," "M.O.," "Statehoods," "Quarter Pattern," and "5th Quarter." Many of the catalogued entries on the main spreadsheet were hyperlinks that opened new pages of further details when clicked.

Nick clicked on Helen Lyman's name, which took him to a series of pictures of her. In addition to the crime scene photos of her body, there were a number of images that looked to have been taken from Facebook and other social media pages. Her DMV photo was there, as were a dozen or so others that looked to have been taken from the Lyman home. There was also a page of vital stats, which included her height, weight, eye and hair color, and build.

Curious, Nick clicked on an underlined blue link titled "Bakersfield, CA." He was rewarded with Google Satellite and Map images of the Lyman home and neighborhood. As he zoomed out, a red "pin" stayed in place to designate where Helen's body had been found, but he soon saw a series of blue pins indicating where each of the other twenty-four victims had been found across the country. Clicking on any of those blue pins opened up the details for that particular case.

Nick was beyond impressed. He brought up the file's "properties" tab and wasn't the least bit surprised to discover Xavier's name as the author of the document. "Way to go, David," he muttered.

He went back to the main spreadsheet and clicked on the "M.O." box for Scott Wainwright. The images of his body, both as it had been found at the scene and several autopsy photos were available. The notes and reports from the M.E. and the Hennepin County Coroner, describing their findings in clinical detail, were also available.

A final column on the main page listed contacts for the lead investigator of each individual task force. Several of those contacts were links themselves—to email, and in a few instances, Skype connections for face-to-face conversations.

It was a brilliant tool that not only compiled and cross-referenced virtually all of the data they had into a single document, but also (and perhaps more importantly) it showed them, at a glance, things they did not yet know—like where they were *missing* files. There were twenty-five completed rows representing each of their victims on the spreadsheet, but where the "statehood" column didn't immediately precede a matching state in the next, an empty row was left between. Thirteen of these blank rows told him they were looking at an absolute minimum of thirty-eight cases, and that assumed they weren't dealing with multiples in the already identified states. It also didn't account for a number of large time gaps. Nick was quite sure they'd need to insert several more rows to accommodate new files as the weeks went on.

Another bonus: they now had confirmation that the heads/tails patterns defined the M.O.s. The code left at each scene corresponded (as David had surmised) to the method in which he would kill the next victim. It was a taunt, Nick knew. The unsub's way of saying: "I'm going to eviscerate someone in Oklahoma (as had been the case with Jolene), and there's not a damn thing you can do about it." If he held true to form, the next victim would be burned to death somewhere in Minnesota and most likely within the next ten days.

Nick closed the spreadsheet with a weary shake of his head.

He frowned at the update at the top of ORION's main page that said he was temporarily unavailable, and that the Bureau wished him a speedy return. A second update indicated that the team was coordinating efforts with LEAs from those states that represented gaps in the spreadsheet and/or timeline. The ViCADETs in those areas were being instructed to look specifically for cases involving the Chaos signature in an effort to get a more complete picture of what they were dealing with. The more cases they could compile, the better the chances that there would be some kind of physical evidence to work with. Chaos was now everyone's top priority.

There were cases dating back nine years, with an average cooling-off period of four to six weeks between kills. But more recent information suggested some level of acceleration—two to four weeks was more the unsub's norm now. Something was compelling him to kill faster. He could be gaining confidence, though that seemed unlikely to Nick after so many years—he'd had plenty of time to perfect his process. So why the sudden escalation? Nick wasn't sure.

But he was sure it was important.

FORTY-FIVE

Minneapolis, Minnesota
Sunday, August 7 2016 8:51 PM

Nick went into the bedroom first, tentative, carrying in the first of several armloads of flowers collected at the hospital. He wasn't sure what to expect. He was relieved to discover there wasn't a trace of blood left anywhere. There were fresh sheets atop a new mattress and a coat of fresh paint around the window. The protein-removing chemicals used in crime scene clean up were wonders of science—the carpet was as spotless as when they'd first moved in. Even the mirror above the dresser had been replaced. Two enormous bouquets in shades of blue and purple adorned each the nightstands flanking the bed. He took a handwritten note from the center of the bed:

Hope the room is okay. Flowers are from the team. Let us know if you need anything. Thinking of you both—Q.

Nick made a mental note to thank Quentin for arranging everything while they were at the hospital.

He went downstairs and found Connie in the kitchen drinking a glass of water.

"It's safe," he told her and helped her navigate the stairs.

Connie undressed, snipped the plastic bracelet from her wrist and put on a pair of loose-fitting sweats that, under other circumstances, Nick would have found sexy as hell. She hesitantly pulled back the sheets on her side of the bed. When she found it unsoiled, she crawled in.

"It might feel a little different. I had them replace the mattress."

She got herself settled in and nodded. "I can tell, but it's comfortable. Be sure to thank them for me. And thank you for thinking to have the place cleaned up." She almost got a smile right. "I was nervous."

Nick sat down on the edge of the bed next to her. "Honestly, I was too," he admitted. He was quiet for a minute, trying to get the words out. "Are you going to be okay?"

She turned her head toward him but didn't quite meet his gaze. "I think so." He watched her eyes fill with tears. "Eventually. It's hard."

Nick took her hand. "I know, babe. I wish there was something I could do."

She swiped at her eyes and swallowed hard. "How are *you* doing?" she asked, giving his hand a soft squeeze.

He sighed and gave her a thin smile in response. "I'll be all right. *Eventually*," he said, echoing her sentiment. "We'll get through it together."

They sat in silence for a few minutes, neither sure what to say.

"I'm sorry," Nick said after a time.

Connie's brow crinkled.

"I…feel like an asshole. The case…"

Connie turned her head toward the new mirror. She was quiet for another long minute.

Nick held his breath and waited for her to lose it.

Finally, she said, "Don't. I understand." She turned her head back to him and looked him in the eyes. "I do."

In that instant, Nick knew they'd be okay.

FORTY-SIX

Zorin circled the perimeter of the Red Carpet Nightclub in his rental car, waiting for the Non to give up his wait and come outside. They'd agreed to meet here tonight after their "chance" encounter on campus on Friday. Zorin wasn't so stupid as to allow himself to be seen with the flamboyant character in such a public place among so many potential witnesses. He wasn't in the habit of taking unnecessary risks.

His target had arrived two hours earlier at their planned meeting time. Since then, Zorin imagined him inside, belly up to the bar in Club Red tossing back caramel apple-tinis and then shots as his anticipation of their date turned into disappointment.

Though the nightclub had quieted over the past hour or so, there were still quite a few university students celebrating their newfound summer freedom. When his "friend" finally stumbled out of the place, there were only a handful of people outside. Half a dozen were clustered in a small circle smoking and talking loudly. A few others sat on the curb with their heads between their knees and puke between their feet, trying to get some air.

No one paid the slightest bit of attention to him.

Zorin waited and watched as his next victim lit a cigarette, shrugged to himself and walked on wobbly legs down the street. It was only then that he pulled to the curb alongside him in his rental car.

"Hey! God, I'm so sorry, man. I was running late and got lost trying to find the club. I'm not from around here."

The young black man looked at Zorin through the car window. He put his hands on his waist and thrust out a hip and lip. "Mmmmhmmm." The man clicked his tongue. "I know you didn't just stand this up," he said running a hand provocatively down his body. "You know I got better things to do with my time than be waitin' for you all damn night. You ain't all that, honey."

Zorin raised his hands from the steering wheel in mock surrender. "I know, I know. I'm an asshole. I really am sorry." He arched an eyebrow. "Don't suppose you're still up for some *fun?*"

The black man grinned at him. "Honey, I'm *always* up for some fun."

Zorin unlocked the passenger door. "Hop in."

There wasn't a soul around to see the exchange or the car. It was as clean as something that had been planned for weeks.

"So I'm Peter. What's your name, baby?" he asked when he got settled.

"Uh, you can call me Dick."

Peter laughed uproariously and slapped the tops of his legs. "Oh, I bet I can. Mmmhmm."

"So, uh, listen—Peter, uh, I don't really do this kind of thing. I've uh, never been—"

"Relaaax, Dick. I'll take good care of you. You wanna smoke?" Peter dug into his shirt pocket and held up a joint.

"Maybe later. So, uh, where can we go to, uh, be alone? You know anyplace we won't be interrupted?"

"Oh, I know just the place. It's perfect. And no one will hear us." Peter put a hand on Zorin's thigh—high and inside—and batted his eyes. "I'm a screamer, by the way."

In the darkness of the car, Zorin's terrible smile was invisible. "I wouldn't want it any other way," he said.

The spot was secluded—perfect really—and Peter was indeed a screamer. But then, who wouldn't be under the circumstances?

There would be no physical evidence, he was sure. Acid was, after all, particularly good at eliminating trace. The coins had demanded burning—how better to do it than both inside and out?

Zorin arrived back in the Twin Cities just after sunrise. It was a quick turnaround, and he was tired, but there was still much to prepare. He allowed himself a moment to revel in his fond new memories of Peter. Then he got to work.

FORTY-SEVEN

The shower did Nick a world of good. His aching muscles from days in the crummy hospital recliner finally loosened, and he felt something akin to relaxation as he leaned against the wall and let the hot water beat down on him. He tried to engage all of his senses on only the shower for a few brief minutes—nothing but the cool tile pressed against his skin, the sting of the scalding water, and the patter as it hit the floor of the tub. He watched plumes of steam curl toward the ceiling and breathed in the fresh smells of shampoo and soap. He opened his mouth and let some of the water run down his face and into his mouth. It tasted clean and bright on his tongue.

Nick let himself slip into a trancelike state of meditation that served to reset his overwhelmed thoughts and emotions. When he brought himself back around, he felt rejuvenated.

Nick was halfway through a cup of coffee when his Blackberry went berserk. Several texts came in at once.

From Quentin: *Turn on your television.*

From Valerie: *How are you and Connie doing?*

From Addie: *Got a name—Dick Cross. Car rentals in Georgia and California. Hotel booked in Maryland in vicinity of Gwynns Falls murder. Timelines all match up. Frenzy here. Data is up on ORION. Looks like he struck again last night/this morning near you. Hope you and your wife are holding up.*

Nick's stomach turned in a strange mixture of dread, excitement, anticipation and triumph. He raced to the living room, turned on the television and switched to a local station. Simultaneously, he booted up his laptop and logged into ORION with Addie's passcode.

"—as yet unidentified. Police discovered the body underneath the University Drive bridge overpass in Riverside Park, just a few hundred feet from the St. Cloud dam after receiving a tip from a jogger who passed through the area. KARE 11 has obtained footage from earlier this morning as the victim was transported from the scene. Be advised, this footage may not be suitable for all viewers."

The screen changed from the blonde newscaster and a chyron containing the words, "Murder in St. Cloud," to a video of two paramedics wheeling a gurney to an awaiting ambulance. They wore heavy silver anti-corrosive gloves. The sheet covering the body was stained with various shades of yellow, pink and black. Nick could hear the roar of the dam in the background, and several voices shouted commands to be heard over the noise. As the camera panned to follow the EMTs, Nick saw Quentin coordinating Lisa Chandler and a few other agents with arm and finger outstretched. Three BCA techs walked up a trail talking to one another. They were pale and looked shaken.

The coverage returned to the newscaster in-studio. "This marks the second murder in Minnesota in just a week. Authorities declined to comment as to whether the murders are related at this time. If you have any information regarding this crime, you are asked to call the

St. Cloud Police Department immediately at the number on your screen. We will have more on this breaking story throughout the day as it develops."

Nick reviewed ORION. Xavier had already updated the Excel spreadsheet with the data from this morning's scene. There wasn't much to see yet, but the date, location, COD, and statehood boxes were already filled.

Minnesota was in for yet another victim. Suffocation next.

Nick texted Quentin back. *Looks bad.*

While Nick waited for a response, he flipped around to the other local stations and found another broadcasting a report of the murder. Footage from an aerial news chopper was onscreen, overdubbed by a reporter describing what they knew so far, which didn't amount to any more than he'd already heard.

Gonna be a bitch to ID this one. Sulfuric acid. Ingested and on the skin. Had to bring in HazMat for God's sake. How are you guys?

Managing. Thanks again for taking care of the house, Bill. It means a lot.

Thank Chandler- she picked everything out. I just delegated. Besides I'd rather buy you sheets than deal with this whackjob.

Nick sighed and sat back on the couch. He wanted to believe that the discovery of their unsub's identity would yield something, but he couldn't convince himself. Things rarely moved this quickly in a serial case. Yes, ViCAD was working—more information meant more leads—which was how they'd been able to ID him so fast. But it didn't make sense that after being so incredibly careful at every crime scene, he'd have been so careless with his name. In any case, the Bureau now had a starting point, and the net was drawing tighter. They'd be relentless in their pursuit of Dick Cross, but Nick suspected it would turn out to be an alias.

He flipped back to Channel 11. As the morning program was drawing to a close, they re-aired the story and again encouraged potential witnesses to come forward.

"Is that him?" Connie asked.

Nick jumped, and his heart slammed in his chest. He hadn't heard her come in. "Hey, hon. You okay? Can I get you something?"

She shook her head. "Is that St. Cloud?"

Despite Connie's understanding, Nick couldn't help but feel a bit like he'd been caught with his hand in the cookie jar. He turned off the television. "Yes. It's him. But it doesn't matter. Quent's got it under control."

"Go, Nick." Her voice was firm.

"Babe, it's fine. I don't need to be there. I *do* need to be here for you."

"I'm all right. Really. Go."

Nick stood and walked around the couch to her. He put his hands on her shoulders. "I'm not leaving you here alone, Con."

"I won't be alone. Mindy's coming over. She can stay until you get back."

"I'm not on the case anymore."

"Will they fire you?" she asked.

"Probably not."

"Then get your ass moving."

FORTY-EIGHT

Nick drove with the windows down and tried not to feel shitty about enjoying the hour plus drive to St. Cloud. After the long days at the hospital, the sunlight and open air were incredibly restorative. He almost felt like himself again. He probably could have carved twenty minutes off of his drive by flipping on his emergency lights and leadfooting the gas pedal, but he chose instead to use the time to gather his thoughts. And, while he was sure Quentin would be glad to see him, Nick was in no particular rush to face the consequences of disobeying direct orders from on high.

More of the fog surrounding his unsub had lifted. Nick now had a reasonably good psychological representation of the man he was hunting, but there were still critical aspects that he couldn't yet make out. Not everything made sense, and Nick suspected that there were answers hidden in what, on the surface, appeared to be illogical and chaotic. Why, for example, would Dick Cross suddenly burst onto the scene two weeks ago after almost ten years of lurking in the shadows? Why would someone who'd been so careful for so long allow his name to be linked to a handful of the murders? And why only some of them? Why the sudden escalation in his timeline? To the best of their (albeit limited) knowledge, he'd never killed three consecutive times in the same state—what was so special about Minnesota? Why the fifth quarters?

Something hovered just outside of Nick's mental reach as he neared the exit to St. Cloud. He pulled to the shoulder before he got to the top of the loop, clicked on his emergencies and put the car in park. He gnawed at the inside of his lip for a minute and fished his laptop out of its bag. He plugged a wireless air card into a USB port and pulled up ORION.

He clicked on the "updates" link and was rewarded with numerous reports from the morning's grisly find. Nick also scrolled through several pages of information on the search for Dick Cross. The Bureau had already run the driver's license number used on the rental car agreements and determined it belonged to a man from South Carolina who was, in fact, named Richard Cross. Agents had contacted his wife, who told them that her husband disappeared without a trace in November of 2012. A missing person's report supported her story. A nationwide BOLO had been issued, and Jasmine Cross was being brought in for questioning.

Nick looked at the photo on the driver's license and wondered if it would be the next image on The Wall at the Academy in Quantico. He zoomed in. Cross was handsome—square-jawed and rugged looking with a mess of chestnut hair. He was 6'1, 205 pounds and wore what looked to be a genuine smile of good humor that crinkled the skin surrounding his large brown eyes. Physically, he fit the profile, but Nick had a hard time reconciling the man in the picture with a vicious serial killer.

Nick frowned and zoomed out again. He hovered the cursor above the "x" to close the window when the small heart symbol on the upper right of the license caught his eye. There was a bold "Y" stamped inside of it, indicating that Cross was an organ donor. Nick knew immediately that Dick Cross wasn't their unsub, but another of his victims. No self-respecting psychopath would voluntarily donate his organs for the sake of others.

"Shit." A low hum settled in his ears, like the constant buzz of an angry insect. A shiver ran through him, and a knot of dread settled in the pit of his stomach. There was something else there—something sinister, but he couldn't yet grasp it.

Nick was focused on the new content on ORION and didn't immediately notice the cruiser that had pulled up behind him. He was startled by the sound of a door closing and looked up and then into his side-view mirror. A young man wearing the distinctive brown hat of a State Trooper was approaching his car with his right hand resting on the butt of his gun.

Nick experienced a sense of vertigo so strong he felt nauseous. His mind was wrenched back more than twenty years.

It's dark—the cherries on the cop car behind him slice through it like whirling, colored blades. A spotlight strikes his side mirror. He recoils, momentarily blinded. He squints and throws up a hand to shield against the dazzling brightness, and sees the silhouette of a police officer shrouded in white light nearing his car—¡Cochino de mierda! As the cop comes closer, his face is illuminated red from the brake lights.

It's his father.

Unable to stop himself, Nick *reaches into the passenger seat and grabs the Colt .45, leans out the window, and pulls the trigger three times. El Singao drops like a stone, but he's still alive and crawling back toward his squad, dragging his leg behind him.*

He opens the car door and steps out, the Colt heavy in his hand. He walks to the fallen cop, stands over him and pops him again in the back of the head. This time he slumps to the ground, a pool spreading like spilled oil in the glow of the squad's headlights.

Oh my God. Oh fuck.

Nick felt the blood drain from his face as his blood pressure plummeted.

"Sir? Is everything okay here?"

The trooper's voice yanked Nick back to the present. He kept his hands on the steering wheel and squeezed to keep them from shaking. It took everything he had to keep his voice steady. "Yes, sir. I apologize. I'm with the FBI. I'm on my way to the dam."

The trooper nodded. "Heard about that. Pretty terrible. Do you mind if I take a look at your identification, sir?

"Not at all," Nick said and retrieved his ID.

"You sure you're all right? You're looking a bit pale, Special Agent…" he looked closely at Nick's badge, "…Keegan."

Nick forced a smile. "I'm good, officer, thanks. Just not looking forward to this scene, you know? I needed to check something on my laptop and thought it would be best to pull over to do so."

Come on, come on…

The trooper handed back his credentials. "If what I heard was true, I can't say I blame you. Good luck, Agent." He tipped his hat and headed back to his squad car.

Nick watched the cruiser pull away. Goosebumps rose on his arms, and he shook from head to toe. He refreshed the page on his laptop before the interruption and saw that there was now a fourth known location where Dick Cross's license number had been used to rent a car: Florida.

Nick felt claustrophobic and trapped. He fumbled frantically with his seatbelt, opened the door and puked onto the blacktop.

In that brief moment that he'd relived his father's shooting, Nick knew everything. Every piece dropped into place, and all of his questions had answers. The fog was whisked away as if on a gust of wind. As outlandish and impossible as it all seemed, his instincts and intuition told him he was dead on.

There was one common denominator to all of the questions he'd asked himself earlier—*him*. Nick himself was the reason that this unsub had just exploded onto the scene. The escalation had begun in Bakersfield where his best friend and college roommate was a Lieutenant with the police department. Every location where the Dick Cross alias was used was of significance to Nick: his home state of Florida; Maryland, where he'd attended college; California, smack in the middle of his friend's jurisdiction; and, of course, Albany, Georgia—the place where the man who had murdered his father had been captured.

But it was the name on the screen of Nick's laptop that had given it all away. In 2012, the unsub had murdered and then assumed the identity of Dick Cross in order to leave Nick a four-year trail of breadcrumbs that only he would understand. Dick Cross—Richard Cross—Richard Cruz.

It was his own father's first name, and the last of his father's murderer, translated from Spanish.

It had been more than twenty years since Umberto Cruz had shot and killed Richard Keegan in the street. Given everything else he already knew, Nick's adversary could only be one person: the son of the man who had murdered his father.

FORTY-NINE

Nick flipped on his lights and hit the gas so hard that his wheels spun, hurling gravel and dirt from the shoulder. He found the first emergency vehicle thoroughfare to cut across the median on 94 and skidded through it at forty-five miles an hour, spewing more dirt and dust. In seconds, he was racing back the way he'd come at nearly one hundred miles an hour.

He pressed the button on the steering wheel that paired his phone to the car. "Call home," he said, on the verge of a shout. His thudding heart sank as each unanswered ring piped through the car's speakers. After four rings that felt like a lifetime each, he tried Connie's cell.

He tried to swallow down the rising panic. Bile burned the back of his throat.

"C'mon, Con. Pick up," he said aloud, swerving around a vehicle traveling half his speed. After six rings, Nick knew.

"Call Mindy's mobile." He could barely get the words out.

"Calling Mindy mobile." That call went unanswered as well. He struggled against a hysteria that clawed at his reason. He didn't have time to lose it. His arms and legs shook uncontrollably, and he refocused his concentration on keeping the wheel steady.

Nick wouldn't allow himself to believe that Connie was dead. He couldn't. But the merciless dread clenching at his heart was enough to convince him that she was in dire trouble. As much as he didn't want to believe it, he had to assume the man masquerading as Dick Cross had her.

He struggled to prioritize what he needed to do.

"Send a message to Connie's mobile."

The car answered, "Please say your message."

"If you hurt her, you will suffer in a way none of your victims ever has. I love you, Connie. Send message."

Nick forced himself to keep it together and instructed the system to call 911.

"911. What's your emergency?" a woman's voice answered.

"This is Nicholas Keegan with the FBI. I need an immediate ping on a cell phone." He gave the woman Connie's cell phone number and carrier and his Bureau information and field office phone number so that she could confirm his identity.

"Hold, please." Nick appreciated her efficiency.

He put his foot down another inch and centered all of his attention on the road while she presumably called the field office in Brooklyn Center, then Verizon. He tried to get his breathing and respiration under control and commanded himself to try to detach and pretend that this was anyone other than Connie. After a few moments his trembling calmed, and he slipped into an adrenaline-induced autopilot.

Dispatch returned to the line. "Agent Keegan, that cellphone is northbound on 35 heading through the Forest Lake area toward North Branch. I have a Verizon rep on the line. Shall I dispatch officers?"

Nick's phone chirped. He had a text from Connie's phone. "One second," he told the dispatcher. "Listen to message number 1."

The car responded in its awkward, clipped female voice, "Oh, how I have waited for this Nicholas. Connie is safe with me for now. We'll talk very soon."

Fuck.

"Miss, send everything you've got. That phone is in the possession of a suspected kidnapper and serial murderer. Tell patrol to proceed with extreme caution. Stay with Verizon, and contact me immediately at this number if there's any change. I'm en route, ETA is forty minutes."

He'd barely disconnected when the siren ringtone on his phone started—Quentin. Nick dismissed the call. There were other, more critical matters that he needed to address before he was prepared to talk to his boss. He made another call instead.

"Jacksonville Sheriff's Office." Nick thought he recognized the voice.

"Penny? This is Nick Keegan. I need to speak to Burt immediately. It's urgent."

"Right away, Nick." She put him on hold.

He waited for fewer than ten seconds.

"Nick?" Burt's voice was tinged with concern.

"Burt, I don't have time to explain, but I need a name. Cruz had a son, didn't he?"

"Cruz?" There was a second's hesitation. "You mean the Cruz who killed Rick? What the he—"

"Burt!" Nick shouted.

"Uh…he had a *stepson* as I recall. Alex or something."

"Alexander Cruz?"

"No. If I remember right, he never took Cruz's name. It would have been his mother's maiden."

"What was it?"

"Jesus, Nick this is ancient shit. Let me look it up for you."

"Call me back when you have it."

"What's this about?" Burt asked.

"It's him."

"What? Who?"

Nick disconnected the call.

FIFTY

Zorin set the cruise control at two miles over the speed limit and kept one hand on the steering wheel while his eyes darted back and forth between the road and Connie's iPhone. It vibrated in his hand and rang out Adele's *Hello*.

"How clever," Zorin said, his voice dripping with sarcasm. Nick's name was on the screen. It was about damn time. He considered answering, but decided against it—let his panic rise for a few more minutes. Instead, he continued to toy with the phone.

Less than a minute later it vibrated in his hand again. A text message this time. He laughed as he read it. He turned and glanced at the woman lying motionless in the backseat. A thin line of drool hung from the corner of her mouth. And was that a tear hanging from her cheekbone? Lovely. He angled the phone toward her and snapped a picture.

"Nick sends his love, Connie," he said, with a smile that had terrorized many. He faced forward again and responded to the message. A tremor of excitement ran down his spine as he pressed send with his thumb. His wait was finally over.

Nicholas Keegan was coming for him.

He worked at Connie Keegan's phone for another five or so minutes, then wiped it down. He pressed a button on the armrest of his door, and the windows slipped down. He checked the rearview. No one was close. He waited until there was a break in traffic coming toward them then hurled the phone out of the passenger side window.

He signaled conscientiously and got over to the leftmost lane. When it was safe to do so, he made a U-turn and drove south again.

Three minutes later, a cadre of police cars with their sirens blaring raced past, heading in the opposite direction.

FIFTY-ONE

Nick was contemplating a call back to Quentin when his phone rang. It wasn't a number he recognized, but the area code was local.

"Keegan."

A woman's voice filled the car. "Agent Keegan, this is Emily with dispatch. We spoke a few minutes ago."

"Go ahead."

"Verizon indicated just a moment ago that the cellphone we were tracking stopped moving on 61 just south of Wyoming.

Shit. Nick's stomach flipped. "Is there anything in that area?"

"No. It's a fairly empty stretch of road. Officers will be in the vicinity any minute. We've sent them the location that Verizon gave us. It should be accurate to within a hundred feet. If the phone is there, it shouldn't be too hard to locate."

Nick prayed it was just the phone that they'd find there and not his wife's dead body. "Thank you. Tell them to bag the phone immediately when it's found. It's evidence in a federal investigation. I'll be there to retrieve it personally within thirty minutes."

Nick threaded the thickening lunch-hour traffic without braking.

"I'll pass that on. Would you like for me to contact you when it's found?"

"Please."

Nick's phone chimed again. It was Burt.

"I have to go, Emily. Keep me posted."

He switched calls. "Go ahead, Burt."

"Before I say shit, are you telling me that Cruz's kid is your serial?"

Nick sighed. "Yes, and he's got Connie."

"What?" he shouted, incredulous.

"Burt, for fuck's sake, what's the name?"

"Zorin. Aleksandr Zorin." Burt spelled it for him. "Born in '83. Second-gen Russian-American. Son of Yelena Zorin-Cruz. She was a prostitute. Probably got knocked up on the job. No father listed on the birth certificate. Are you sure he's got Connie?"

"Yes. Listen, Burt. Pull everything you have on him. Dad's case, all of it. Get some people out to look into what happened to him. Call Indra Tandon at BAU, and send her everything and anything you find."

Nick's phone beeped again.

"I'll call when I can, okay?" Nick said.

"Go. I'm on it."

Nick jumped over to Quentin. "Go ahead, Bill."

"What the *fuck* is going on, Nick. I got a call from the field office saying you're requesting resources from State Patrol."

"Connie's been kidnapped."

"Cut the bullshit, Nick, it's been a terrible day."

"I'm serious as a heart attack. Our serial has her. His name is Aleksandr Zorin. He's the stepson of the man that killed my father twenty-three years ago."

There was silence on the line for a few long seconds. Nick braked hard and swung around the loop onto 35W North. Gravel and dust ricocheted off of his undercarriage as he swerved onto the shoulder of the on-ramp to maneuver around someone driving a reasonable speed.

"Quent, I know this sounds nuts, but I need you to get everyone on this. Now. Jacksonville PD is sending everything they have on Zorin. You need to have the cops drive by my place. Connie's sister was there with her this morning."

"You're not kidding?"

"Jesus Christ. Why would I make this shit up? I'm on 35 doing a hundred and ten trying to get to where Connie's phone was last pinged." Nick wrenched the wheel to the right to rocket around a Kia. The sound of his tires squealing apparently convinced Quentin that he was serious.

"Okay. I'll pull a team together." His voice was punctuated by brief bursts of static, and Nick realized he was running. "I'm still in St. Cloud, but I'm on the way. Be careful, Nick. The last thing we need is you slamming into someone driving like a goddamn idiot. Check in with me every twenty. And once you've got Connie's phone, get your ass home. You're not working this case."

Nick heard a car door slam and an engine turn over in the background. "Bullshit I'm not." Nick shouted over the high-pitched shriek of his own engine. "Zorin is after me. He'll make damn sure I'm part of this whether I'm authorized or not."

"We'll talk about it later."

"Bill, you're my boss and we're good friends. I respect the hell out of you, but I will knock you the fuck out if you try to stop me."

"Just get home as soon as you can." He hung up.

Nick pushed the pedal down the rest of the way and started laying on the horn. The tachometer needle redlined. Under his sweaty hands, the steering wheel shuddered with the speed. Though he had to fight his instincts, he backed off a little bit.

The needle slipped back beneath one-twenty.

FIFTY-TWO

A heavyset State Trooper brought Nick an evidence bag with an iPhone inside. Even though he knew what to expect, he shivered and swallowed hard when he recognized Connie's gold rubber case. He took the bag and held it up to the light at different angles, checking for any visible prints. He couldn't see much through the thick evidence bag.

"I didn't see any on there," the trooper told him. "Maybe he wiped it first?"

"Probably," Nick said. "Anything else in the vicinity? Blood?"

"Not that we found. There's a small chip on the phone's glass. I'd guess it was chucked out the window of a moving vehicle. Emily at dispatch wanted me to let you know that she checked the traffic cam feeds from MNDOT. No help."

Nick frowned and nodded. That was a long shot, but he appreciated her thoroughness. "Thank her for me. She's been tremendous today." He signed for the evidence bag.

"Will do. Good luck."

"Thanks. I'm going to need it," Nick said and jumped back into his car.

A few minutes later, he pulled into a BP station. His hard driving had emptied his tank. He was also crashing hard from a monster adrenaline rush, and his entire body trembled with fatigue. He pumped his gas, then went inside and bought a huge coffee and a few bottles of 5 Hour Energy and started trying to replace his body's natural high with a manufactured one.

The iPhone's capacitive touchscreen interface was a masterful feat of technology. He remembered when he and Connie had gone to Valley Fair and rode Thunder Canyon on a sweltering summer afternoon. They'd both put their wallets and phones into a Ziploc bag to keep them dry. It was then that Nick learned something interesting about Connie's new iPhone. Because electrical impulses are able to pass through semi-porous materials like plastic, the touchscreen still functioned perfectly *inside* the baggie.

He hadn't expected prints other than Connie's on the cell phone itself, but Nick did think that Aleksandr Zorin might have tried to communicate with him in another way. And he should be able to find that out without tampering with the evidence bag.

Nick pulled away from the gas pump and parked. He took a deep breath, trying to brace himself for the worst and keyed Connie's security code. He first opened her Photo Stream. The most recent image had been taken about forty minutes earlier and was a zoomed shot of Connie lying on her right side on a gray fabric backseat. She was completely expressionless. Her eyes were open but focused somewhere beyond the camera. The photo was grainy, and Nick couldn't make out any other surroundings.

Nick pinched out on the screen to increase the image size and looked closer at his lovely wife. She appeared uncharacteristically ragged from the traumas of the last several days, but she was still so beautiful to him that it hurt. He fought to stay detached and looked for anything that might indicate she was alive. He pulled the baggie tight against the screen and looked at the photo closely. A shiny string of drool dangled from Connie's lip to the seat on which she lay, and a single tear hung frozen in place on the bridge of her nose. Proof of life.

He touched the image through the plastic as if he could brush her tear away.

Nick exhaled a massive sigh of relief and closed Connie's Photo Stream. If Zorin wanted her dead, he would have already killed her. That meant she was bait, and he'd keep her alive until he'd firmly set the hook and reeled Nick in. It also meant Nick had reason to hold out a sliver of hope.

The "Notes" app had dozens of entries that Connie had never deleted, but the topmost note had a timestamp of 11:40 AM. It read: *"Send thank you cards for all of the lovely flowers."* Nick thought about it and realized he had no idea who had sent many of the bouquets that Connie had received during her hospital stay. Zorin could easily have sent something that he'd overlooked.

Stupid, he thought. *Careless.*

Next, Nick opened Connie's calendar app and began clicking on the dates marked with a dot. There were many—Connie used her iPhone calendar religiously. Most of the entries were immaterial, but he did find one entry set for the following evening at 10:00 PM that read, *"Alone time with Z."* The location spot contained only a question mark. A reminder alert had been set for two hours before the event.

Via Connie's phone, Zorin had left him proof of life, a date and time, and a warning to come alone. Nick suspected he'd find more instructions in one of the floral arrangements at home—perhaps a location for their meeting.

He scrolled through Connie's other applications looking for any other messages Zorin might have left him. He tried the Voice Memos app and was rewarded with a six-second entry labeled *"To N."* He upped the volume and held her phone close to his ear.

"See you soon, Nicholas. I can't wait."

Nick replayed the recording several times, memorizing the voice and inflections. It seemed familiar somehow, but he couldn't place it. Aleksandr Zorin had no obvious accent, despite having grown up in the south to a Russian mother and Hispanic stepfather. His speech was smooth, confident and engaging. His tone was charming and warm. And yet, as Nick played it back again, he was reminded of the pictures on The Wall at the Academy. He heard a thrum of excitement in Zorin's voice and a hint of the viciousness he was capable of. In just those seven words, Nick could hear the chameleon in him. It was the part that could make you believe that the contents of your hi-tech safe might save your life. The part that could persuade you to invite him over for dinner. The part that could deceive a woman so completely that she'd ultimately bear his child.

Nick had another thought. He opened Connie's contact list and swiped his way though the names of her colleagues, friends, and family. As he'd surmised there might be, an entry for Richard Cross was in the directory. He touched the name and the detail screen opened. Under the name Richard Cross was the name Aleksandr Zorin.

And   beneath   that   a   homepage   entry   read: http://www.enterthemaelstrom.com.

FIFTY-THREE

Nick clicked on the web address. A new page opened. At a glance, it appeared to be Zorin's personal blog. He resisted the urge to explore the full extent of the site, but after skimming a few of the entries, he was convinced it was authentic. One of them in particular, titled, "Aquarum Cicutae" described—in disturbing first-person detail—the poisoning of Amanda Taylor in Albany. Another, "Domus Dulcis Domus," confirmed Burt's earlier assertion that Yelena Zorin had been a prostitute and reflected on Aleksandr's childhood with candor. Nick saw several more entries recounting murders that he had no doubt would be confirmed in time. The website would have immense evidentiary value if Zorin were ever caught, and it would be priceless insight for BAU. It was a look directly into the mind of a psychopath.

Nick emailed himself copies of everything he'd found in Connie's iPhone. He hesitated only briefly before deleting the note about the flowers. The consequences of tampering with evidence could be severe, but Nick knew he needed to get to Zorin's message before anyone else did. He left everything else for the FBI to discover, including the calendar entry. He had a suspicion that was misdirection anyway. It was too easy, and Aleksandr Zorin was far too careful to be so obvious about his intentions.

Nick pulled out of the BP parking lot and raced toward home at only a slightly more reasonable speed. He snaked in and out of traffic and commandeered the shoulder when he didn't have an option to pass.

He gave the voice command to call Quentin's cell.

His boss sounded pissed. "You're late. You get her phone?"

"Got it."

"Anything?"

"Later," Nick said. He was jittery and irritable from the caffeine and had to fight to keep his mind from straying to a million things other than the road in front of him.

"How far out are you?"

"Ten minutes. No more than fifteen."

"I'm about the same. Ramsey County Sheriff's just did a drive-by at your place. They said everything looks quiet. Blue Nissan in the driveway."

"That's Mindy's Rogue. Fuck."

"How do you want to play it? Breach or wait?"

"Ten minutes probably isn't going to make a difference at this point. Have them stand by. We'll breach when we get there."

"If you get there first, wait for me."

"Yeah." Nick disconnected. His stomach was turning again, threatening to expel his liquid lunch. He wasn't sure what he was going to find at home, but the quaking in his gut told him that it almost certainly wasn't going to be good.

Nick swerved into his development at breakneck speed. The tires screeched and slipped on loose gravel, and he just avoided slamming into the curb. He got himself straightened out and finally gave the gas pedal a reprieve. He made the turn onto his street and pulled in behind a Ramsey County squad idling in front of his house. Nick jumped out. A heavy-set man of about forty with short black hair got out of the car to meet him.

"Don Leonetti. What are we looking at here?" He had just a hint of a Brooklyn accent, mostly phased out by years in the Midwest.

"Nick Keegan." He showed Leonetti his FBI credentials. "No idea. Could be nothing. There's a chance that the owner of the Rogue is incapacitated inside somehow."

Leonetti checked his notepad. "Mindy Peterson? You know her?"

Nick nodded and turned toward the sound of an engine running hot. A black Ford Escape veered onto his block, lights strobing from the grille. Quentin. "She's my sister-in-law," Nick said without elaborating.

Quentin parked, jumped out of the SUV, and jogged over.

Nick said, "Officer Leonetti, ASAC Bill Quentin."

Leonetti and Quentin exchanged nods. "How many points of entry?" Quentin asked, wasting no time.

"Four," Nick said. "Garage, main door, rear patio, and deck. One man at the patio should be able to cover the deck door also. Leonetti?" Nick looked at the officer.

"You expecting someone to come running out of there?"

"No, but better safe than sorry."

"You want me to get more backup over here?" Leonetti said.

Quentin gave Nick a questioning look.

Nick shook his head. "I don't expect hostiles. We should be fine."

"All right, give me a minute to get into position," Leonetti said and started an awkward, waddling jog along the side of the house.

Nick and Quentin drew their Glocks and approached the house.

"Both on the front door?" Quentin asked.

"Yeah. If you hear the garage open, peel off."

Quentin nodded. "What are we going to find in there, Nick?"

Nick gave him a serious look as they took up positions to the left and right side of the door. "My sister-in-law. Dead."

"Fuck," he muttered.

Nick slipped his key into the lock and gave it a silent twist. He put his hand on the knob and gently turned it in his hand. He looked at Quentin, who gave him a nod. Nick pushed the door open.

Quentin swept the room quickly and stepped inside. Nick followed, pivoting toward the corners and spaces where someone could hide.

"Clear," he said quietly. They worked their way from room to room while covering one another's movements silently and automatically.

Nick stepped into the kitchen with Quentin right behind him. Two plates of uneaten scrambled eggs sat on the island's granite top. He saw blonde hair spilling from behind the center island. "Dammit," he said and tilted his head to draw Quentin's attention. He peeked around the island and found Mindy's body lying in a supine position. Her face was pale and her lips a shade of blue that told Nick she was beyond saving.

Nick hesitated for a split-second, recognizing immediately that something wasn't quite right. He dropped down to his knees next to her and put his fingers to her throat as he'd done with Connie just a few days earlier. Her skin was cool to the touch.

"Oh, Mindy," Nick whispered. "I'm sorry."

Quentin backed away and left him to clear the rest of the house.

In an instant, Nick realized what was wrong with the scene. Mindy didn't have four quarters over her eyes and in her hands like the others. There was just one, placed in the center of her forehead, obverse side up.

Nick leaned closer. A portion of George Washington's profile was discolored—a pinkish-magenta. He reached out without any real thought and picked up the coin and held it to the light coming in through the window. His eyes drifted down to the date. 1990P.

His breath hitched. "No," he said aloud. "No, no, no."

Nick turned it over, looking at the familiar pattern of staining. "No," he said again. It wasn't possible. And yet he had no doubt whatsoever that it was.

From upstairs, Quentin shouted, "Clear!"

His voice snapped Nick out of a fog. He gently put the quarter back on Mindy's forehead.

Nick stood back up and had to steady himself against the island. His eyes stung with unshed tears. He holstered his Glock with a trembling hand and looked down at his sister-in-law's lifeless body.

He let out a bellow and swept his arm across the island hurtling dishes and egg through the air and into the far wall. The plates shattered. A fork clanged off one of the shards.

Mindy was dead. Zorin was long gone.

And his wife's life hung in the balance, entirely dependent upon the decisions he would make in the coming hours.

FIFTY-FOUR

Nick sat on the curb outside his house with his head in his hands and willed himself to keep it together. His only hope of saving Connie was for Zorin to underestimate him.

He remembered her on their wedding day. She'd been as flawless and radiant as ever, and wore just the slightest hint of makeup. He recalled the stark contrast of her dark, almost black curls against the brilliant white of her dress. She was as near to pure perfection as Nick had ever seen before or since. He saw her in that moment—so alive, confident, and full of purpose.

After her father had tearfully handed her off to Nick at the front of church, she'd looked at him with such love and commitment, such belief and pride. He could only describe it as utter and complete faith. And he had failed her.

Oh fuck, her parents...

As easy as it would have been to let those thoughts force him into an emotional meltdown, Nick instead wrought them into a barely restrained rage. He stood and paced like a caged animal unable to find a place to direct its fury.

Quentin approached, his hands shoved into his pockets. He looked uncomfortable. "Walk with me," he said and led Nick away from the house toward their cars.

"COD yet?"

Quentin shook his head. "No blood, no contusions. It doesn't look like she was strangled."

"Have him check for needle marks. The paralytic could have caused suffocation."

Quentin's jaw tightened, and Nick immediately realized he'd made a mistake. "How do you know she was suffocated?"

Nick returned his boss's hard stare, saying nothing for a moment. Eventually, he turned his gaze back to the house, the first to surrender. "I've got to find her, Bill." He didn't like the way his voice broke or the pleading he heard in it.

"I know. And *we* will. Everyone's on it. Right now we need to take a breath and figure out what the fuck is going on."

Quentin was right. Nick nodded and leaned against the fender of his Charger, every muscle in his body taut like thick ropes of tension wire. Every fiber of his being wanted—*needed*—to be doing something. Anything.

"Where were you this morning?" Quentin asked.

Nick hesitated again.

Quentin sighed and held his hands out with his shoulders raised. "Have I ever given you a reason not to trust me?"

"No," Nick admitted, and turned his head.

"I'm going to find out, Nick. And you know that if I wanted to burn you, I've already got plenty, right?"

Nick watched as a grey squirrel nibbled on an acorn next to the large oak in his front yard. "I know."

"Okay, so let's try again. Where were you?"

Nick sighed as the squirrel bolted up the tree. He turned back to his boss. "On my way to St. Cloud. We saw the news reports and Con told me I should go. I waited for her sister to get here and left a around quarter of ten."

Quentin nodded as if he'd guessed as much. "How'd you figure it out?"

"I got word about the Dick Cross connections this morning."

"From whom?"

"There are some things I'm not going to tell you, Quent." He flashed him a dangerous glare. "You know full well that I know LEOs on several of these cases. I'm not about to sell them out after they helped me. And if they hadn't, you still wouldn't have a fucking clue about Zorin."

He held up his hands. "Okay, Jesus. Sorry I asked. Go on."

"I was almost to the dam, but something was bothering me. I pulled over to think about it, and a Trooper pulled up behind me. I told you about my dad, right?"

"Yeah. Over beers after you got out of the hospital when that Somali kid knifed you in the side."

Nick nodded, remembering. "Well, I descended into Cruz as I watched the trooper walk up. It hit me like a ton of bricks. The name, the locations where he used the alias were all significant to me."

"Whoa, slow down. You lost me. What about the name?"

"My dad's name was Richard, and the man that killed him was Umberto Cruz." Nick raised an eyebrow and gave him a second to figure it out.

"Cruz is Spanish for Cross," he said, nodding. "Son of a bitch."

"I called Jacksonville and had them pull the name on Cruz's stepson. Aleksandr Zorin."

"So why's this guy got a hard-on for you?"

"Cruz offed himself in jail. Aleksandr was stepson to an infamous murderer, and his mother was a prostitute. It's a pretty safe bet that his home life was filled with abuse and neglect, and I was the local fallen hero's son. We were big news for about a month—painted as the 'perfect family before tragedy struck,'" Nick said, making quotes in the air with his fingers. "Donations were collected for us, the whole nine. That was in '93."

"That's a long ass time to hold a jealous grudge."

"I think there's more to it than just jealousy. My dad dies on the job and becomes the local hero—we're plastered all over the news, and people fall all over themselves to give us money. *His* dad dies, and they don't get squat. He'd have a deep sense of injustice and resentment."

"Why would he blame *you* for his father killing yours?"

"I don't think he does. If that were the case, he probably would have killed me years ago. I think he feels like we're connected. We both lost our fathers that night. Because of that, and in his own way, he probably even identifies with my loss. He's a psychopath and he's obsessed, but I don't think he holds me personally responsible."

"So why take Connie, then?"

Nick realized that Quentin was helping to walk him through it. They'd done this together while working cases several times before. Nick appreciated it, but reminded himself that he was still talking to his boss. He needed to stay cautious.

"He's been trying to get my attention since at least Bakersfield. He's left behind clues that only I'd understand. He's disappointed in us. In *me*. Now he's making it personal."

"Why? What's the endgame?"

Nick shook his head. "I'm not sure, but he's matching wits with me—trying to prove he's smarter than me. As for Con, I don't know." He shrugged and looked at Quentin. He hoped his eyes didn't betray the terror and hopelessness that he felt. "Maybe he doesn't think I've suffered enough?"

Nick didn't mention that he also thought the murder in St. Cloud was specifically intended to draw him away from Connie. He was ashamed that he'd allowed himself to be baited so easily.

"What did you find on the phone?"

Nick opened the car door, leaned in, and retrieved the evidence bag containing Connie's phone from the passenger seat. He handed it to Quentin. A photo—proof of life. A contact entry for Richard Cross with his real name. A web address that links to a blog. It looks legit. At least one of the entries references a case we already knew about. A voice recording saying he can't wait to meet me. And a calendar entry for tomorrow night at 10:00. It's all still there."

If Nick had given him nothing, Quentin would have known he was hiding something. He wasn't stupid. Instead, he'd given Quentin *almost* everything in the hopes that he wouldn't press any further. One of the things Nick knew without a doubt was that Zorin wouldn't hesitate to kill Connie if the Bureau got involved.

"I think it's safe to assume that this Zorin is using Connie as insurance or leverage for something."

"I agree, unless he's just trying to pull my strings," Nick said, trying to downplay it.

"Okay." Quentin frowned and turned Connie's phone over in his hands a few times. "You're staying with Gina and me until your house is processed and we know more."

Fuck, Nick thought. He hadn't anticipated that proposal, but he knew if he accepted, Connie was as good as dead.

"I appreciate the offer, Bill. But I'm dead on my feet. I'd much rather grab a room at the Best Western just up 10 and crash for the night. I'll stay available."

Quentin looked at him long and hard.

"What?" Nick asked testily. "Are you going to arrest me?"

"Of course not."

"Listen, he's not going to make a move until tomorrow night, and he's certainly not going to make it if I'm surrounded by agents. There's no goddamn way I'd go after this guy without backup. He's too dangerous. If I hear from him, you'll hear from me. No tails, Quent. If we spook him, he'll kill Connie."

Quentin stared into the distance with a frown. When he turned back to Nick, he nodded reluctantly. "Fine."

"I mean it. If I think someone's on me, I'm in the wind. I won't risk it. I won't risk *her.*"

"*All right,* Nick. I fucking get it. I just hope you know what the hell you're doing."

"Me too, Bill. Me too," Nick replied as they walked back toward the house.

FIFTY-FIVE

Quentin managed to get Nick a few quiet minutes alone in his bedroom to pack. He quickly dumped the contents of the duffel bag onto the bed and threw a few pairs of jeans, socks and shirts into it. He tossed the toiletry bag back inside, then rose and looked around the room at more than a dozen bouquets of flowers. *Where to start?*

Nick shook his head and was about to begin going through them all one at a time, when it dawned on him that he knew exactly which arrangement Aleksandr Zorin had left for him. The Bureau had bought flowers, but they'd almost certainly not splurged for *two* arrangements. And whoever brought them would almost certainly have placed them on Connie's nightstand.

Zorin would have left his "gift" as close to Nick as possible.

He went to his nightstand and lifted the rectangular vase out of the small wicker basket that held them. There was nothing in the basket itself, but he found a small envelope taped to the underside of the vase. Nick slipped it into a pocket and replaced the flowers.

A chill ran down Nick's spine when he realized Zorin had been inside his home. Had he broken in?

I didn't need to, the voice from Connie's phone whispered in his mind.

Nick realized just how careless he'd been. "Christ," he said to the empty room. He'd left the basement door unlocked when he'd run in to get to Connie on Friday. Zorin had walked right in.

He grabbed his bag and went downstairs. Quentin was waiting for him.

"You ready?"

"Almost," Nick said. He ducked his head inside the kitchen and checked the spot where they hung the spare keys. The extra house key was gone. *Shit.* He made a mental note to have the locks changed when he returned to the house again. If he ever did.

"I need to call them. Her parents." Nick said, though it was the last thing on earth he wanted to do.

"You should let me do that," Quentin said.

Nick shook his head firmly. "I need to do it." He'd failed. He deserved to carry the full weight of their sorrow.

Nick went out onto the deck, careful to avoid any areas of the house that the BCA had yet to process. He took out his cell phone, took a deep breath, and dialed.

Quentin stood watching him just inside the sliding glass door, perhaps concerned that Nick might throw himself over the deck's railing. If Connie wasn't currently at the mercy of a psychopath, he might have considered it.

"Hello? That you, honey?" Marianne Peterson asked.

"No, it's me, Mom," Nick said. Tears welled in his eyes.

His mother-in-law must have picked up on the gravity in his voice, because her own arced into a much higher pitch that bordered on panic. "Oh no. Is it Connie? Were there complications?"

In the background he heard Paul asking what she was talking about.

"Mom, you should really have Dad pick up too."

"Is my baby okay, Nicholas? Tell me. What—"

"Mom!" he interrupted. "Just put Paul on speaker or whatever. I can't do this more than once."

"Oh dear God," she moaned.

He heard a click.

"Nick, what's going on?" Connie's father asked.

He tried to swallow a monstrous lump in his throat, and ended up making a choking sound instead. "I have no idea how to tell you this, it's—" He could already hear Marianne sobbing on the other end of the line.

"What's happened?" Paul asked in a quiet but controlled voice.

"Mindy's dead," Nick said.

"Mindy?" Paul Peterson sounded confused. "What? No. We just talked to her this morning. She… How?"

"She was here. At our place. Earlier. Visiting Con. I went out. Uh—" Nick found it difficult to articulate himself. "She was, um, murdered. Early this afternoon. In our house."

His father-in-law gasped, and Marianne let loose what Nick could only describe as a despondent howl punctuated by sobs.

"I'm so sorry. I wasn't here, and—" he choked. "He, uh—"

"How?" Paul repeated. His voice was just above a whisper. "He who?" Of the three of them, he was the only one maintaining some semblance of control.

"She was murdered. The case I'm working—"

Marianne's sobs became a long gasp followed by a broken, tremulous wail that Nick knew would haunt him until the day he died.

Paul's voice was now trembling as well. "What about Connie? Where was she?"

Nick broke out into a sweat and thousands of sharp pinpricks raced up his arms and back. He felt dizzy. Saliva backed up his throat. He leaned over the rail of the deck just in time and vomited bile onto the grass below. He shivered in the heat of the late afternoon and retched twice more. He heard the sliding glass door open and felt the wood beneath his feet shift slightly as Quentin joined him outside.

Nick wiped his mouth with a forearm and cleared his throat. "Uh, hem. She was… here."

Marianne howled again. "Oh, Jesus! No. Please God, not both of my babies!"

"Marianne, stop!" Paul shouted.

The screams became more muffled, but didn't cease.

"He's got her. He's got Connie and Mindy's dead. I shouldn't… I should have—" He couldn't breathe and was on the verge of hyperventilating.

Quentin put a hand on Nick's shoulder and took the phone from his shaking hand.

"Mr. and Mrs. Peterson, my name is William Quentin. I'm an agent with the Bureau field office your son-in-law works for. I'm so sorry for your loss."

Nick could only hear the one side of the conversation, but it was easy enough to figure out what was being said.

"No, he's still here. He's understandably overwhelmed right now and can't talk at the moment. I'll try to answer your questions as best I can."

He paused. "Unfortunately, yes. We're sure. Nick identified her body."

He paused again. "No, I'm sorry. We don't know for sure how she died yet. That might take some time to determine."

Pause. "We're not entirely sure. It seems likely she was kidnapped by the same man that killed Mindy."

Quentin signaled Nick with a tilt of his head toward the door. He went inside to finish the call.

Nick dropped into a plastic chair and pressed the heels of his hands into his eyes. Bright white explosions painted the back of his eyelids. He breathed slowly but deeply until his chest stopped hitching. By the time Bill returned, he was at least quasi-functional.

"They're coming," Quentin told him. "They're taking a red-eye from Phoenix and should be here at six tomorrow morning."

Nick nodded.

Quentin studied him closely. "You gonna be all right?"

Nick shrugged. "What choice do I have?"

"You look like shit."

"I'm exhausted. I need to sleep." It felt like a week had been pressed into the last ten hours.

"C'mon. I'll take you to the hotel. I don't want you driving right now."

"It's five minutes away. I'll be fine. And I need the car. I have to pick up Connie's parents from the airport tomorrow."

"It's not a suggestion, Nick. I'll come and get you in the morning and bring you back here to get your car. Or we can send someone to get them."

"Trying to keep me out of trouble?"

"Let's just say I'd be more comfortable knowing you won't be out on your own hunting this fucker tonight."

Nick rolled his eyes.

"Hey, I'm covering both our asses here."

Nick nodded. "I get it."

"Let's get going. You look about ready to pass out."

FIFTY-SIX

The drive was brief and quiet. Nick noticed none of it.

When they pulled into the hotel lot, Quentin tried again. "Let me put someone on you, Nick. You won't even know they're there."

Nick reluctantly lifted his head from the rest and shook it. "No. It doesn't matter if *I* know they're there. If he knows, Connie's dead. Let it go. You know where I am. I have no car. I've got my cell, and I told you I'd let you know if he contacts me."

Quentin pulled under the awning and stopped in front of the door. He stared out the windshield. His mouth moved as he gnawed nervously at the inside of his cheek.

"We've got until tomorrow night," Nick said. "I trusted you with that, Bill. I could easily have kept it from you, but I didn't. I'll come in tomorrow after I get Connie's parents settled, and we'll come up with an action plan."

"This is against my better judgment. I don't like it."

Nick nodded. "I know. But it's my decision, and if shit hits the fan it's on me. Not you." If things went south, he didn't expect he'd be around to face the consequences anyway.

"I'll be here at five to pick you up."

Nick got out of the car and retrieved his duffel and laptop bag from the back seat.

Before pulling away, Quentin lowered the passenger side window and leaned over. "I'm serious, Keegan. If you try to fly solo on this, hand to God, I'll kill you myself. Don't be a hero."

Nick went inside.

He checked in and went to his room. Once there, he took out the envelope from his pocket. The flap had been tucked in. Of course. There would be no DNA to pull from saliva on the adhesive. Inside was a black card with bright red lettering, the color of freshly spilled blood. The penmanship was impeccable:

N,

By the actions of our fathers twenty-three years ago, our truest selves were born. Soon our own actions will determine the remainder of our lives. Connie's fate depends entirely on you. I will be in touch.

I believe this belongs to you...

Z

Nick turned the envelope upside down over his hand, knowing exactly what he'd find. A quarter fell into his palm. 1988D. Stained, like the one Nick found on Mindy's forehead. He had no doubt whatsoever that it was one of the bloodstained quarters that Burt had returned to him with his father's personal effects. One of those that he'd pressed into the blue folder that disappeared from his dorm room in college.

Another revelation. Aleksandr Zorin had attended UMD College Park at the same time Nick had been there.

It was only at that moment that Nick fully understood the scope of his own role in the case. He wasn't merely Zorin's fixation, or even his obsession. He was his *source*—his catalyst. Zorin's design, his entire *paradigm*, was based on Nick—a fantasy built upon the anticipation of the moment that their paths would converge again. His elaborate signature had originated with the blue booklet of coins he'd stolen more than a dozen years earlier. Built around something that was important to *Nick*.

"Jesus fuck," he muttered to the shitty painting on the wall as an invisible fist clenched his heart in a vicious death grip. He slipped a hand behind his head and tried to squeeze some of the tension out of his neck and shoulders then crashed down on the bed, which was about as hard and unyielding as his trapezium muscles.

Nick unpacked his laptop. He navigated to Zorin's blog and entered the mind of a madman.

A vibration startled Nick's eyes open. Whether it was his phone or his empty stomach, he couldn't be sure—both were rumbling like crazy. He'd not eaten anything since early morning, and he'd lost that to the side of the road in St. Cloud. Sleep could wait until he had Connie back. Fuel, however, was a necessity.

Nick sighed and checked his phone. He had texts from Addie in Quantico and Harris in Bakersfield, both expressing shock and condolences that he had no time for. He plucked the old quarter off of the comforter next to him. "Miss you, Dad," he said and slipped the coin into a pocket. Zorin's note he set atop the small table beside the bed. He resituated his rumpled clothes, ran a hand through his hair and walked down the hall to the conveniently attached Green Mill restaurant.

A pretty hostess seated him in a large, lonely booth that he'd once shared with Connie. When his waitress came over he ordered a plate of Langostino Lobster and Shrimp—one of his favorites—and a whiskey neat.

While he waited, he sent Addie a text: *he went to UMD College Park in '03.*

Nick flirted with the tantalizing idea of getting shitfaced; instead, he nursed the liquor until his food came. It took him minutes to finish the pasta, and he was busy mopping up the white sauce with bread when his waitress returned.

"I'm gonna guess you'd like some dessert, darlin'?" she said with a warm smile. Her southern drawl, and the smell of a smoker fresh off a cigarette break reminded him of Valerie.

Nick returned a weary smile, and shook his head. "No, I'm good." He leaned toward her and whispered, "But I'd kill for a smoke."

"I think I can arrange that for ya," she whispered back and dropped him a wink. "Another Jack?"

"Why not?"

"I'll be right back for you, hon."

Nick watched as she walked over to the bar and then headed back into an area marked "Employees Only." His hands trembled a bit with anticipation. After a minute she returned with a fresh rocks glass for him and slid a Marlboro and lighter next to his plate.

"You're an angel," he told her.

She smiled at him again. "Just wave if ya' change your mind about dessert."

"I will. Thank you so much."

This time, Nick drained his glass in one long swallow. A fiery snake slipped down his throat and ignited into an inferno in his belly. He felt its warmth spread almost immediately to his extremities.

He slipped three twenties under the edge of his plate and stepped outside. It had been more than a decade since he'd last had a cigarette, yet he salivated at the mere thought of it. It was frightening to realize that he still experienced the same conditioned response after so long. The first drag was fierce. Dopamine flooded his system, and his eyes rolled back slightly in his head. Even so, he found it didn't quite measure up to his expectations and memories.

The parallels were ironic, Nick thought through his chemically induced high. The euphoria of his first cigarette could never be entirely duplicated. No other smoke would ever be as good, as fulfilling, or satisfying again. Precisely like a serial killer, eternally doomed to try to recreate a feeling forever lost. They'd go bigger, more elaborate, more often, take bigger risks. And no matter how satisfying, they'd still always be a little bit disappointed. Killing was as much an addiction as anything else.

Nick was taking another long pull off the smoke when he felt the pinch of the needle in his side just above his left hip. He smiled. He took one long, last drag then calmly dropped the cigarette onto the walk and stubbed it out under his shoe.

"Zorin." He said it without turning around. "I thought I might see you tonight."

"I did say I couldn't wait." It was the voice from Connie's phone.

Zorin's warm breath against his neck made Nick's skin crawl. "Yes, you did," he said through his disgust. "I'm going to take my phone from my jacket pocket and drop it into the garbage can by the door. The FBI will be monitoring it. It's on silent. But if it starts moving or if I turn it off, they'll swarm. I suspect there are teams nearby."

"I have no doubt," Zorin said. "Slowly, Nicholas."

Nick retrieved the Blackberry and held it out to his side as he walked to the trash receptacle. He could already feel the drug starting to coalesce with his exhaustion and the Jack Daniels. Vaguely, he realized that the sound of his phone striking the metal bottom of the trashcan probably signified the end of his career, and quite possibly his life.

"Walk," Zorin instructed. "You only have another two minutes or so."

"If even," Nick replied, his eyelids heavy. He tried to catch a glimpse of Zorin's features but his eyes wouldn't focus properly, and the psychopath was conveniently cloaked in evening shadows.

"To your right," Zorin said.

Nick obeyed, but swayed unsteadily on his feet. He felt like he was moving through a thickening syrup, and he was having a hard time convincing his legs to cooperate. After another three steps it was more like liquid lead. It became difficult to raise his feet off the ground, and he nearly fell forward twice before Zorin finally grabbed him. He slid his head under Nick's armpit, put an arm around his back, and steadied him the rest of the way.

Even through his dimming consciousness, Nick appreciated the cunning of the ploy. If anyone happened to see them, he'd just look like a stumbling drunk being helped through the parking lot by a buddy. It wouldn't trigger the slightest bit of suspicion.

By the time Zorin had helped him into the back seat of the car, Nick could hardly move at all. After a few blank seconds, he heard a door open and felt the car shift. A slam followed immediately after.

From his position behind the wheel, Zorin turned and removed Nick's Glock from the shoulder holster inside of his jacket and set it on the passenger's seat.

Nick tried to focus his vision, but reality was blurry and fading fast. "Nnnneee."

"She's fine for now."

"Lllluu"

"I understand."

Then everything winked out.

FIFTY-SEVEN

Unknown
Tuesday, August 9 2016 4:13 AM

Nick came up into a tenuous awareness long before he regained any kind of motion control. He was confused. His brain couldn't compile enough information to make sense of his situation. Every time he started to remember, he was overwhelmed by another insurmountable wave of weariness and pushed forcibly back into the black. It went on that way for another ten or fifteen minutes as the sedative continued to metabolize. Eventually, he was able to fight back fatigue enough to call it consciousness.

At first, he thought he might be blind. He thought he'd opened his eyes, but everything remained dark. He struggled against a rising panic until he realized he could sense light beyond his eyelids, and some recollection of the night came back to him.

Nick took stock. He was lying on his back. Drawing breath was unusually difficult. He felt pressure around his mouth and nose, and cold, clean air. Oxygen. Though he couldn't move, he didn't feel anything restraining him. It was then that he remembered the Pancuronium Bromide and its paralytic effects. Knowing he was chemically bound didn't help. If anything it was worse. He felt an overwhelming claustrophobia that sent his heart racing.

"Hello, Nicholas," Aleksandr Zorin said, his voice close. "Try to relax. Your pulse just went through the roof."

If anything, it quickened again with Zorin's words.

Nick felt a finger on his eyelid, and then he was blinded by brightness. He tried to look away, but couldn't. He went through the same thing with the other eye. He saw very little but silhouettes and shadow in the brilliance. He heard a repeating hissing sound and felt something constricting around his upper arm. It took him a second to realize it was a blood pressure cuff.

"Your BP is coming back up, and your pupillary response is good." Zorin told him. "It won't be too much longer."

After a few panicked minutes, a quiet sense of inevitability overtook Nick.

Zorin said, "Very soon, you'll start to regain control of your movement a bit at a time. You should be able to open your eyes and wiggle your fingers and toes. Extremities first. When your breathing is easier, the Pavulon will have mostly worn off. Be cautious, though. You won't have complete command of your muscles right away, and the tingling is a bitch—like everything's been asleep. Which, I suppose, it has."

Nick tried to talk and got little for his efforts except for a low quiet growl.

"Take your time. We have plenty." Zorin sounded eerily calm. "I'm going to set some ground rules for our time together while you're coming around. Your gun is on a coffee table to your right, in front of the couch you are lying on. You may reclaim it whenever you are physically able. The choice to use it is yours. However, know that if you do so, Connie will die."

Nick groaned, this time a little louder, and he thought his eyelids had fluttered just enough to let in a sliver of light.

"No, she's not here," he said, as if Nick had spoken the question aloud. "That would be far too easy and hardly conducive to a productive chat. I will tell you that she's someplace where she won't be found unless I tell you where to look. My wellbeing is the price of her return to you. Once I am safely away, I'll provide you with her location."

Nick concentrated on moving the fingers of his left hand through what felt like a billion red-hot needles searing every nerve ending. The numbness and pain that accompanied it was excruciating and crept slowly along his arms and legs. He tried to keep his mind occupied with other things, but it was impossible. The sensation was a constant, torturous agony that he couldn't escape. He drew several short sharp breaths, and his heart slammed and raced in his chest. He tried to bite back a moan, not wanting to give Zorin the satisfaction, but didn't quite manage.

"It's a bit like being stung to death by fire ants, I know," Zorin said. "I was kind and gave you a sedative, so you slept through the worst of it. It will pass."

It dawned on Nick that at some point, this sick fucker must have dosed himself with the Pancuronium and had this very experience. After a period of several minutes that felt like days, it slowly began to dissipate. Nick knew he couldn't hide where he was in the recovery process, as Zorin would see it plainly from his normalizing pulse and blood pressure.

Nick was anxious for it to begin. He *wanted* to talk to Aleksandr Zorin. There was a chance he could be tricked into giving up Connie's location. But it was more than that. Nick needed to understand Zorin's fixation with him and couldn't deny his curiosity.

And as much as he hated to admit it, now that he knew who Zorin was, Nick felt connected to him in a way that he couldn't explain. There had always been a dangerous, roiling undercurrent inside that allowed him to navigate the darkest and most disturbing corners of the most violent of minds. Perhaps as he'd wavered on the knife's edge when his father had been killed, he'd glimpsed just enough of the oblivion beyond to understand them.

Nick thought about his options as he flexed his wrists. None were promising. He could play by Aleksandr's rules and trust the word of a psychopath who had already killed dozens of people. He could take him into custody and hope that the full force of the Bureau could come up with enough evidence to find his wife. And there was the possibility, however slim, that Zorin could be *coerced* to talk—but Nick wasn't entirely sure he was prepared to go to that dark place.

"I think you've had plenty of time to consider your dilemma," Zorin said. "Open your eyes, Nicholas."

He did so, slowly. The dim lamplight of the room was impossibly bright. He squinted and blinked several times until his eyes found their focus and the shadows started to take on shape and form. It was still difficult to breathe, but Nick felt much better and tried to reach for the oxygen mask to remove it. His arm twitched several times, but he was unable to lift it more than a few inches off the couch he was lying on.

"Fuck," he whispered. The clear plastic of the oral-nasal mask fogged with his breath.

"You'll get there," Zorin said calmly. Nick heard a waver of exhilaration threaded through his words.

Nick turned his head slightly toward the voice, but could only make out a vague silhouette.

"It was a long drive, and I had to give you a maintenance dose along the way. An IV would have been better, but I've learned to do without such luxuries."

Nick saw the shadow across the room shift slightly. A shrug.

"Amazing stuff, Pancuronium. It took me a while to get the dosage just right. Too much causes respiratory arrest, too little and people tend to wiggle and squirm. I've had a few..." he paused, "...shall we say, less-than-perfect attempts. I've also gotten very good at estimating my victim's weight over the years. 195, yes?"

Nick blinked hard several more times and tried again to get the mask off. Coordinating his fingers was still a challenge, but he was finally able to push it off with the heel of his right hand. There was also a plastic clip on the middle finger of his left hand that had been monitoring his heart rate and probably his blood oxygen. He managed to nudge that off as well, but the blood pressure cuff would have to wait a few more minutes.

Nick made an effort to sit up, but his arm buckled at the elbow, and his hand slipped from beneath his weight. His eyes, however, were finally cooperating, and he took a minute to look around. He was in a small room. There was a coffee table in front of him, and his Glock 17 was indeed there, the clip lying next to it. A glint of copper suggested it was still loaded. Nick marveled at the confidence and audacity it took Zorin to leave it there. Then again, he *was* a psychopath. They were often fearless and exhilarated by the thought of taking such risks.

On the opposite side of the table, about eight feet away, were two comfortable looking armchairs. Aleksandr Zorin sat in one of them. He gave Nick a small wave and a smile that was all teeth. It was the Cheshire Cat grin of an excited kid on Christmas morning. He was bald, with bright-green, intelligent eyes and broad shoulders. His features were similar to those in the DMV photo of Richard Cross, but more than a cursory glance at the driver's license would have given him away. He wore blue jeans and a dark blue polo that strained against a muscular chest and bulging arms. There was also something unusual about his appearance that Nick couldn't identify. Nonetheless, he knew him.

"Friday morning," he croaked. "The runner."

Zorin applauded slowly. "A convenient way to surveil."

Nick wondered how long he'd been watching them. He continued to take in his surroundings. Beyond Zorin were a tiny kitchenette and a hallway that presumably led to the bedrooms. There was a large stone fireplace to the right of the couch he was lying on, and a sturdy-looking stained oak door was on the wall opposite. He guessed they were in a small cabin.

"Nice place. Yours?" Nick asked with a dry, raspy voice and tried to focus on the man across from him.

Zorin smiled. "Borrowed. You don't *really* believe I would bring you to a place of my own, do you?"

"Never know." Nick said, breathing as deeply as his diaphragm would allow. He was starting to feel better. At least the horrible prickling had passed. "Dumber things have been done."

"Not by me, Nicholas."

"Everyone makes mistakes. Should we talk about Lindsay Lyman?"

Aleksandr tipped his head slightly. "That was… unexpected. But hardly a mistake. Helen Lyman brought you into the picture, did she not? Your friend's confusion. That was her great purpose. To be honest, I've been rather disappointed it's taken you so long. I hoped for better."

Nick made another attempt to sit up and this time got there. He fought off a furious bout of lightheadedness, and balanced his elbows on his knees. He eyed the gun on the table.

Zorin followed his gaze. "I doubt your fine motor skills are up to it, but you're welcome to try. I'm not afraid to meet my end if that is what today brings."

"Bullshit. You've killed how many people, and now you're prepared to die?"

"Well, it's not really *quite* so simple as that, is it? If you were to kill me, you'd also be killing your pretty wife. Your torment would be never-ending, Nick, and in its way, that would provide me a kind of immortality. Every time you thought of dear Connie, you would also remember me. But let's be realistic. We both know that's not how this is going to play out."

"Do we?"

"Of course we do. You're one of *them*." Zorin said the word with a roll of his eyes, his voice tinged with disgust. "You don't have it in you to kill me here today, because you'd have to sacrifice the life of someone you care about. Your emotional attachments make you vulnerable. It's a weakness. A chink in your shining armor.

"I've waited the great majority of my life for this moment. I've planned for it with great care. I've envisioned it hundreds of times. I already know how this will end."

"So that's what's driving you? Immortality? I've got to say that's pretty unoriginal. I guess *I* hoped for better."

Zorin was imperturbable. He stood and turned his back on Nick and the Glock in a display of casual confidence and went to the kitchenette. He retrieved two bottles of water from the refrigerator, returned, and slid one across the table to Nick.

"I'd say my immortality is already fairly assured, wouldn't you?" he asked, and took a long pull from his bottle.

Nick chose to not stroke the fucker's ego and said nothing. Instead, he worked at the Velcro holding the cuff to his arm. It still took him a minute to manage. He tossed the device on the couch next to him.

Zorin tipped his bottle toward Nick. "Drink. It will help." He changed the subject. "How many have you found?"

Nick knew exactly what he was asking. "Too many."

Zorin looked disappointed. "Is it really necessary to be difficult?"

"Counting my sister-in-law and Richard Cross, twenty-seven, last I saw. But the gaps indicate there are at least forty. More were coming in daily. How many are we missing?"

"We'll get to that."

"Now who's being difficult?"

"I'm not trying to be evasive, Nicholas. We'll discuss it."

Nick's limbs still felt heavy, but he forced himself to stand and took a few tentative steps. His calves and thighs trembled, but held him up. As he walked off the shakes, he looked closely at Aleksandr Zorin. It finally dawned on him what it was about him that was so unusual. He wasn't only bald—he had no hair whatsoever. His arms and face were perfectly smooth. It was extremely disconcerting, and once Nick had noticed it he couldn't stop seeing it. That helped explain the lack of physical evidence at the scenes.

"So, why am I here?" Nick sat back down, cracked the water, and took a sip with a quaking hand. "Why the infatuation with me?"

"I don't know that infatuation is the right word. Curiosity, certainly. Kinship, maybe."

Nick laughed. "Right. Sure. My long lost brother. You're fucking insane."

Zorin shrugged, unperturbed. "By the definition of some, yes. But that isn't really relevant to this discussion."

"Oh, I think it's absolutely relevant. Can I take a shot?"

Zorin grinned. "I'd be disappointed if you didn't, but you won't tell me anything I don't already know." He gestured for Nick to continue.

"You grew up in an incredibly difficult situation. Your mother was a whore, and the only father you ever knew was a violent and aggressive tyrant that ruled by fear and fist and probably drugs. You came to both hate and deify him. Then one day he went out for some booze and never came back. You were devastated and lost. You were abandoned by someone you worshipped, and a terrible rage built inside of you. Your mother got worse. I'm guessing she molested you. How am I doing so far?"

"Very well." Zorin seemed unfazed by Nick's analysis. "But you could have found most of that profile in *The Maelstrom*."

"I didn't bother reading it," Nick lied.

Zorin smiled again. He knew better. "My mother never told me what happened to Cruz. She wouldn't allow me to watch the news during that time. I only learned the truth when WTLV did the follow-up piece about your college gift six years later."

Nick nodded. "My mother and I got all the attention and money, and you got nothing. My dad was called a hero and yours was portrayed as a monster. I bet that was hard for you. I imagine finding out that your mother kept it from you all that time made it worse."

"That's ancient history. I don't deny what I am." Zorin leaned forward in the chair. "I do find it interesting that you feel so compelled to ascertain all the reasons, assign blame—to find out what makes us tick. Maybe the bomb just ticks because it's a bomb." He raised his hairless brow. "Bombs explode, Nicholas. It's what they do. I feel no need to justify my actions."

"There is no justification for what you do. But I find it more than a little ironic that you've slaughtered a lot of innocent people because the only role model you had was an abusive piece of shit, and yet, when he killed my father it caused him so much guilt he strangled himself with his jumpsuit."

"Guilt is pointless and pathetic." Zorin waved his hand dismissively. "And innocence, like insanity, is subjective. It requires a set of rules that govern right and wrong. But the rules are written by a flawed species that defies its own nature. I don't bother denying myself. When I'm bored, I hunt. When I'm hungry, I feed. I've long outgrown any influence that Cruz might have had on me. He was little more than a match to my fuse, but he was a coward. He was weak."

"Did you know that I was one of the last people to ever see him alive?"

The withering look Zorin gave him seemed to drop the temperature of the room several degrees. It was the first time Nick felt he'd found an opening.

"The night before he hung himself. I went to see him. We had a nice little chat. We talked about you, as a matter of fact."

Across from him, Zorin said nothing but looked at Nick expectantly.

"I think he was disappointed that you and your mother hadn't come to see him. He felt abandoned, Zorin. Alone. He acted tough, but I saw it in his eyes."

Still Zorin said nothing. His jaw was set. A vein throbbed on his temple.

"I think seeing me must have reminded him that he had a family that didn't give a shit about him. I've always thought maybe I was the reason he did it. For a while, I even felt a little bit guilty about it.

"But I got over it. I probably did the world a favor—hell, I did *you* a favor. He was a bully. He preyed on those that were weaker than him. He even tried it with me. It made him feel powerful, but he was really just a coward."

Zorin looked off into the corner of the room. When he looked back, he'd regained his composure. The smile he gave Nick was terrible. "Well done. You've managed to surprise me. That doesn't happen often. But it doesn't matter. *I* am not weak. And I am not a coward." He nodded toward the Glock on the coffee table as if it proved his words.

"That's bullshit and you know it. The gun doesn't mean anything as long as you have my wife."

"Unless I've underestimated you," Zorin said, his eyes gleaming.

"You mean *over*estimated. If I do take you out, it means I'm a little less human than you give me credit for."

"Semantics. It all depends on the point of view, doesn't it? I can't deny that this is the most excitement I've experienced in a long time. Betting your life on someone else's actions is…exhilarating." Zorin rubbed his groin. An erection strained beneath the fabric of his jeans.

Nick refused to give him the satisfaction of a reaction. "So, what? You've been harboring some kind of grudge against me for all of these years? Is that what this is about?"

"Not at all. But I will admit that you intrigue me. I consider you almost an equal. I've followed your career closely. Did you at least discover that I attended UMD while you were there?"

"Yes. The quarters."

Zorin nodded. "I dormed next door to you and Jim Harris for a semester, though that took a bit of…finagling."

Nick didn't ask what that meant, but he suspected someone had died suddenly so Zorin could bunk in a neighboring room.

"In a way, your father gave birth to me and Cruz to you. Finding your quarters was fortuitous, Nick. Symbolic. We are really two sides of the same coin."

"I'm nothing like you," Nick said with disdain.

Zorin smiled slyly. "That isn't really what I said, but it would seem I've struck a nerve. How about this, then? We are opposites, but struck by the same die at the same moment. We're made of the same stuff."

Privately, Nick conceded the analogy, but he refused to perpetuate Zorin's philosophy openly. He said nothing.

"We're intelligent, driven, dedicated, relentless, and exceptionally good at what we do. We just happen to be on opposing sides. We are one another's balancing force."

"Many people have those characteristics. You could be describing hundreds of my colleagues and friends."

"But they don't share our past, do they? They haven't experienced what we have."

"*We* don't have a past. Your father put four slugs in mine. It was tragic. We were both dealt shitty hands, but we have nothing else in common."

Nick leaned over and took his gun and the clip from the table. His hands still shook, and it took a few seconds to slide the magazine home and chamber a round. He aimed a wobbling hand in Zorin's general direction.

The lunatic across from him didn't even flinch. In fact, he grinned.

"Where is my wife?" Nick said.

Zorin sighed. "Don't be tedious. We've already talked about this."

"And why should I take the word of a psychopath. My wife is as good as dead, if she isn't already. Am I supposed to believe that you have some measure of honor?"

"I won't lie to you, Nick. I'd much prefer you not have Connie as a distraction—she gives me an unfair advantage. But if you wish to play with a handicap, that's your decision. In the end, it makes things easier for me."

"This isn't a fucking game, goddamn you."

"Isn't it?" Zorin asked.

"I have access to the most sophisticated and capable criminal justice teams and systems on earth. You will be caught. It won't be long, one way or another. We know more than enough to find you."

Zorin smirked. "You know only what I've allowed you to know."

Something about his confidence shook Nick. He decided to play the only card he had left. "Really? What about your daughter?"

Zorin's brow creased for the briefest of seconds, and Nick knew he'd been right.

He pushed. "How old would she be now?"

Zorin recovered his composure. "It won't help you."

"We know who you are now."

"Do you really?"

"Someone will know you. Her mother, someone."

Zorin's eyes glimmered in the lamplight, and he leaned forward in the chair again, clasping his hands together in front of him. "Oh, Nick." He sighed like he was dealing with an ignorant child. "Let me level our playing field a bit for you. You really should know what you're up against.

"Yes, I was once Aleksandr Zorin, but it has been a very long time since I've used that name. No one really has any idea who I am. There are perhaps a dozen identities that have lived between then and now. I might as well be a ghost. You may find a few records, but then my trail will go cold.

"I started killing when I was sixteen. I've done so one hundred and sixty-three times. I remember all of them. Vividly."

Nick's blood ran cold, and his stomach cramped. It was as if Zorin had punched him in the gut.

"Many of my victims will be revealed to you as your ViCADETs continue to enter case files. And, by the way, I must admit that was a brilliant idea. ViCAP was terribly ineffective. I exploited its weaknesses intentionally and often. In any case, there are many bodies that you will never find. And many more still have absolutely nothing to do with the quarters—with *us*. *Chaos*, I believe you're calling it?"

Stunned, Nick lowered the Glock and set it on the couch beside him. His hands shook so violently he didn't trust his aim even at the mere three yards that separated them.

"I've been using our signature specifically to gauge how much the FBI knew. And for you, of course. Much of the time I don't bother with a signature at all. Standing on the edge of the Else is all the release I need. It is always quite an incredible experience."

Zorin's gaze was far away, and a sneer played at his lips. His eyes were filled with an indescribable mixture of cruelty and ecstasy that went beyond what Nick thought he knew about the dark places of the mind. It was something primal and ragged that could never be sated. It was something worse than psychopathy or even malevolence. It was rabid.

Finally, the full magnitude of the situation set in.

Nick had to consider the very real possibility that this man might not ever be stopped. He was a virtual shape-shifter and could change almost anything about himself—his eye-color, weight, build, hair and facial hair. The danger of letting Zorin leave this room was incalculable. If what he'd already confessed were true, hundreds more could be left floating in his vicious wake.

"Jesus Christ," Nick muttered and rubbed at his wet, stinging eyes. He now thought he understood the purpose behind all of the subterfuge. Despite the lack of malice and almost casual conversation, Aleksandr Zorin's sole desire was to place him in an emotionally impossible position. He'd painstakingly planned every detail for years and was prepared to die to see it through to its end. Just as he enjoyed experimenting with the limits of the human body, he was now doing the same thing with Nick's mind.

If Nick were to sacrifice Connie for the sake of justice, he'd have to live with that torment for the rest of his life. If instead, he were to let Zorin leave the cabin alive, that too would be an impossible burden for him to bear. He would harbor the guilt for all of Zorin's future victims. And Connie's life would still be at the mercy of a madman.

Zorin seemed to read his thoughts and smiled at him again, almost warmly. "So, shall we get to it?"

Nick could barely speak. Tears streamed down his face. "I can't make this decision. You know that."

The look in Zorin's eyes was nothing short of euphoric. Nick thought he saw him shudder.

"Ah, but see, you don't really have a choice. In a few moments, I am going to walk out that door. You can allow me to leave. Or not. I've really made it rather simple for you."

Zorin stood and looked down at Nick with ice in his stare. "Now we will find out just how different we really are." Then he smiled. It was a broken thing that didn't make it to his empty eyes. "This has been everything I always hoped it would be, Nick."

Nick's mind raced at impossible speeds. Images, voices, thoughts, memories, and even sounds flashed by as if from a hundred dreams.

Connie on their wedding day, her eyes shining with tears.

How long would she have? Two days? Three at most?

Could he find her in time with all of his Bureau resources?

His father's tickling game at night.

"Cochino had it comin."

Would Zorin keep his word?

The peal of church bells as confetti and rice rained down around them.

Connie's bright blood on the bedroom floor.

What would *she* want him to do?

"Take him down, and we'll call it even."

Harris breaking down after finding Helen and Lindsay Lyman in their kitchen.

"I've done so one hundred and sixty-three times."

Connie twisting her naked body and giggling as he blew raspberries on her stomach.

How many more before he was caught? *If* he was caught?

The sharp edges of his father's badge cutting into his hand.

Could he be broken?

A seemingly never-ending slideshow of crime scene photo after crime scene photo.

"Go get that sick son-of-a-bitch."

Marianne Peterson's heartrending wail.

How would he live with himself?

"Oh, yes, I very nearly forgot," Zorin said, turning back. "There's a sandwich and more water in the fridge for you. You'll want to get your strength back before you leave. There's no phone here, and it's several miles due east to the next cabin. Until next we meet, Nick. The pleasure has been mine."

Zorin opened the door unto a soft sunrise diffused by millions of green leaves on thousands of trees. It would otherwise have been a beautiful morning pierced by birdsong and a light breeze that smelled of dew. Nick quivered like a plucked bowstring, watching as Zorin took a measured step over the threshold.

Behind him, Nicholas Keegan raised a shaking arm, issued a pained, guttural scream and put precisely 5.5 pounds of pressure on the trigger of his gun.

A dark cloud of startled birds burst silently from the trees, the sound of their wings lost in the echoes of the shot.

THE END

An excerpt from the forthcoming second book in the Chaos Series…

ONE

Shoreview, Minnesota
Monday, October 31 2016 5:48 PM

The bedroom curtains billowed like full sails against a chill Halloween wind. They popped and snapped as the occasional gust hissed through the screen. Outside, flurries, crystalline and shimmering, blew in faint swirls against a darkening sky. Inside, Nicholas Keegan sat with his back to the wall underneath the open window, absently guarding a fifth of Jack Daniels from the flailing fingers of the drapes. The bottle had little more than a single swallow left at the bottom.

He hadn't slept in the bed across from him in weeks, but the sheets were mussed and untucked and stank of sweat and booze. And probably puke. The room was cold, but Nick couldn't feel it. He couldn't feel much of anything thanks to Mr. Daniels, and that was fine with him. A few stains spotted the floor around the space where he sat. He saw them without seeing them, and couldn't remember and didn't care how they got there.

Nick had no idea that it was Halloween. It wouldn't have mattered if he had. His house was positioned adjacent to a small wooded grove at the end of a long, out of the way block. If he had trick-or-treaters at all, he'd probably be able to count the rings of the doorbell on one hand. He wouldn't have answered anyway.

He tipped back the last of the Jack and tossed the bottle into the corner. It landed on a small mountain of other empties that clattered and clanked as the pile shifted to make room for a new-fallen comrade.

On the dresser, Nick's Blackberry buzzed. He ignored it, but knew it was his boss Bill Quentin checking in. 6:00, like clockwork, every day. Nick was on leave, but the job just wouldn't leave him alone. That was the FBI. But Quent was also a friend, and Nick would have to pay him a response soon, or he'd have unwanted company. Skipping mandatory psych sessions was probably not the best idea either, but the Bureau wasn't high on his priority list at the moment.

The warmth in his belly bloomed into his head and took him deeper into the fog. He was plenty drunk now and a blessed blackout was soon on the horizon. He waited for it to take him. His head swayed a bit, and his mind drifted dangerously to the top dresser drawer. Almost as soon as the thought came, it was forgotten. His brain was having trouble holding onto things. It wouldn't be long now. That was good.

Nick was pretty sure he imagined the first scream, but it snapped his lolling head back to attention. Goosebumps crawled up his arms. The second scream seemed a bit more distant. A woman. Probably one of his neighbors having sex, her cries carried on the wind. The third scream had shape and form. A single word: "Help!"

He had zero desire to move, but something instinctive propelled him. Nick somehow managed two flights of stairs without killing himself and opened the sliding basement door to the outside. It seemed too warm for the snow, but maybe that was just the booze and adrenaline. He had no idea from what direction the screams had come. The wind did peculiar things to sound here, and it was snarling tonight.

Nick fought an almost overwhelming urge to sit down, and instead closed his eyes and listened. He swayed on his feet, and had to set his shoulder against the doorframe for support. A small gust brought the sound of a hushed voice in the distance and the hiss and crunch of dead leaves. He clenched his teeth and opened his eyes. Things were soft and hazy, but he thought he could manage to get to the woods and through them, if need be.

He started slowly, but as the wind kicked up the broken sounds of a struggle and a woman's muffled sobs he picked up the pace as much as he was able. At the point where the woods began, Nick met up with his usual running path. The trees on either side were mostly barren, but some brown and orange leaves fluttered from their branches in unyielding defiance of autumn. Others lost their battles and dropped around him as he stumbled along the pavement.

The moans and cries seemed to be getting louder. Nick tried calling out, but his voice was carried away on a gale. He upped his speed into what could almost be called a run and immediately paid the price. He wiped out hard, ripping his jeans at the knees and tearing up his palms as he broke the fall on the asphalt. The jolt gave him a brief moment of sobriety, during which his mental self asked, *what the fuck are you doing?* while his physical self jumped up and bolted forward.

A despairing whimper came from up ahead and, he thought, to his left. He reached unconsciously toward his left armpit for the Glock still tucked in his dresser and scanned through the trees as he ran. Beyond a small stream and behind some heavy brush, Nick spotted movement and a splash of pink that jumped out against the rust and grey colors of fall in the woods. He took the next hundred yards or so by the path, then cut diagonally into the woods on a course that would avoid the stream.

Fallen twigs and leaves cracked and broke underfoot—*bare feet*—Nick realized vaguely as he crashed toward the brush. Branches stretched for his face and arms, stinging as they scraped skin. He could see two people ahead now, maybe another fifty yards away. A burly man was straddled atop the waist of a young woman, his body weight pinning her down. Her pink jacket and blouse was open, her blonde hair fanned out on the leaves. As he neared, Nick could see that the girl was straining her neck to escape a hand covering her mouth. Her booted feet kicked and pedaled at the ground, looking for purchase or leverage—anything that might give her a chance. The man's right hand was at the girl's bare chest.

"Hey!" Nick yelled without slowing, marveling that his thunderous approach through the woods hadn't yet been noticed. "The fuck off her!"

This time, his shout was heard. The girl focused on Nick with wide eyes and the purest look of gratitude he'd ever seen.

Her attacker turned to gauge the threat before relinquishing his prize. He was bigger than Nick originally thought, flat-faced and probably in his early twenties. His eyes were wild and he didn't look overly concerned by the man running toward him.

Nick slowed his approach. Barefoot, in stained t-shirt and torn jeans, scratched, cut, and just shy of shitfaced, he wasn't particularly menacing. More than two months of heavy boozing didn't help matters. The sallow shadows around his eyes weren't only from the looming darkfall.

"Screw off, asshole," Flat-Face said. He shifted his weight in preparation for an attack, but didn't get off the girl. He obviously hoped he could intimidate Nick into leaving him to finish what he'd started.

Nick was close enough now to see bruises on the girl's breast. She was maybe nineteen. Mascara stained her temples, and she shook like the leaves in the wind. Her stomach heaved with sobs.

Whatever drunk Nick still felt was replaced with white rage. His fists opened and closed involuntarily. His lips twisted into a sneer. His eyes never left the man in front of him, but he spoke to the girl. "When he gets off you, run. Don't stop."

"You're dead, motherfucker," Flat-Face said and rose cautiously. Nick shrugged, then laughed and pointed at the bulge in Flat-Face's sweatpants. "Were you gonna rape her with that, or tickle her?"

Less than a second later Nick was on the ground. Before the first blow connected with his face, he saw a pink flash racing through the trees, quick as a gazelle.

TWO

Forest Lake, Minnesota

Monday, August 8 2016 2:47 PM

"You've had a hell of a time lately, Connie. I'd apologize for my part in that, but I don't have the capacity for regret, and I won't insult your intelligence by pretending."

Connie Keegan lay on a dirty mattress in an otherwise empty room. The sting in her extremities was almost unbearable. With intense concentration, she could just bend a fingertip. She still couldn't blink. A single tear slipped from her eye. She heard it hit the mattress with a soft *plop*.

She was coming back to herself after what seemed like an eternal torturous nightmare. A few minutes earlier, she'd just started regaining the ability to move. A few hours earlier her sister was killed in her kitchen. A few days earlier she'd lost a baby—no—*all babies*. Forever. A few weeks earlier, she was happy and content. It seemed impossible to go from so much to so little in such a short period of time. It seemed unendurable. A soft moan from deep in her chest tumbled over her lips. Another tear fell. *Plop*.

And then there was *him*. He sat on the floor a few feet away from the mattress directly in her line of sight. She still didn't have enough muscular control to look away or close her eyes. For the time being, he and the dirty mattress were her entire world.

"It will wear off soon," he said. "Unfortunately, we don't have the luxury of much time together today. Perhaps another."

Connie hated that the next noise she made sounded like a whine.

"Yes. Frustrating, isn't it?" He checked his watch. "You should be right as rain in a few hours. You'll be able to talk again in about half that." He smiled. "Right now, it is very important that you do nothing but listen. There are things that you'll have to remember, one way or another."

Plop.

"I imagine you'd like to know who I am." He paused and then nodded at her as if she'd answered. "I am Aleksandr Zorin. I haven't used that name in a very long time, but it is the one that will matter to your husband. I have to admit, I am a bit disappointed that it has taken him so long to figure this out. I expected better. Perhaps I overestimated his abilities."

Connie's lips, fingertips and toes somehow felt both detached from her body and overwhelmed with the prickling of a thousand sharp needles. The sensation was maddening and terrible, like that of a body part fallen asleep but many times worse. The constriction around her chest had finally loosened enough for her to gasp a little. If they could have, her eyes would have rolled back with this new agony.

Plop, plop, plop.

Zorin watched her with the hint of a knowing smile. His eyes gleamed. "Awful, isn't it? I imagine it's a bit what Hell would feel like, were it real. If I could recreate that particular suffering at will and make it last, I'd have no need for any other tools."

There was nothing but this agony. It was her entire existence. Connie couldn't tremble, or scream. Her mind did both. She prayed to pass out before it drove her insane. The only comfort she could create for herself was in the form of a low continuous hum.

"Hnnnnnnn." *Oh Jesus, oh God.* "Hnnnnnn."

Plop.

"It will pass. It will seem like an eternity, but it will pass. Do what you must to get through it, Connie. But you must also listen. I can't wait with you. I have plans for Nicholas later this evening."

Nick. She tried to think about him, tried to remember his green eyes gazing into hers and the easy, mischievous smile that was hers alone. She tried to think of the feel of his thick, brown hair running through her fingers. It helped, but only for a second. She tried to imagine him putting a bullet in the forehead of the smirking bastard sitting in front of her. That was intensely satisfying in its way, but didn't provide any relief from her torment.

Fuck. "Hnnn." *God, make it stop. Make it stop. Make it stop.* "Hnnnnnnnn."

"I'm a killer, Connie. And I am exceptional at it. I don't say that to boast. It's a fact. By the definition of many, I'm a sadistic psychopath. I take pleasure in the suffering of others, and I'm unhindered by the things that make mankind weak. I don't experience guilt or remorse, love or pity. Evolutionarily, I am the end of the line—the perfect predator."

Connie finally blinked once. If not for the horrors the rest of her body was experiencing, it might have been heavenly. Zorin blurred. Every light source in her line of sight shattered into dazzling starbursts as tears covered her corneas. *Plop, plop. Plop, plop, plop.*

The more tolerable sting of crying replaced the dryness she'd felt for the past three hours. Her nose burned and began to run. She hardly noticed. It was just one more in an endless stream of discomforts.

"Your husband hunts predators like me. By all accounts, he is exceptional at it. He is my opposition. But he and I have much more in common. We go way back. He won't remember me, but we went to college together in Maryland for a few years. We even took a few of the same classes." Zorin tilted his head to the right, and raised his eyes to the ceiling with the recollection. He ticked them off with his fingers as he recited them. "Adult Psychopathology. Psychology of Criminal Behavior. Forensic Psychology. Criminal Investigation. Contemporary Criminological Theory. Intro to Criminalistics. Intro to the Study of Deviance—" He looked back down waggled seven fingers at her and smiled. "That was my personal favorite, but I've found them all quite useful over the years."

Connie's calf began to spasm, the beginnings of a wild-eyed charley horse snorting and hoofing angrily at the ground. There was apparently no end to the litany of agonies she would have to endure. As it built, more tears fell from her eyes and her low moan quivered. *Oh Jesus fuck, this hurts.* Between the pain and the incessant needling, she thought for sure her mind would shatter.

"But Nick and I go back further still. I'm sure you know about the death of his father, the ..." Zorin made quotes in the air and rolled his eyes. "...heroic policeman that was killed in the street during a traffic stop. What you and he *don't* know is that the man who killed him was my step-father."

Connie had no way to convey her confusion. If she could have squinted in surprise, she would have. Instead she just continued to stare at the man in front of her and tried to will herself to blink again.

Zorin continued, as if he sensed her puzzlement. "His name was Umberto Cruz. He married my mother when I was still on her tit. He was not a nice man, Connie. He taught us both with his hands." He smiled like he might be remembering a pleasant childhood memory. "He used to pinch." Zorin scooted himself up to the edge of the mattress and squeezed the fleshy skin just forward of Connie's right armpit between thumb and forefinger. "Here," he said and gave a vicious twist.

It felt like an electric shock. Connie gasped and squeaked out something that would have been a scream under normal circumstances. More tears fell from her eyes as she blinked a second time. She hoped she would soon be able to close them on this waking nightmare.

"Hurts like a *bitch*, doesn't it?" He slid back to his original spot and crossed his legs beneath him. "I had a permanent bruise there until he vanished when I was nine."

THREE

Quantico, Virginia
Monday, October 31 2016 9:28 PM

Addison Lange sat on the floor of her room at the FBI Academy. Her fingers rocketed over the keyboard of the battered laptop in front of her. Black command windows appeared on the monitor, filled with long strings of white text and winked closed, and were immediately replaced by others. To her right, a MacBook sat open, the screen filled with a strange and hazy image of a boy's face. A number of red lines marred the upper portion of the picture, stretching from various points to others, bisecting and connecting features. A graphics tablet lay on the floor within reach of her hand. Every few minutes Addison stopped typing, and made an adjustment with the tablet, very subtly sharpening sections of the blurred face staring out from the Mac. Only the boy's eyes were in perfect focus, just a shade bluer than graphite.

The image was actually a composite of three pictures lain one atop another like transparencies, which accounted for the blurriness. Addison didn't consider photo editing among her strengths, but she'd found Photoshop filled in the blanks for her nicely. Digitally speaking, she didn't even need to blend the faces to accomplish her task—most of that was already done—but she was curious to see the finished product.

The room was silent but for her fingers moving on the keyboards and the faint whirring of the fans cooling the strain she was putting on the laptops.

Normally, cadets would spend at least part of their training housed at a local hotel, but budget cuts and strict hiring limits at the Bureau meant that her class was able to stay at the dorms for their entire summer to fall session. Addison's room was immaculate. The beds were made with perfect hospital corners and tight tucks, more than adequate to pass a military quarter bounce test. Counter to probably every other dorm at the Bureau, no clothes littered the floor. In fact, all of her clothing was in the wardrobe, hung or folded just as crisply as the bed sheets. A white glove inspection would yield no dust—not even (and perhaps especially) atop the doorframe, a place her father had been notorious for checking when she was growing up.

The FBI would never admit to giving special treatment to anyone, but Addison was one of only a few to have not had a roommate during her seventeen weeks at the Academy. Even before the first dropouts from the fitness test and "Reality Check," she'd had this dorm to herself. It was really the only accommodation she'd allowed them to make for her. She preferred her privacy and it had allowed her to work on this project without curious or prying eyes. It also meant that no one else knew about her particular skillset, which, for all she knew, was just how the Bureau wanted it.

Addison's father was USMC Colonel Thomas Lange. In and of itself, that fact would have had no bearing on his daughter's time at the Academy. But because he was also the base commander at Quantico, where the nearly 400-acre FBI Academy was located, a certain amount of deference might have been afforded her. Colonel Lange was also on a very short list of expected nominees for promotion to Brigadier General. And although no one would have spoken any special requests aloud, the Marine Corps and the Bureau were very much political beasts where favors (and the lack thereof) were never forgotten.

Addison pushed aside a small wave of guilt at the thought of her father. He would not approve of what she was doing. She reasoned he would almost certainly never find out in any case, and if he did it would only be because she had discovered something that he couldn't possibly be upset with her about. Or so she hoped. Her father's disappointment was the one thing she couldn't bear. A monstrous swarm of butterflies took off in her stomach as she completed one last long string of indecipherable code on the bulky old laptop. For better or worse, it was done. Before she could change her mind, she plugged in a wireless air card and booted the new program. In a few seconds it was off and running. Addison closed that laptop and fiddled with the graphics tablet for a few minutes, sharpening the image on the MacBook's monitor.

"Hi, Tommy," she said to the face staring back at her.

www.ingramcontent.com/pod-product-compliance
Lightning Source LLC
Chambersburg PA
CBHW031213120726
47905CB00002B/321